1

# Thoughts Harrowing
# Edge

## A Psychological Thriller

R. C. Smith

Other books by Randy C. Smith
Open Window Reflections in Poetry
Gnarly
Sequel to Gnarly
The Return of Mudge
and Moose Trapped

Isbn- 978-0-9983775-0-6

## Acknowledgments

There have been many family members, and friends, who have given of their valuable time and knowledge to the writing of "Thoughts Harrowing Edge." I would like to acknowledge them, for they have contributed to this story in one way or another and I am very grateful.

Cheryl Smith, Josh and Stacey Smith, Sarah and Jared Martin, James E. Sanderson Jr, Elisabeth Middleton, Cheyne Dougan, Angie Hudson, John Burke, Jimmy Walker, Mandy Watkins, Michelle Hansen Savell, Carol Simmons Hunt, Kristi Robertson, Jeff Blackard , David Hart, Jennifer Koch, Rutha Freemen, Leslie Wave Mori, Bobby Villareal, Shelley Sosebee, Melinda Wish Gould, Ellie Black, Angie Richardson, Joann Lynch, and Jennifer.

Reading Circle Publishing

U.S. copyright © 2017,

Cover design by,

Productions

Jared Martin Photography

# Thoughts Harrowing Edge

## Chapter 1

It was just a thought, perhaps an old thought, or the ragged edge of memory from long ago. Who could say for sure? The thought came and went of its own accord, leaving Jason Brennen exasperated and quite confused. It was persistent, lingering on in his mind, ever nagging, prodding him into action. But what kind of action Jason didn't know. Sleep had been scarce, and when he did manage to fall asleep, it was only in snatches; the thought would invariably shake him wide awake from his stupor, coming as a vague knowing. It was the feeling that comes just before awaking, as though from a dark hidden place somewhere between dreams. The vagueness had him puzzled, but it didn't seem to be a forerunner of doom, at least not that Jason could tell. There were no real feelings of apprehension, only a persistent nagging that wouldn't go away. It was as if the thought was trying to talk, trying to tell a story, wanting to reveal a secret. Jason's rough appearance and lack of alertness at work were beginning to turn heads. It wasn't long before he was told that he should go see a doctor. After much persuasion an appointment was finally made.

Jason was embarrassed as he spoke to the doctor. He tried to explain what had been going on, but the doctor didn't seem too concerned. He was prescribed a sleep aid and told to try it for a week.  If that didn't help then he should make another appointment. Taking drugs was not what Jason had in mind, but there wasn't much choice. He needed his sleep, and so he gave it a try.

Sleep, blissful sleep!  How nice it was to rest through an entire night and awake refreshed. As for the thought, it seemed to have disappeared into unreality. Jason was relieved that it was gone. It would have been better if he had known what the troubling thought was about. It was a moot point at best, so Jason tried to forget about it. He was relieved that it had departed his mind.

Jason's life returned to normal avenues. He felt renewed and stopped taking the sleep aid after a few days, feeling that it wasn't needed.  His old vigor had come back, and each task assigned at work was completed with abandon.  It was good to get back into the normal groove of things again.

During the haunting episode with the thought, Jason had unfortunately neglected his routine exercise, but now felt compelled to continue the practice. He did so, exerting more effort than normal, and began to feel driven as if there was a greater goal to be attained. This had never happened to him before, and Jason's body responded in a greater measure. It seemed as if there was some force pushing him, and he just couldn't help himself. At the back of his mind a wariness was being aroused; a feeling of caution. Jason began to sense that the thought wasn't finished with him yet.  But so far all was tranquil, and his mind seemed undisturbed.  As the days went by, he just couldn't find true relaxation. Then a day came when the thought returned and tried to regain its influence over him, forcefully probing its way into his mind, exerting pressure, wanting to control him.  Jason wanted to run and hide, but there was no escaping. He was often driven to careless ponderings and began to consider other avenues of release. The sleep deprivation was slowly returning, and the sleep aid had little effect. What few hours he did get weren't enough. Then the nightmares started. He would jerk awake in the middle of the night, terrified by what he had dreamed. He tried to shake off the premonitions of the nightmares. Jason felt as if his sanity was slipping away; he was helpless to hold on. He felt that he was standing on the brink, ready to plunge into an abyss of he knew not what. He was afraid to go to sleep, but exhaustion overpowered him.

It was just turning dusk when Jason found himself in a wooded ridge. He was standing on the edge of a great cliff with his arms spread wide. Far below, the expanse of a valley opened up before him. There was a white farmhouse nestled among some trees, and he could see a winding road off in the distance. It was as though a drama were unfolding. It wasn't a familiar place, and it was very cold. The wind had begun to blow, picking up dry leaves from off the ground, shaping them into an unworldly apparition that began tugging at him, urging him to fly, to jump into the abyss below. Then the face of a frightened woman appeared in the apparition. She was very beautiful. As Jason watched, she disappeared over the edge of the bluff; her tormented screams filled his mind. Then the thought came, looming large on the horizon of his consciousness. Jason felt very desperate and powerless. Swept away by panic, he leaned forward into a descent and pushed off into nothingness, trying his best to rid himself of the thought. The cold, shivering sensation of the free fall overcame him. Rocks and scrub brush clinging to the sides of the cliff went racing by at breakneck speed as Jason tumbled downward. He heard himself cry out as the earth and death reached up to claim him. Jason jerked awake; he was sick in the pit of his stomach and was trembling all over. The misery was upon him again, and it seemed with a vengeance! His mind was racing, causing fear to go careening around inside. The nightmare was so real, so vivid, so terrifying! It was 2:00 in the morning. Luckily for Jason it was Saturday, and there was no work. He had been shaken by the nightmare, and so he lay still listening to his heart pushing blood through the veins at a frightful rate. It took some time to calm down, and when he finally did, Jason drifted off to sleep again. It wasn't a restful sleep, and when the dawn broke bright and clear, the warm rays of the sun were shining through the window, lighting up his familiar bedroom. Slowly emerging from his slumber, Jason lay still, letting the sounds of morning into his weary mind. It had been a rough night and the scene from the frightful nightmare lingered; it was as though it had really happened. He felt extremely exhausted from all of the tossing and turning in his bed. The vestiges of the nightmare and of the vague thought followed him throughout the entire day. He knew that the thought and the nightmare might not be real, but the torment was real enough, and there was little relief from it.

It was the second month of his ordeal, and things weren't getting any better for Jason. Try as he might, he just couldn't shake the tormenting thought. He seemed to be falling apart at the seams. There were times when he would tremble, and he was losing his appetite. His coworkers were becoming alarmed. They took it upon themselves to mention that perhaps he should go back to see the doctor, but this he was unwilling to do. He had no desire to become a slave to pills. The sleep aid had worked for only a short while, and he was afraid that if he went back to the doctor he would prescribe a stronger medication. So, day by long miserable day, Jason struggled with the torment, stubbornly plodding on with his life, such as it was until one day, while making his usual rounds working at the Mayfair Chronicle, doing research for the newspaper articles, he collapsed in a heap on the floor. Fortunately for him, a coworker was nearby and rushed to his aid. An ambulance was called, and Jason was taken to the hospital.

"Where am I?" Jason looked around to see what was going on. He was shocked to see that there was an IV in his arm and a nurse standing by. When the nurse saw that he was awake, she spoke to him in a soothing tone, "Well, Jason, I'm glad to see you have finally come around. How do you feel?"

He replied, "Very sick. What happened?"

"I'm afraid that you passed out at work," she said, "and you will have to rest for a while, if the doctor thinks you are strong enough, you can go home this evening." But he ended up staying three days instead.

Jason didn't like being confined to a hospital bed, but his body had been weary from the lack of sleep and he was malnourished. He was still a little weak when they released him, but at least the hospital stay was over, and he could get on with his life.

The next day he went back to work and thanked everyone for their concern and for watching out for him.

Mister Griswell loudly proclaimed, "Well, look, the ghost is back! How are you holding up Casper?" Jason just smiled, knowing that this seemingly sarcastic remark was only Mr. Griswell's way of saying he had been concerned. It also meant that if you were able to come to work, that maybe you should do just that. Jason did not hesitate, but got his marching orders and proceeded to do what was asked of him. His coworkers questioned him about how he felt and asked if there was anything they could do to help. Jason assured them that he was okay and thanked them for the offer, but said that he would make it just fine.

What he hadn't told them, though, was that the doctor in the hospital had told him that he should go to a psychologist. He seemed to think that Jason's problem was psychological. This had disturbed Jason very much, and he adamantly denied that he was having that kind of a problem. Jason began to doubt the wisdom of confiding in a doctor. He had only wanted to get his problem off his chest and was looking for a sympathetic ear. But the doctor had insisted, and hadn't let up on him, and had even recommended a psychologist. Jason finally gave in saying that he would think about it, but that he wasn't going to make any promises.

For the first week out of the hospital, everything went just fine until he had to do some research on a back article. The longer he researched, the more nervous he became, and he couldn't figure out why.  He began to think that he was having some kind of reaction to the ink on the newspapers, but he had handled them time and again and nothing like this had ever happened. Then the old feeling of dread started to creep into his mind, and suddenly his old nemesis, the thought, was there. He just stood where he was, trying to ignore its presence. But it was a powerful thing, and Jason could feel it tugging at his mind, pulling him into he knew not what. In desperation he fled the research room, trying to escape his tormenter. He went into the bathroom, entered a back stall and moaned, "I really thought I was through with this thing!" Jason was shaking all over, and it was all he could do to keep from running out the door and going home, but he somehow drew on his reserve of courage and calmed down enough to make it through the rest of the day.

Jason was wrung out from all of the work he had done and from struggling with the thought. If there had been any doubt that he needed to see a psychologist, all of the doubt completely vanished. Jason was convinced that he couldn't handle the problem on his own. All he needed to do now was to make the call and set up an appointment. When he got home, he got the card with the doctor's name and number. It read, "Doctor Jillian Freemont, Psychologist." Without any hesitation, Jason dialed the number. A pleasant female voice said, "Doctor Freemont's office, how may I help you." "Yes, this is Jason Brennen," he replied. "I would like to see about getting an appointment with the doctor."

The receptionist gave him the day and time available, and before he knew it, the appointment had been made.

Jason felt a sense of relief. Even the tormenting thought seemed to have let up on him, and he actually got through an entire night without being disturbed.   The next day he went into work feeling refreshed and relaxed. This seemed rather strange to him after having been deprived of sleep for so long. He wondered if it would last. Jason couldn't help but be on his guard as he went about his work while trying not to dwell on his nemesis.

It was toward the end of his shift when Jason remembered that he hadn't finished the research that he had abandoned the day before. If he didn't turn it in, Mister Griswell would, without any doubt, be breathing down his neck, wanting to know why. Jason didn't know if he was more afraid of Mister Griswell, or more afraid of the thought. He knew what had to be done, and so he set his fear aside and went into the research room, taking up where he had left off.

When Jason was doing research on articles from the past, he found one that held a tragedy. The more he studied it, the more he realized that he had read it before. The thought came alive, and it pressed him to continue reading. Jason was alarmed by this and once again tried to reassert control; but it persisted, pressuring him to give in to its demand.  Jason couldn't stand it, so rather than be driven mad he gave in and began to study the article a little farther. When he did this, the thought let up on him and began to soothe his mind, and as he read, it retreated into the recesses of his sub-consciousness from whence it came.

When Jason finished all of the research, he contemplated long and hard about the tragedy in the article he had read. It was vaguely familiar to him, but he couldn't quite put his finger on it. One thing that he was sure of was that he had been moved by the tragic event. It bothered him that he couldn't understand why it troubled him so. Jason tried to put the disturbing article out of his mind long enough to finish his delayed task so that he could turn it in on time.

It was 3:45 when Jason entered Mr. Griswell's office with the finished article. He placed it on the desk and turned to leave.

"Wait just a minute Jason; Sit down!"

He had said this in a rather gruff voice. Jason winced at the tone in his words and expected the worse. He sat and waited for Mr. Griswell to begin. Finally, Mr. Griswell looked at Jason over the top of his glasses and just stared at him for a moment; then he said, "Jason, you might not think that I haven't noticed you struggling to get your work done on time, but I have noticed. Even with all that you have been through, you still try to be diligent in your work, and I want to thank you for your effort. It must be hard on you trying to get a grip on things and still showing up for work. I wish I had more like you. I see that you finished the article I asked for. You made it just in time. Now get out of here and go home before I make you work over!" "Yes sir, Mr. Griswell," he said.

Jason couldn't believe what he had just heard. It wasn't like Mr. Griswell to hand out compliments. Jason thought that he had been hiding his problem, but it was obvious that he hadn't been hiding it very well at all. Jason was just glad that he didn't get a chewing out for being a little late with the article. He felt a little better, knowing that Mr. Griswell had taken notice of his work and hoped that his problem wouldn't continue to interfere.

# Chapter 2

"Doctor Jillian Freemont, Psychologist," the card read. Jason couldn't believe he was going to a shrink! Something had to be done soon though, for the thought was getting the best of him, and he was half afraid to go to sleep for fear that the nightmare would come again.

When the day for his appointment came, Jason drove around awhile before finally turning onto Shady Oak Lane. It was a secluded, tree-lined street in the north part of town. When Jason arrived at Doctor Freemont's office, he found that it wasn't the modern building he thought it would be. Instead, what he saw was a Victorian house nestled among ancient oak trees. The house and grounds were prim and proper, everything in its place. It looked as though an elderly spinster lived there, not a modern Doctor of Psychology. And, in keeping with the surroundings there was a sign or as it used to be called, a shingle that proudly announced: Doctor Jillian Freemont, Psychologist. There was an old-fashioned rocking chair on the porch, so Jason ensconced himself in the rocker, hoping to get his nerve up before going in for the appointment. He still couldn't believe he was going to a shrink. The appointment was for three o'clock. It was ten minutes till so Jason kept his seat, rocking back and forth, killing time, trying to relax his nerves. Aren't people who go to a shrink mental? Jason wouldn't admit that he might be mental, but he did have a problem that wouldn't go away. As a matter of fact, the pesky thought was nudging him again, irritating his mind, setting him on edge. No wonder he was nervous about seeing a psychologist; anything might happen.

Jason nervously glanced at his watch. It was three o'clock. He reluctantly got out of the rocker, opened the door, and stepped inside Doctor Freemont's outer office. It was surprisingly pleasant, not what he had expected. The room's pleasant appearance reflected the theme of the Victorian era but was somehow very modern. The flowered carpet was new and there was a grandfather clock in one corner. The furnishings were new also, and once again reflected the Victorian style. The setting was very pleasing to his senses and Jason's apprehensions began to very slowly melt away. This was not the sterile environment he had thought it would be, but he still couldn't help being just a little nervous.

"You must be Jason," someone said. Jason looked up from his reverie to see a petite, pretty young woman with dark brown hair and an engaging smile sitting behind a desk. He hadn't really noticed her before, being caught up in his ponderings. Jason replied that he had an appointment with Dr. Freemont at 3:00.

"My name is Molly, Doctor Freemont's receptionist; and I have a form for you to fill out. Make yourself comfortable and Doctor Freemont will be with you in a few moments." she told him. It didn't take long to fill out the form and when he returned it to Molly she began drawing him into a little small talk. It was a tactic that was employed to make clients relax and maybe get them to open up. Jason felt at ease with Molly and he couldn't help but notice how cheerful she was. As she talked, she habitually ran her fingers through her hair, as if she couldn't talk without doing so. After the usual comments on the weather and the latest news, Molly said that she would see if Dr. Freemont was ready for him. She got up from her desk, walked quickly across the room, and entered Doctor Freemont's office. A few minutes later Molly announced that he could go in.

14

Jason entered Dr. Freemont's office. When Molly closed the door behind her, it had the sound of finality to it. Jason's apprehensions began to rise within him; he felt awkward and unsure of himself, but there was no need. Doctor Freemont greeted him warmly and invited him to have a seat and relax. Standing before him was a slender woman of medium height. Her long black hair framed her soft features, and her deep blue eyes seemed to be assessing him. Jason saw right away that Doctor Freemont wasn't the Victorian personage he had imagined, and he could feel her self- confidence.

"Now then" she asked, "Jason, what can I do for you today? What seems to be the problem?"

At first Jason was a little reluctant to unburden himself to a complete stranger, but the more he conversed with the Doctor, the more the words flowed. From time to time Doctor Freemont would ask a question or two and make notations in her book, and then tell Jason to proceed. At one point she asked Jason about his personal life: What kind of work he did, how often he went out, and what his friends were like. Was he dating anyone? Jason didn't see what the questions had to do with his problem, but then she was the doctor, and so he answered them as best he could.

Doctor Freemont, looking at the subject before her, saw a very disturbed person. Jason was not disturbed mentally, but was in mental torment. In her notes she had written, "Subject is not really having a full psychotic breakdown, but is very close to the edge, and something must be done about it." The thought and the nightmare he had related to her was alarming. It was as though Jason believed that the nightmare was an event about to happen. Another notation read, "Jason would bear watching." Doctor Freemont advised him to write down the nightmare as he remembered it and try to recall any recent events that might be connected. She also questioned Jason about the recurring thought and what he believed its role might be in all of this, but Jason confessed that he didn't know for sure.

After the long session with Doctor Freemont, Jason felt relieved. It had been good to finally be able to unburden himself. It was as if a heavy load had been lifted. The Doctor wanted to see him again in one week to see how he was getting along, to discuss any possible reason for the cause behind the nightmare, and to see if they could work out a solution to his problem. Jason left Doctor Freemont's office lighter in step and with a confidence he hadn't felt in quite a while. Now maybe things will start getting back to normal, he thought.

Jason spent quite some time in trying to recall the details of the nightmare, and when he did, it all seemed so real. But the ridge and the bluff didn't seem familiar to him, and he began to wonder if there was such a place. If there were, and it could be found, it might help to open the meaning of the nightmare. In his spare time Jason began to systematically search for the bluff. At first he studied topographical maps of the surrounding area, but to no avail. The maps didn't give all that much detail about location, so he decided to expand his search by driving into the mountainous regions not far from town. There was a place or two that looked promising, but when he examined them, the feel just wasn't right. Jason was getting a little discouraged; he had spent a good deal of time searching, and it seemed to no avail. He was about to give up on the idea, but decided to give it one more try. His appointment with Doctor Freemont was the next day and he wanted to prove, once and for all, that either the nightmare was indeed just a nightmare, or that something plausible was going on.

After work Jason drove his car onto a dirt road that led out of town and into the hills. He had only gone a mile or two when the thought suddenly returned to his mind. The feeling of somehow knowing began to rise within, and his pulse quickened. Jason could see an old farmhouse nestled among some trees that sat off the road a few yards. On the mailbox was the name Rallings. It evidently had been there a very long time, for it was a bit rusty and showed much use. Jason pulled into the driveway and was immediately met by an old hound that began baying in a deep, course voice, challenging any who dared to trespass! The farmhouse looked as warn as the mailbox and was in need of a coat of paint. Scattered about the yard were parts of old tractors and farming implements. Jason had made up his mind to pull out of the driveway and try somewhere else, but the thought suddenly got stronger, and so he sat there a moment or two longer to see if anyone was home. As he waited, the old hound nosed its way back to the house. The front door opened, and a wizened old man with white hair, wearing faded blue jeans and a red and black checkered shirt with suspenders, stepped out on the porch. He was leaning on a cane for support. His demeanor seemed friendly enough, for he was telling the hound to quiet down and to go back to sleep. The old man then motioned for Jason to come on in. Jason cautiously got out of the car and made his way to the house. The old hound once again took up his hoarse barking, and then began sniffing the air and, with a snort of unconcern, returned to its resting place.

The old man waiting on the porch said, "Come on in, I don't get much company now days. By the way, I'm Jeb Rawlings. What is your name?"

"Jason Brennen," he said. "I'm pleased to meet you. What is the dog's name?"

17

"That old hound is Rouser. He isn't much use hunting wise, but he makes for good company. Do you drink coffee? I've got a pot on. I keep it going most all day. There is nothing more comforting than a good hot cup of coffee, especially when fall weather sets in. My old bones can't take the cold like they used to."

Jason was beginning to like this old man. His demeanor was disarming and down to earth.

The interior of the house was much different from the outside of the house. The wall paper looked original but the house was clean and neat. The furnishings were simple, but ample for someone living alone. Soon the pair entered into a discourse on the weather and other familiar topics. Jason began easing the conversation around to the real purpose of his visit, finally finding a spot to breach the subject.

"Mr. Rawlings," he said, but Jason was brought up short by Mr. Rawlings' curt reply.

"Let's get something clear," he said. "You don't have to call me Mr. Rawlings. I'm not use to it. Everyone around here calls me Jeb. That's my name. You call me Jeb, and we'll get along just fine."

Jason had to smile to himself at this old man's friendliness; his trusting manner made Jason feel right at home. He could see it would be no trouble at all to get the information he wanted. Jason began by asking what the terrain was like in the area and that he was looking for a cliff or steep bluff that overlooked a valley that had a white farm house in it. Jeb didn't answer right away, but poured another cup of hot coffee and paused between each sip as though pondering Jason's question. Setting his cup down, Jeb looked at Jason and replied.

"Yes there is such a place as that not far from here. It's a dangerous place though, not safe at all. How did you come to know about it?" he asked.

Jason didn't want to go into a long discourse about the nightmare, so he said he had been asking around about unusual landscapes to take pictures of, and someone had told him of the one up here and that he would like to take a picture of it. He hadn't really heard about it, but he had been driving around searching and had just happened upon this place. And as for taking pictures, Jason had indeed brought his camera along in case he did find what he was looking for. Jeb began to relate stories of the bluff and how more than one person had come to his death by falling over the edge.

He said, "Folks still go to see the view of the valley and the surrounding hills, but it isn't really all that well known. It is an out of the way place, about a half a mile off the road. Most folks don't want to hike through the brush and trees to get there." The description of the area stirred Jason's curiosity; it sounded just like the cliff and valley in his nightmare. When Jason asked how far away it was, Jeb replied that it was only about three- quarters of a mile.

"There is an old logging road on the left with a rock fence that is partially torn down. Just stay on the logging road and you will come to a ridge top. The cliff faces southwest. You will have to go slow because it gets over grown in there, and if you aren't careful, you might walk off the bluff! The wind constantly blows, and that's another reason to be careful. As I said before, it can be a dangerous place!"

Jason asked if he could park his car in the yard if he went to take a picture of the cliff and the valley, for he might make a day of it. Jeb replied that he didn't mind as long as he took his advice and looked after himself. He then said that there was a place to park his car up there if he didn't mind driving down the old logging road. Jason thanked him for all the information and for the coffee and got up to leave. Jeb followed Jason onto the porch, said his goodbyes, lingered there a moment or two and then watched as Jason drove away. He reached down and scratched old Rouser's ears, and said out loud, "Rouser, something ain't just right about this."

Instead of going up to the top and looking for the bluff, Jason decided to explore a county road he had passed at the bottom of the hill that looked like it might go past the bluff, or at least close to it. Jason turned onto the dirt road and followed its winding course down and around into a valley that gradually opened up into an ever widening vista. The road continued its winding course around the hills until it finally flattened out onto a broad expanse of a fertile plane. Much to Jason's delight he saw an old white farm house up ahead and farther beyond was the cliff face jutting out from the mountain side. It couldn't be more than a mile or so, he thought. Jason went a little farther until he came to a driveway with a mail box that had writing on it: C. R. MacAfee. Jason sat in the car pondering whether or not he should drive up to the house. It was getting a little late in the afternoon, and he really didn't want to get caught in the hills after dark. Then the thought suddenly entered his mind and began spurring him on to explore a bit farther. Jason tried to push it out of his mind, but it quickly pounced on him for his reluctance to investigate farther, but Jason stubbornly refused to give in. He sat for a few moments longer looking at the bluff, and then turned the car around and headed back to town.

Jason's return home from his wandering adventure had been somewhat productive, and the results played upon his mind. The steep cliff and the white house in the valley had gotten his attention, and that was all he could think about.

Before he went to bed that evening he tried the sleep aid once more. He took two tablets this time, rationalizing that he would sleep sounder. It did help, and he soon slipped into a fitful slumber.

It is said that when you dream your body is at full rest. And when dreams do come to you, they are, in reality, quite unexpected. No one is really prepared for a dream. But the thought was prepared!

The moon was casting its silver glowing light upon the ground, and long dark shadows of the leafless trees stood out in stark contrast against the backdrop of the ridge. Jason was standing in the midst of these trees, staring up at the bright moon above. An indefatigable wind was swirling the leaves around and around until the apparition of the former nightmare formed. Jason, startled by its sudden appearance, began backing away from this specter, but to no avail. He soon found himself at the bluff edge, teetering on the brink of destruction! Far below he could see the white farm house nestled in the valley, and then the thought was with him in the forefront of his mind. It seemed to be whispering to him, as though trying to make him understand. The spectral apparition was floating before his very eyes. It seemed to be the embodiment of the thought, forming into the likeness of a person. Jason felt a cold tingling sensation enveloping his body. He began to quake from the fear more than from the cold. He tried to move away, to run and hide, but he was transfixed, unable to flee. Jason had no choice but to give in, to fasten his eyes upon the scene unfolding before him. The face of the apparition, that was transparent at first, slowly materialized as the face of the woman from before. She was a beautiful young woman with flaxen hair and fair skin. Jason was awestruck at what was transpiring. As he watched, her beautiful countenance took on a look of shock and disbelief.

The image began moving to the edge of the precipice, as though it would throw itself into the abyss below. Jason heard himself cry out in horror.

"No! Don't!" He tried to reach the image in an attempt to save her, but he could not. He watched as the beautiful apparition tumbled over the edge and was gone. The screams of her agony filled his mind and then faded away into nothingness! Jason slowly awoke to the sounds of his own groaning. Fear was fresh in his mind, and the images of the night were still strong upon him. Jason was perspiring and trembling all over, and he was exhausted from the struggle with the nightmare. It seemed the thought had won the battle to take over his mind. He was tumbling over the brink of the precipice, and into the void of insanity.

When Jason went about his assignments at work the next day, he acted as if all were well. He smiled at everyone in pretense, going about as best he could, trying to keep up appearances. Fortunately it was Thursday and he had another appointment with Doctor Freemont at five o'clock. Jason was very doubtful of the outcome, because so far he couldn't see where she had helped him all that much.

At five o'clock Jason pulled into Doctor Freemont's parking lot and reluctantly got out of the car. He took time to look around him. He breathed deeply, taking in the fresh air, observing the pattern of the fallen leaves that were strewn upon the ground. They seemed to reflect the confused patterns of his emotions. He felt drained, and was becoming weary of mind and body. He knew that a confrontation was at hand, a battle for his sanity!

Jason sauntered into Doctor Freemont's office. There was Molly with the same cheerful smile on her face and the same warm greeting.

"Hello, Jason," she said," It's good to see you again. Have a seat and I'll see if the Doctor is ready for you."

Molly, who was well versed on human behavior, could tell that Jason was having an emotional struggle with himself and advised Doctor Freemont of the situation. After a few moments Molly emerged from the consulting room and said that he could go in. Jason slowly arose from his seat and entered the consulting room, took the seat beside Doctor Freemont, and just stared at the floor in defeat.

Doctor Freemont, using as soothing a tone as possible, said, "Would you like to tell me about your problem, Jason?"

Jason, who by this time was ready to blame anyone or anything for his misery, began to wring his hands, and said, "What is the use? Why bother? Let's face it, I'm going out of my mind! I can't shake this thing. What have you done to help me," he asked. "All we seem do is talk, talk, talk, talk, and I'm no better. In fact, I feel much worse!" Jason said with sarcasm.

Doctor Freemont, upon hearing this tirade from Jason, just sat quietly and continued to write in her notepad. She didn't let Jason's outburst bother her. After a few minutes of pondering, and when Jason had settled into silence, Doctor Freemont began asking him about the last few days' events. "Had the thought returned? Had there been any other nightmares? Were there any other things she should know about?" Jason was surprised that Doctor Freemont would be willing to continue the session after his outburst of frustration, but she seemed calm and serene as ever. He was here, and had paid his money, so he might as well make the most of it. If the Doctor is willing to continue, he thought to himself, so am I. Jason apologized for his act of frustration; now he was more than ready to answer any questions. It was embarrassing to have had an emotional breakdown, all his pent up emotions had to be released somehow; Jason just couldn't hold them back anymore.

Doctor Freemont addressed Jason with a statement rather than the question he expected. She said, "The mind is a deep well and at times hard to fathom. Jason, I feel that there is more to your episodes with this thought than you realize. There are times when our subconscious minds pick up on things going on around us. And sometimes those troubling things aren't very easily explained. We must listen to our inner voice and try to understand what is being said. When we have a dream or nightmare, many times it reflects things that we have experienced throughout our lives. With this in mind, I would like for you to tell me the latest nightmare you have had and give me your own thoughts on it. If we compare notes, it is just possible that we can analyze the dream, and come up with a real solution."

Jason felt more confident than when he first entered the office; it seemed as if things were about to change. He started off by saying that he had found the place of the bluff and the white farm house in the nightmare. It wasn't all that far from town, but that he couldn't remember ever being there. Jason said that when he hadn't gone to see the bluff right then, the thought pounced on him for not going. It was as if it were alive. When he went to sleep that night, he had another nightmare, and the woman was in it and fell to her death! Jason began to relay all of the details from the nightmare that he could recall, trying to make sure none of the important points were left out. At this juncture of the interview, Doctor Freemont could tell that he was speaking the truth, as he knew it, and that with some care and encouragement, Jason would overcome his mind's afflictions. This newest nightmare now included a more precise description of the woman. As Jason related certain details of the nightmare to her, Doctor Freemont began formulating an idea that might possibly bring about the answers Jason was seeking. The woman was perhaps a person he had met, or maybe he saw her photograph and his subconscious mind was bringing the memory to the forefront. Jason, without realizing it, may feel the need to protect her from some kind of harm. Doctor Freemont continued encouraging Jason to speak freely and said not to hold anything back. It could be that the dream was only a vehicle the mind was using to eventually bring about the truth. The image in Jason's nightmare could possibly be a real person. "There is more to his dreams than he realizes," she wrote. Doctor Freemont admonished Jason to call her, especially if he happened to see anyone who resembled the woman in his nightmare. Jason was a little doubtful of her request but said that he would do as she asked. When the session with Doctor Freemont had ended, he stood outside her office looking up at the tangled tree limbs. Although this last session had been intense and seemed productive, he couldn't get away from the fact that all was not well. His mind felt as tangled as the tree limbs, and it was as if a cloud of darkness were closing in. There was no escape. The thought still lingered, waiting for another opportunity to renew its efforts to pursue him. Jason could feel its presence haunting him, challenging him, and he didn't know why. Then a line from a verse came to mind. The complexities of our sojourn are but a mystery, the answers hidden from our eyes. Jason, puzzled about the outcome of the troubling events, wanted nothing more than to return to a normal life, to get away from the torment in his mind. Things might never return to normal, and he would have to continue to walk forward into the unknown, but his visit with Doctor Freemont had helped him to face the challenge before him. Everything was still an emotionally tangled web, but at least he had been able to discuss it with someone instead of keeping it bottled up inside. When he laid his head on the pillow that night, sleep came a little easier.

It was Saturday morning, and the day dawned bright and clear. Jason had slept through the entire night without any interruptions and felt rested and at ease in mind and body. There was a feel of freedom about the day, and Jason could sense a coming change, a change that he could almost touch. The apprehension of the day before had vanished. It felt very good to be able to get out of bed refreshed and relaxed. The dread had disappeared, replaced by anxiousness for him to get going, to start searching, but, searching for he knew not what. There was one thing Jason understood though, and that was that today things would be different. Something had changed. Somehow he knew the thought was going to guide him through the misery that had become his life. It was a bit too early to go exploring, so he went about the morning preparing for the events ahead. He waited until eight thirty before deciding it was time to depart, and the first thing he did was to go to a restaurant for breakfast. He hadn't wanted any company in quite a while and had avoided contact with people as much as possible because of the very strange situation he was in. Now, everything was beginning to seem normal, and he relished company. He hadn't felt this way in a long time. It was very refreshing; he felt human again. After having sat in the restaurant enjoying his repast and joining in on the bantering conversations with those around him, Jason exited the restaurant and pointed the car towards the hills outside of town. Everything looked fresh and clean. The cool fall air was invigorating the day inviting. There was no telling what was in store or what event would unfold before the day's end.

As Jason headed out of town, he already knew where he would go first. It was to the old farm house in the valley. The first time he had gone there, the thought had tormented him for not going farther, but it was not that way now. Instead, he felt it as an encouraging presence urging him on. As he drove up into the hills, Jason began observing the landscape and the beautiful color of the leaves that were scattered around. The trees, for the most part, had lost their foliage and stood out dark and somber against the blue sky, but to Jason, it was a lovely scene. He hadn't looked at the world in this light since the episode with the thought had begun; Jason finally felt confident that there was a new beginning ahead of him.

Turning onto the country road leading to the old farm house, he pondered upon what might lay in store for him. Perhaps this was really just one long nightmare, and he would soon awaken to find that all had been imagined. But the car seemed real and the clouds in the sky looked real, and it was obvious to him that the clouds of dust swirling around the car were real also. Jason pushed any negative thoughts out of his mind and let himself become engrossed in the beauty of nature as he rode along.

It wasn't long before Jason saw the mailbox with C.R. MacAfee written on it. He didn't hesitate about going up the driveway this time but drove straight to the house, parked his car in the driveway, and got out. He walked down the stone sidewalk, stepped up onto the porch, and knocked on the door. There was no answer, but there was a note on the door that said, "I'm out back, come on around." As Jason exited the porch and walked around to the back of the house, he began to wonder what kind of a situation he was walking into. It could be anything at all.

When Jason turned around the corner of the house, he couldn't find anyone; he thought that whoever had left the note must be gone and had forgotten to take it off the door. But upon closer examination, he saw that someone was sitting in a chair a good distance from the house. Whoever it was seemed to be taking in the view of the bluff face. Jason couldn't help but stand transfixed as he looked upon the thing that had been foremost in his mind. The subdued thought suddenly began to make itself known again. Its sudden urging to do something returned. He was very reluctant to suddenly walk upon someone unannounced. So, Jason made himself known by saying hello, and hoped he didn't frighten whoever it was sitting in the chair. The individual got up and turned to see who had spoken, then started walking towards him. Jason immediately recognized who the person was. It was the beautiful woman in his nightmare. He couldn't believe his eyes. The winsome individual whom he had seen fall off the bluff was now standing before him! At first he was taken aback and wasn't sure how to proceed. Then, Jason began to remember exactly what Doctor Freemont had admonished him to do if he happened on a woman that looked like the one in his nightmare. But he was at a loss as how to proceed. Then the thought took control of the situation. Jason didn't feel any apprehension, just gentleness, urging him to say something. Jason introduced himself and said that he had been looking for this particular landscape and wanted to know if he could take a few pictures.

The young woman said, "I don't see why not." She then introduced herself as Sarah MacAfee and told Jason to take all the pictures he wanted to. Sarah MacAfee's pleasant friendliness encouraged him, and any uneasiness completely melted away. After a few short moments of pleasantries,

Jason and Sarah walked over to her painting easel. It was obvious that she was a fine artist, for she had painted a picture of the bluff face and the surrounding foreground of the valley, capturing the very essence of the fall season. Sarah asked him if he would mind walking closer to the bluff to take a few pictures. He gladly complied and made his way over to it, stopping at various vantage points, snapping a few frames. Jason finally walked up to the bottom of the bluff and took a picture looking straight up. It was a frightening experience to be standing at the bottom of such a mammoth structure, especially since it was playing such a large part in his life. He had forgotten about the thought until now, when it suddenly made itself known. Jason began to feel apprehensive about being there, and he wasn't quite sure what to do about it. And then something terrifying suddenly happened. A large boulder tumbled down from above! Jason barely had time to jump aside before it crashed to the ground just a few feet away. If it hadn't been for the thought's warning, he might have been killed! Sarah came running over to see if he was alright. Jason assured her that he was just fine but that it had scared him. He took one last picture and then moved to a safer vantage point. Jason and Sarah stood looking at the bluff discussing the near mishap, and after a few anxious moments, they went back to the easel to see what Sarah had captured there. She had started painting the figure of a man that was standing before the bluff, steadfastly gazing upward, peering into its craggy ridges. Jason pondered upon the lone figure and wondered what the final outcome of his adventure might be. The struggle with the thought had been very trying, and his mind was still a bit confused. There were times when Jason felt like he was walking around in a fog. But deep down inside he knew that the end was near, or at least it seemed to be.

Jason, trying to keep the conversation going, asked Sarah if she lived in the old farm house. As it turned out, she did stay there from time to time but it was mostly used to store her art work. About once or twice a year, Sarah said that she had an art show and invited other artists to display their work also. She said that the farm was the perfect place to study her craft because it was close to town, and yet secluded enough that she could concentrate on her paintings without distractions. Jason commented on the rugged terrain, and the beauty of the landscape, and wanted to know if he could do a little exploring, and perhaps go to the top to see what the view was like from there. Sarah MacAfee hesitated before answering, but agreed that it would be okay for Jason to do some exploring but that he should be careful, for it could be a dangerous place.

After discussing the merits of the landscape, Sarah, who had been studying Jason, could tell that he was a person that could be trusted; his pleasant demeanor revealed his personality. Sarah then asked Jason if he would like a tea break and perhaps to take a look at some of her paintings. Jason said that he didn't want to impose, but Sarah said that she had been painting for a while, and could use a break, and so they went into the house.

The interior of the old farm house was cozy and inviting. There was a hearth in one corner of the living room with the accouterments for making a fire. The furnishings were rustic, and Jason couldn't resist the temptation to make himself at home, so he sat down in an old rocker and began to relax. He could hear Sarah out in the kitchen as she prepared the tea, and he relished the moment, listening to her preparations.

After a few moments Sarah brought a tray of tea and cookies.

"I see you have found a place to sit," she commented. "That particular rocker was my granddad's favorite. He spent many hours in it. I don't get all that much company; and it's good to see someone besides me sitting in his rocker for a change. You know, I really miss my grandparents. Sometimes when I stay here, I half expect them to come walking out of another room. There are times when I think I can hear them puttering around in the house and even imagine them carrying on a conversation. This old house creaks and moans, and it gets a little spooky sometimes, especially when the wind is blowing hard. If I didn't know better, I'd say it was haunted. But if it is, it's a good haunting."

Jason, upon hearing this, began thinking about his own haunting. Sarah's situation was similar to his. It seemed they had something in common. He almost told her of his own experience but decided that she might not understand. Instead he said, "Sarah, do you happen to have a picture of your grandparents? I would like to see what they looked like and perhaps get a feel for them."

Sarah retrieved a picture from the mantel and gave it to Jason. It was easy to see from their picture that they were simple folk. Their dress was a little homespun and was worn with simplicity. Jason could tell where Sarah got her good looks. Her grandmother had evidently been a beautiful woman, but she was still lovely when the picture had been taken. Sarah's grandfather looked like a very rugged, strong individual, and yet you could see the mischievousness on his countenance, and there was a twinkle in his eye.

Sarah, "I can tell that you favor your grandmother; and your grandfather seems to be a strong personality. It's no wonder you feel them here. I wish I could have known them. I lost my grandparents when I was very young. I don't remember them at all, and I lost my parents when I was a teenager. I don't really have any family connections."

"Well Jason," she said, "I'm sorry for your loss. You are welcome to come out and explore the property any time you wish. Maybe it will help give you a needed connection and hopefully will help fill in the gaps of the missing memories."

Jason was glad for Sarah's very generous offer and thanked her profusely. Then the thought moved into his subconscious mind. It was an encouraging presence, as though it was well pleased with the day's events. Jason, emboldened by this feeling, asked if he could see some of her paintings. Sarah was glad to comply and ushered him into her studio.

Sarah had converted one of the former bedrooms into a useful studio/gallery. There were several nice pictures of landscapes, all done realistically. Jason noticed there were paintings of the bluff, done in different nuances. Some were very dark and foreboding. Others were done in grey shadow. It seemed Sarah had an obsession with it. Or perhaps it was only a convenient object to be put on canvas. There was another painting of the bluff that captured its true essence. It was done in full daylight, with the rays of the sun causing the structure to gleam. The trees along its edge were in full leaf and they seemed real. It was a breathtaking picture, one that shouldn't be hidden away in an old farm house. Jason related his thoughts on the portrait to Sarah and asked why she didn't sell her work. She replied that there wasn't much call for paintings out here in the sticks. But when she opened the gallery in the spring, she would send out invitations. Then her art work would be sold.

"Sarah," he said. "I noticed that you paint the bluff a lot. Is it significant to you?"

"Yes Jason, it is. It has been a part of my life and has great meaning for me. I remember playing out here on this farm when I was a little girl. Even then I would do sketches of it. I was fascinated with it. The bluff has dominated everything around it."

"Do you ever go up there?" Jason asked. "No," she replied in a half whisper.

"I haven't been up there in years." Sarah's voice trailed off, and Jason detected a touch of apprehension in her. He started to question her a little farther, but Sarah quickly changed the subject. "I have more artwork in another room if you would like to see."

Jason didn't want to probe into Sarah's fascination with the bluff, even though the thought pushed him to do so. He shoved it to the back of his mind and replied that he would like very much to see more art work.

Jason followed Sarah into the next room and was not at all surprised to see other paintings of the bluff; some of them were unfinished. It was as though Sarah was searching for answers through paintings. He wondered what the answer might be. Jason didn't try to bring the subject up, not wanting to intrude into Sarah's private life even though he would like to know more. Instead he just took time to admire her work. There were pictures of other landscapes too. They were very good, and appealed to the eye. Sarah was a true artist. But there was something that he just didn't understand. Jason was now beginning to think that the paintings of the bluff weren't the only dark study tucked away in the old farm house. There was something very mysterious and compelling about Sarah MacAfee.

Sarah and Jason continued their conversation for a while longer, discussing the merits of her work, enjoying each other's company. Jason felt at ease around her but also just a little bit apprehensive. The thought on the other hand reemerged, tormenting him to delve just a little deeper into Sarah's past, but he didn't want to ruin any chance to get to know her better.

Jason decided he had better take his leave before he gave in to the thought's persistent nagging, and said, "I had better be going. I really don't want to wear out my welcome."

"Jason," she replied, "Come back any time you want to. If I'm not here, you can go exploring. Bring a lunch and spend some time looking around." After a few more moments of conversation, they said their goodbyes, and Jason got in the car and headed back to town.

Jason felt elated at the idea of visiting with Sarah again; he had met someone that would be worth getting to know better, but it was difficult to keep things straight in his mind. Sometimes he felt like running and screaming, anything to get rid of the thought. One time it would be a soothing presence, and the next time a torment. His patience was wearing thin, and he didn't know how much longer the charade could go on. Jason knew that things would have to come to a head sooner or later. The thought was forcing him to the edge of insanity; and any moment he might fall into its dark abyss. Jason could hardly wait to get back to town and call Doctor Freemont.

As Sarah watched Jason Brennen drive away, she began to wonder what had really brought him out to the farm. Maybe I'm blowing things out of proportion, she thought. And it's only a chance meeting. Jason's few innocent sounding questions were probably just what they sounded like, innocent. But in Sarah's curious mind they were enough to awaken an unwanted memory, or at least she thought it was a memory. Something seemed to be hidden behind a shroud. Sarah walked behind the house and once again began working on the painting of the bluff. She didn't really want to pursue this particular subject, but adding Jason to the painting gave it a new dimension. Sarah visualized him looking up at the bluff, his eyes fixed upon it, wondering, pondering. Pondering upon what? Was it just a coincidence that Jason had asked those questions? As Sarah worked, she tried to put as many of her pent up feelings into the rendition of the bluff as possible. The vague memory still lingered in her mind, but she continued painting anyway for it seemed linked to the bluff in some way. Her efforts were not unrewarded for as she became lost in her work, the expressions of her true feelings became apparent on canvas. The chance meeting with Jason had awakened deep emotions. It caused Sarah to create one of her best artistic efforts. The shroud of the past was slowly being lifted and it frightened her, but there was no turning back from the inevitable. It seemed that another piece of the puzzle had fallen into place. "But how many times must I paint the bluff," she thought." I'll be glad when the puzzle is complete. Then maybe the mystery of the vague memory will be revealed." Sarah MacAfee had suffered much, and there were times when she wanted to give up her pursuit of the baffling dilemma. But there could be no stopping, and she knew it. Sarah worked on the painting until the light became too dim to continue, then gathered her things together and headed back to the farm house; all the while pondering upon the day's happenings.

# Chapter 3

"Doctor Freemont's office, how may I help you?"

On the other end of the line, Jason said, "I must see Doctor Freemont right away. This is Jason Brennen, and I have found the woman of my dreams!" Jason had said this with enthusiasm.

Molly was a little taken aback by this bold statement, and she just couldn't help but laugh and teasingly said, "Well, Jason, I'm glad that you have found her, but I don't think that Doctor Freemont can help you with that. It sounds to me like you are doing alright on your own."

Jason had to stop a minute and think about what he had just said. He could hear Molly giggling, and so he started again.

"No, wait, you don't understand. In my last session with Doctor Freemont, she said that if I happened to come across someone who looked like the woman in my nightmare, that I was to let her know. Well, I found her, and it really was the woman in the dream, I need to know just what I am supposed to do next."

Doctor Freemont, who had just come out of her office, heard Molly laughing and wondered what was going on. She stood in front of Molly's desk and waited. Molly looked up to see her standing there, raised her hand, and mouthed, "it is Jason Brennen."

Doctor Freemont said, "I'll take the call in my office," and went to her desk.

Molly said, "Jason, I'll transfer you to Doctor Freemont. I think that she should hear what you have to say."

"This is Doctor Freemont, Jason, how can I help you?"

Jason related his story about meeting Sarah MacAfee and asked what he should do next. Doctor Freemont was very pleased at this turn of events and was a little surprised that things were happening so quickly. She asked about Sarah MacAfee's background, and when Jason told her that she was an artist and that she had a studio in town, Doctor Freemont could see that her job was going to be a bit easier. She could hear the excitement in Jason's voice and also some concern. She reassured him that everything was going to work out alright, and that all he had to do was not to be pushy and not to start asking Sarah MacAfee too many pointed questions but to let everything flow in a natural way. Doctor Freemont told him to come in if he felt the need for a consultation, and she would work him in. Jason replied that he was okay for now, but that it had been a shock to find the woman in his nightmare, and that he was beginning to wonder where it was going to lead. When Jason said this, Doctor Freemont suggested that he go ahead and come in for an appointment if he thought that it would ease his fears. Jason replied that he would like to come in after all, for the thought began prodding him into doing something. He said that he had fought back, trying hard to push it from his mind. But it wouldn't give up and kept pestering him, pushing him until he felt like screaming. He was glad when it was time for the appointment, and when Jason headed out the door the thought suddenly disappeared from his mind as if it had never existed at all. That alone about drove him crazy. One moment he felt sane, the next felt unhinged. He would be glad when the nightmare was finally over.

When Jason went into Doctor Freemont's office, Molly greeted him as she usually did and immediately ushered him into the doctor's office. Doctor Freemont told him to have a seat and to try and relax. But right now relaxing was the farthest thing from Jason's mind. Doctor Freemont was not unaware of this, for she could tell by his features that he wasn't at ease.

She started the session with,

"Jason, look at me." Jason looked her in the eyes and said, "Doctor Freemont, I'm in big trouble! The thought keeps haunting me with images of the bluff, and I can't get them out of my mind. What am I going to do?"

Doctor Freemont knew exactly what Jason needed to do, but convincing him to do it might prove to be a little difficult. Jason would have to follow her instructions to the letter if he wanted to overcome the torment. She told him to listen carefully, and that if he did, it would help him break through. Jason didn't answer her right away, but shook his head in acknowledgement and listened to her instructions.

Doctor Freemont began with, "Jason, I know that you fear for your sanity. But I also know that you must face your own fear. I think that somehow the thought is in reality your subconscious mind looking out for you. My advice would be for you to go up to the bluff and face that which you fear. I think you will find that if you give in to the thought's urgings, everything will work out. Jason wasn't so sure about her instructions, for the fear of the bluff gripped his heart and mind. But by the end of the session he had decided to do whatever it took to get away from the torment. When Doctor Freemont had finished, Jason got in his car, but instead of going home he went out of town and straight to Jeb Rawling's house up on the mountain. He figured that he had better not put off the inevitable, for sooner or later he was going to have to face the bluff.

After having found out just who the woman in Jason's nightmare was, Doctor Freemont began to wonder if there wasn't more to the situation than Jason realized and would like to learn more about Sarah MacAfee in order it see if she really was the woman in Jason's nightmare. It wouldn't be exactly ethical to probe into someone's life that wasn't her patient, but if it helped Jason realize his healing, it might be worth bending the rules just a little. As long as she was discrete and didn't interfere with Sarah MacAfee's personal life. It wouldn't be much different than a police investigation. Doctor Freemont felt that there was much more going on with Sarah MacAfee than what was seen on the surface. She could feel something sinister in the background, and it worried her. So, rather than looking into Sarah MacAfee's background, she thought it prudent to call her friend Brian Ferguson who was a detective. He would know for sure how to proceed. It wasn't that she didn't know the letter of the law concerning situations such as this, but her intuition told her that something was amiss, so she picked up the phone and called him.

"Detective Ferguson, How may I help you?"

"Hello, Detective."  This is Jillian Freemont."

"It's been a while. How are you doing?"

"Oh I'm doing as good as expected. How about yourself?"

"It's good to hear from you."

They exchanged pleasantries for a little while, and then Detective Ferguson said, "Jillian, I'm sure you didn't call me just to say hi. What can I do to help you?"

Doctor Freemont wasn't the least bit surprised that Detective Ferguson knew she wanted something. He was a very good detective and knew his craft. She then related to him everything that had been going on with Jason Brennen. They discussed the ethical aspect of the situation and decided that there didn't seem to be any criminal intent on Jason's part or on the part of Sarah

McAfee. Detective Ferguson said that it did seem a bit odd that things were progressing in such a way and that it wouldn't hurt anything if it were looked into. He had solved crimes on less evidence than that.  He also said that there was a case that had come up that was in her line of work, but for now they were in the dark about it, and if he had the time to spare, he might do some discreet investigation for her. Doctor Freemont thanked him and said she would be glad to help in any way she could and to call her office anytime he needed to.

It was a week or so later that Detective Ferguson called Doctor Freemont.  He thought that there was a possible link between the case he was working on and what they had discussed earlier, and thought that it would be all right for her to do some investigating on her own, but that her research should be as discreet as possible and that he would be in touch.

Doctor Freemont, after having her conversation with Detective Ferguson, wanted to start investigating into Sarah MacAfee's background. It would be worth looking into; but that would have to wait until later, for she had other cases to attend to. Perhaps she could send Molly to do some scouting around, she thought. Molly might get some results. Doctor Freemont set the notes on Sarah MacAfee aside and got ready for the next appointment. She already had a busy day and was pressed for time.  Sarah MacAfee would have to wait until the next day when things weren't quite so hectic. According to her calendar, she only had a patient or two in the afternoon and that should free Molly up to do some investigating for her. Doctor Freemont made a note of this, and then put Jason Brennen's problem out of her mind and tried to relax a little before the next appointment.

# Chapter 4

Jeb Rawlings was sitting on his front porch soaking up the sunshine. The fall weather had really starting setting in. It had turned a little cooler, especially up in the hills. The leaves were very brilliant in color and had begun their descent to earth, being scattered hither and yon by the wind. He was contentedly snoring away when Rouser, who had been napping at his feet, began to emit a low growl. A car was winding its way up the steep grade. The sound of the car's motor had reached Rouser's ears and had awakened him. As the car approached, it began to slow down and then turned into the driveway. Rouser emitted a hoarse bark, and Jeb awoke with a start.

"Hush, Rouser, you toothless old hound. What are you going do, gum someone to death? Lay back down." Rouser growled a few more times and then grew silent.

Jeb peered out from under his bushy eyebrows, trying to see who it was that had come to visit. He wasn't sure who it was at first, but when Jason got out of the car, he knew.

"Come on in, son," he proclaimed. "I'll put on a pot of coffee, and we'll have a yarn." Jeb got out of his rocker and went into the house. Jason sauntered up to the porch and sat down in one of the rockers.

"What brings you out this way?" Jeb asked.

"It is my day off," Jason replied. " I thought that I would come and visit you for a while."

"Well, you picked a good day for it. I'm glad you stopped by." The screen door opened with a screech, and Jeb came out of the house. He had a plate of muffins with him.

"Have one," he said.

The coffee will be done shortly."

Jason leaned back in the rocker and listened to it squeak as he rocked back and forth. A calm sense of contentedness washed over him. He hadn't had a feeling like that in a very long time.

Jeb broke the peaceful silence of the moment with, "What have you been up to, son?" he asked.

"Oh, just working; staying busy. You know how it is. I have to earn a living. But since it was my day off, I thought I would come up here and do a little exploring."

The thought suddenly awakened in Jason's mind and began nudging him. Its presence wasn't menacing, but rather soothing, as if it were rewarding him for saying that he wanted to go exploring. Jason, rather than try and push the thought to the back of his mind as he usually did, said that he would like to go up on top of the bluff and look around for a while

"Well," Jeb commented. "If you go up there, be very careful. That place is quite dangerous. It isn't a place to go fooling around in!"

"Oh, I will," Jason affirmed. "I have no intention of getting too close to the edge."

"Just the same," Jeb insisted, "don't forget yourself. Stay on your guard. You might take a lot longer walk than you intend!" Jeb raised his eyebrows to emphasize the danger of going there.

The aroma of freshly brewed coffee wafted its way out onto the porch; Jeb went inside and poured Jason and himself a cup.

"Here ya go Jason," he said. "This will settle your nerves when you go up to the bluff." Jason began munching on the muffin and sipping his coffee. He was pleased with the way things were turning out. It was a beautiful day and what better time to go exploring? Giving in to the thought had helped, and it seemed to have slipped out of his mind.

As the pair sat and talked, Jeb began reminiscing about old times and started telling his stories of the past. Jason didn't interrupt but remained silent, knowing that it would do Jeb good to tell his stories. "I remember one time," Jeb was saying,

"a fellow went coon hunting up along that bluff. I think his name was Wayfield, Silas Wayfield or something like that. But anyway, his dogs got after a coon and treed it right next to the bluff. They made an awful racket. You could hear 'em carryin' on for miles. Well, Ole Silas couldn't get a clear shot at the coon, so he decided to climb a little way up into the tree. He got his gun and commenced to climbing. But what he didn't know was that the tree had shallow roots, seeing that it was growing on the edge of the bluff." At this juncture of the story, Jeb stopped the story telling and reached for his cup of coffee, took a drink, and continued. "Now then, where was I? Oh, yea, I remember." Well, old Silas got about half way up that tree when all of a sudden it started to lean and commenced to uproot itself. He was in a real fix! There he was a- hangin on for dear life. The tree didn't break loose right away, cause there were one or two roots still attached to the ground that kept it from swinging over the bluff edge. By this time mister coon had had enough. It ran right across Silas Wayfield's back, jumped out of the tree, and hit the ground a- running. Them coon dogs just went crazy. Away they went a- howling and cutting up something fierce, hot on the trail of that coon. About that time the tree began to shake, and Wayfield started inching his way back down the trunk. Every time he moved, the tree dropped a little lower. He finally got to where he could get ahold of a big rock stickin' out from the bluff and climbed onto it. Just in time

43

too, because the roots broke and the tree fell off and went crashing down to the bottom. Let me tell ya, Silas Wayfield was shook up. He never did get that ole coon."

Jason had become engrossed listening to Jeb's tale, but he was suddenly awakened out of his reverie by the thought. It began tugging at his mind again, urging him into action. He tried to ignore it, but it wouldn't let up and became more insistent that he do something. It was no longer a calming presence, but became demanding. Jason repeatedly pushed the thought aside, but it just wouldn't go away; he finally had to give in to its urgings. Then he remembered that Doctor Freemont had said to give in to it. He didn't really want to relinquish control, but the torment in his mind was alarming. So he finally gave in and told Jeb that he had better be going if he was to get a look at the bluff. Jeb again admonished him to be extremely careful.

Jason had become caught up in Jeb's story and could just imagine what it must have been like to be that close to death. It reminded him of his purpose and decided that if he was going up to the bluff, he had better do so before long. He again mentioned this to Jeb who hated to see him go so soon and told him to stop by when he could. Jason stayed a while longer, but finally told Jeb that he had better get going. He thought about leaving his car and walking to the top, but Jeb said that it would be better if he drove.

He stated, "It is only about a quarter of a mile as the crow flies, but a mile if you walk; plus it is very steep. Better take the car. Now when you get up there, you will see a road on the left. Take that road for about four hundred yards or so.

44

The bluff will be on the left. I forget just how far it is, but if you walk through the woods you will walk right up to the edge of the bluff. Now when you get in there, don't go climbing any trees!" Jeb grinned at his own comment and once again told Jason to be careful.

Jason went back to his car and started up the road. The farther he went, the steeper it got. The road had several hairpin turns that were difficult to navigate. He had to slow down to avoid going over an embankment. After getting to the top, he began looking for the road that Jeb had said to take. He finally spotted it on the left, went a little way along it, and parked in a small clearing. He didn't get out of the car right away but sat still trying to convince himself that going to the bluff was the right thing to do. A bit of fear began rising within his mind, and he started to doubt his motive. The thought, on the other hand, had become very persistent again. It was almost suffocating. He fought against it as long as he could but finally gave up the struggle and surrendered.

After Jason got out of the car, he took stock of his surroundings, trying to find the best way to proceed. It was obvious that others had been there before because the grass was trampled, and there were tire tracks in abundance. This was encouraging to see, and he didn't feel quite so alone. As he observed the woods, he noticed a trail that led through the trees. The moment that his feet touched the path, the thought came alive again, urging him onward. Reluctance still lingered fresh in his mind, but Jason eager to expel his fear, went down the path.

At first it looked like he had gone the wrong way because the path was steep and overgrown with weeds, and it was becoming hard to navigate the rough terrain. Soon, though, he came to the top of the incline. He was still in the wooded area, but the undergrowth was not as thick. In fact, someone had cleared some of the brush; it looked as though they had camped there. The flat that he had come upon was a rather large area, wooded with oak, hickory, and pine trees. There was another path that wound around through them in a southerly direction. Jason paused only a few moments to get his breath and then plunged forward onto this new path. After having gone a short way, the trees thinned out, and he found himself looking out over a large expanse. He had walked right up to the edge of the bluff. It made him feel giddy, and he began to panic. Jason didn't stand very long but sat down on a nearby rock and took in the frightening scene.

Far below he saw the old white farmhouse nestled among some trees in the valley, and he could see a road winding along through the distant hills. It was a long way down to the bottom. As he sat there, he noticed that the wind had begun to blow. It picked up the leaves that were strewn round about and began to swirl them all around him, churning them into odd patterns. Suddenly the memories of the nightmare came into his mind again. The thought began agitating him, insisting that he watch. Jason got off the rock and backed away from the bluff edge. Then the wind began forming the leaves into the apparition from his nightmare. He stood transfixed, unable to move from the spot. It was as though he were being held against his will. The memory kept repeating itself over and over in his fearful mind. The thought, though no longer tormenting, was nonetheless insistent that he watch. Jason remembered what Doctor Freemont had said about giving in. He wanted to run and hide from what he was seeing, but instead of running away, he made up his mind to see it through to the climactic end.

In his mind's eye, he saw himself at the edge of the bluff looking down into the valley below. Once again the wind began to blow, picking up the leaves that lay strewn round about the ground and shaping them into the unforgettable apparition from his last nightmare. Then he watched as the spectral form moved toward the bluff, taking on the features of the beautiful young woman, and then move out into the nothingness of space. Jason saw himself leaning out over the bluff edge trying to reach the apparition, but it was too late; he just couldn't reach her in time. He saw her plummeting downward, and he could hear his own voice crying out in fear and disbelief.  Suddenly Jason came out of the dreamlike trance. The screams of the young woman were still fresh in his mind after watching her fatal plunge to death. Jason sat down on the ground too weak to stand. The harrowing experience had shaken him to the core. But now he was more certain of the purpose of the thought and the reason for the nightmares. He was glad that he had listened to Doctor Freemont's explicit instructions and had followed them through, even though it had shaken him to the core.

There was no doubt in Jason's mind that the woman in the nightmare was Sarah MacAfee. He wasn't sure how it all fit together, but somehow there was a tragedy that must be avoided. His purpose was clear to him now. He knew that he must become better acquainted with Sarah MacAfee and try to gain her confidence. Jason didn't know why the thought had chosen him for this purpose. Perhaps it was divine intervention; it was hard to tell. All he knew was that the entire scenario was very much out of the ordinary and that it must be seen through to the end.

Jason got up off the ground and ventured to the bluff edge again. The fear that had once dominated him was no longer there. It had vanished as soon as he had given in. Standing, looking down into the valley, Jason began to admire the raw beauty of the scene laid out before him. It was breathtaking.

The wind began to blow again, coming in sudden gusts. Jason knew that it was a natural phenomenon that occurred and that there was nothing haunting about it at all; it was not to be feared. He lingered about the bluff for some time enjoying the view, and then made his way off the mountain and finally went back to town, confident in his purpose.

## Chapter 5

When Molly went to work the next day, Doctor Freemont had already been in the office and had a fresh pot of coffee made. She poured Molly a cup, brought it over to her desk and offered it to her, asking, "How are you feeling this morning, Molly? Alright, I hope. There is a lot to do today, and I thought you might want a cup of coffee to perk you up before we get started."

Molly had worked for Doctor Freemont for a good while and knew her moods pretty well. Greeting her in this manner the first thing in the morning was quite unusual. Doctor Freemont had always treated her well, but this was a little different. So she said, "Well, Doctor Freemont, you must have something very special for me to do today. How can I assist you?"

Doctor Freemont sat down and explained what she wanted Molly to do, stating that she should take her time and that it didn't matter if it took all day long or even if she had to work over. Molly was given Sarah MacAfee's name and said that she was an artist and "told" that it was pertinent to Jason Brennen's case. Molly was more than happy to comply with Doctor Freemont's wishes. It would get her out from behind the desk for once. After Molly reminded Doctor Freemont of her appointments, she got the local phone book out and searched for local arts and crafts stores. There were three businesses listed. One was in the mall, while the other two were located downtown. She decided to go to the mall first and look there.

Upon arriving at the mall, Molly cruised around until she spotted a sign that read "Arts and Crafts Galore". It was a likely looking place, and she was intrigued with the thought of reconnoitering. She didn't waste any time but went into the store and casually looked around.

The store was stocked with art supplies of all kinds. There were paint brushes, art paper, and various colors of paint, none of which she knew anything about. She took her time walking up and down the aisles as though searching for just the right product to buy. Finally, a gentleman came from behind the counter and asked if he could be of assistance.

"Oh, I'm just searching for a present for a friend of mine," she coyly replied. "Well. Take your time; look all you want," he said. Molly only stayed in the store a few moments longer, then left, disappointed. There had been plenty of art supplies in the store and a few prints, but no real artwork. It wasn't likely that Sarah MacAfee owned Arts and Crafts Galore, and it was doubtful that she even worked there. "Strike one," she said to herself. "Better luck next time." Molly turned her attention to the downtown area to continue her search there.

The back streets of the old downtown were quaint, and they were tree lined. The leaves were very beautiful to look at. Molly had a perfect day for exploring, and she took full advantage of it. Doctor Freemont had said to take her time, and she did. The store fronts of the shops were decorated in order to attract the attention of potential customers, and it was hard for her to resist going into each one. She did venture into a few, but not too many; there was, after all, her duty to perform. Molly wandered up and down the old streets keeping an eye out for art studios when she suddenly came upon a store front that had some paintings displayed in the window. The store was called "The Gallery." As she entered, the doorbell rang. It was a soft gentle tinkling that was very pleasing to the ears. The atmosphere was inviting, and there was soothing music playing in the background.

"This is a classy place," Molly thought to herself. "This is a true art gallery.

Then someone asked, "How may I help you? Are you looking for anything in particular?  We have many high quality paintings or prints to choose from. I would be glad to help you make a choice from our collection."

Molly turned and saw a dark-haired, middle-aged woman approaching her. She was dressed to the hilt. The woman's grey eyes looked Molly up and down as though trying to determine if she were serious about artwork. "This woman belongs in an art gallery," Molly thought. Molly felt a little intimidated in the presence of the person. "A true stuffed shirt, a highbrow, no doubt," she thought to herself. But Molly was surprised when the lady introduced herself.

"Hi, I'm Anna. Look around all you want. Just take your time. If you see anything in particular that you like, I would be more than glad to help you." Anna beamed on Molly as though she was truly pleased to serve her.  She wasn't the stuffed shirt she seemed to be.

 Then Molly replied to Anna, "Well, I have a friend who is having a birthday, she lied.

"Going to have a birthday, sooner or later," she said under her breath. "I'm looking for something really special." Then a thought occurred to her. She asked, "Do you happen to have any paintings by local artists?"

Anna's face lit up.

"As a matter of fact, we do carry some paintings by an exceptional local artist. Her name is Sarah MacAfee. She has her own gallery, and her work is very good. We consider ourselves fortunate to be able to display her work."

"Pay dirt!" Molly mused.

"Would you like to see one of her paintings?" Anna asked. "I think you would be pleased. Of course, it all depends on your friend's taste."

"I would love to see something by her," Molly replied. "I might find what I am looking for."

Anna directed Molly to the center of the gallery where several pictures were prominently displayed.

"This one is done in oil on canvas," Anna began," and is signed and dated by the artist. As you can see, the artwork is exquisite."

The particular painting that Anna was referring to was a forest scene. It was called "The Glens." It was very fetching and made Molly feel as though it were real and made her want to go there. She related this to Anna, who replied that she believed Sarah MacAfee had painted that particular scene in one of the mountains nearby, and that a person could go there if they knew the location. Molly studied the painting a while longer and thought that it would be nice to own it, but she almost choked at the price. The price of "The Glens" was twenty-five hundred dollars, far too rich for her blood. She thanked Anna for showing her the art work and said that she would like to shop around before making a decision.

"Come back anytime," Anna said. "I would be more than happy to help you."

With that, Molly left the gallery and resumed her search for Sarah MacAfee. So far she was very pleased with the results of the search. The only thing she had neglected to do was to ask for directions to Sarah MacAfee's studio.

Molly leisurely made her way, peering into the store front windows as she went, occasionally making a small purchase as she continued looking for Sarah MacAfee's art studio. On a side street Molly spied a sidewalk café; she went inside and ordered a raspberry ice tea and sat down at one of the tables. She sat sipping her refreshing drink, pondering her dilemma. She studied individuals as they entered the café, but there was no way to determine if one of them was an artist. She really needed to get on with her search for Sarah MacAfee, but her feet were getting sore from all of the walking, so she decided to linger for a while longer before resuming the search.  Presently the waitress came to her table and asked if she required anything else. Not wanting to refuse, she asked for a raspberry ice tea to go. Susan brought the refill of tea, and then Molly casually asked if she knew of an art gallery nearby. Susan paused for only a moment and said, "Yes, there is an art gallery nearby. As a matter of fact, the artist comes in here quite often. Her name is Sarah MacAfee, and she is a very good artist. Her studio is only about a block farther up the street; you can't miss it."

Molly felt encouraged by this, so she left a tip, paid for her drink, and once again took up the search.

Sarah MacAfee had just returned from her car and was placing a painting on an easel. She had finally decided to display a painting of the bluff, rationalizing that if the painting sold, she might rid herself of the continuous urge to paint it. It had been a hard decision for her. Sarah knew that doing paintings of the bluff provided a kind of therapy and knew deep down inside that the bluff held a secret, a secret that had hounded her all of her life. It often caused her to grow weary and despondent, and there were times when she wanted to give up on life. The despair would well up inside, and it was all she could do to keep from going to the top of the bluff and throwing herself off the edge. But then the urge to paint one more picture would take control, and so she would force herself to paint it over again.  It always left her wondering why she must do so.

Sarah stood looking at the painting of the bluff and almost took it off the easel to get it out of her sight, but then the doorbell rang. She came out of her reverie and turned to see who had come into the studio.

Sarah quickly pulled herself together and asked, "May I help you?"

Molly could see right away that something was not right with Sarah MacAfee. It was obvious that Sarah MacAfee's mind was in great turmoil. Her eyelids were twitching, and she was wringing her hands. Molly didn't let on, but only stated that she had a friend who was in the market for a painting and that she was helping her to find just the right one.

"Oh, um, well," Sarah managed to say. "Look around all you like, and if you have any questions, I will try to answer them for you."

Molly made a pretense of showing interest in one or two of the paintings until she saw the painting of the bluff. It was a dark and foreboding work. The artistry itself was very fine and detailed in every way, but the rendition of the bluff was frightening. It seemed to pull the observer into the scene. Molly shivered a little and then asked, "Are these your paintings?"

"Yes," Sarah's replied. "I have a studio out in the country where I do most of my work. Sometimes I do portraits, but I do those here in this gallery. Are you interested in something in particular?"

Sarah was beginning to feel a little better now that her mind had been distracted by the conversation with Molly, and she soon settled down and focused on the potential sale.

"Yes, I am," Molly replied. "A friend of mine is searching for a painting of a mountainous scene. I see that you have a picture of a bluff. It might be just what she is looking for, but

I notice that it doesn't have a price. "Is it for sale?" "As a matter of fact," Sarah said, "I just brought this painting into the studio and haven't priced it yet."

"Well," Molly proclaimed, "this could be the very one my friend is looking for. If you will tell me what you have to have for it, I will tell her about it."

Sarah hadn't even had a chance to think about a price for the painting. She wasn't sure what to ask. It had been all she could do to bring it to the studio, let alone set a price for it. "Perhaps," she thought, "If I can sell this one, some of the distress will go with it." Then and there Sarah decided to let it go for a reasonable price, a price that a customer couldn't refuse. The money wasn't all that important to her, but release from the torment was.

Sarah said, "Tell you what I will do. I'm a bit over stocked just now, and I need to move some of my paintings. I would normally ask fifteen hundred dollars for a painting like this, but I am feeling generous today. Tell your friend that if she wants the painting, she can have it for five hundred dollars. I don't usually sell a painting for so little, but, as I said before, I'm overstocked."

Molly acted excited about the great bargain Sarah was offering her. She said that her friend was sure to be pleased and that she would tell her to stop by and look at the painting for herself. Molly thanked Sarah for showing her around and then left the gallery to return to the office. She was sure that Doctor Freemont would be pleased with what she had discovered.

When Molly left the gallery, Sarah had to sit down for a while. The ordeal with the painting was almost too much to endure. It was so personal, like selling a part of her, but Sarah hoped that it would sell. Practically giving it away would be worth it to have some relief of mind. Sarah tried to shake off the feeling of apprehension and the nervousness that had been welling up inside, but it wasn't an easy thing to do. She had to force herself to work on a portrait that needed touching up. But once she started, the bad feelings began fade away. Staying busy always seemed to work for her, and she knew that going forward was a must if she were to overcome her dilemma. Sarah reasoned in her mind that painting the bluff was indeed going forward. The problem was, though, where would it all end?

Doctor Freemont was listening intently to Molly's report on Sarah MacAfee. She knew, of course, that without encountering Sarah MacAfee in the proper setting, there wasn't much she could do. From what Molly had observed of Sarah MacAfee's actions, there seemed to be indications of something gone awry with her. If only she could find a way to get her to come to the office. But at this point Doctor Freemont knew that it wasn't about to happen, at least not by any conventional means. She reasoned that for now, the best thing to do was to go to the art gallery and observe Sarah MacAfee for herself.

It was just about five o'clock when Doctor Freemont pulled up in front of Sarah MacAfee's studio, got out of the car, went up the sidewalk, and stood reading the gallery sign. "Art-Impressions, Resident Artist, Sarah MacAfee." In the window were various paintings. All of them were of excellent work. Doctor Freemont was impressed.

She started to open the door just as Sarah MacAfee was coming out.

"Oh, I'm sorry," she said. "Were you about to close for the day?"

"Well, yes." Sarah said. "As a matter of fact, I was. I close at five, but I can stay open a little longer if you wish."

"That is very gracious of you," Doctor Freemont replied. "I have been searching for a certain type of painting, and my friend told me about your gallery. I would love to see your work. Perhaps there is something I would enjoy."

"Oh, yes, I remember your friend. She said that you might drop by. I'll show you the painting she thought you might like." Sarah directed Doctor Freemont to the painting of the bluff and stood by quietly, waiting for her response.

Upon seeing the very dark rendition of the bluff, Doctor Freemont asked, "Did you paint this yourself, or do you display other artists' work as well?" "Yes," Sarah answered, "I did paint this and all of the others, also."

"My," Doctor Freemont proclaimed. "What a dark study it is. How did you ever capture it in such a way?"

"I hope that you like it," Sarah returned. "Being able to paint it this way has to do with mood setting, and of course, the right lighting. This piece was done at night with a full moon shining through a break in the clouds. The setting was stunning to say the least. I guess it is rather dark and foreboding though, but you would have had to be there to fully enjoy the experience."

Doctor Freemont said, "I love the way you have captured the moonlight reflecting off of the bluff edge, and I like the long dark shadows of the trees. Very impressive! Have you any other renditions of this scene?" Doctor Freemont knew that it was a leading question, but it was the only way she could think of to draw Sarah out, to try and get some kind of reaction from her. She got what she wanted. Doctor Freemont could tell right away that she had hit a nerve. Sarah started wringing her hands and began to fidget with the buttons on her blouse, and she could sense panic beginning to rise in her. Doctor Freemont quickly changed the subject. There was no use in making her suffer any further, so she asked. "How much did you say this painting was?"

"Well, um, let me see," Sarah stammered, trying to gain her self-control. "I think that I had priced it at five hundred dollars. But, well, umm, that is, perhaps I could do better than that if you were really interested in it." Sarah could barely get the words out. Doctor Freemont's unexpected question had thrown her for a loop.

Doctor Freemont exclaimed, "Oh, I love this painting. I do want it. What is the price?" She was trying to bring Sarah back into focus, wanting to draw her away from the great struggle going on in her mind. When Sarah finally got her nerves settled down, she hesitated a moment and explained that there were indeed other renditions of the bluff, and that was why she was selling this one at such a discounted price.

"If you want to buy this one today, I will let you have it for three hundred seventy five dollars," she replied. "This painting would normally sell for fifteen hundred."

Doctor Freemont wasn't about to dicker over the price. This painting had already cost the woman dearly. She said, "Wrap it up. I'll take it."

Sarah took the painting into the back room and neatly wrapped it. A flood of relief flowed over her. The anxiety began to slip away, and she felt overjoyed at the thought of unloading a part of her long carried burden.

Doctor Freemont was sitting in her office, studying the painting. It was indeed a very dark and foreboding scene and was just a little bit disturbing to look at.

"Now, I wonder," she said out loud, as if the sound of her voice would somehow open a door into the mind of Sarah MacAfee. "Why would someone want to paint such a thing?" Other artists have painted scenes just as disturbing, she thought. But she could feel the emotion that seemed to be tied to this particular painting. As she scrutinized the image, a sense of despair seemed to emanate from it. Doctor Freemont didn't like the vibes she was receiving and knew that a deeper research into Sarah MacAfee's past would have to be done if there were to be any satisfying results. She continued her study of the painting a while longer, but without coming up with any real answers, she finally turned away and sat in deep contemplation, trying to understand.

When Jason Brennen had first come to her, she had no idea that things would develop into such a twisted turn of events. It was plain to see that Jason and Sarah had been destined to meet and that somehow their two dilemmas were actually one. It was obvious to her that she was going to need help with this puzzle, and so with her mind made up, Doctor Freemont called Molly into her office.

Molly, had been correcting errors in Doctor Freemont's casebook, and was glad for a diversion from the paperwork. The only thing bad about being called into the office was that it probably meant more typing. She got up from her desk and went to see why she had been summoned. Doctor Freemont was sitting in a chair by one of the windows and appeared to be deep in thought. Even though she had been called for, Molly patiently waited, knowing that the Doctor would speak her mind when she was ready.

Quite a few moments passed before Doctor Freemont finally asked, "Molly, how would you like to do a little more investigating for me? I'm really stumped over this painting by Sarah MacAfee. There is a lot going on here, and I need to know some more about Sarah's background. I want you to see what you can find out about her family. Where are they? Does she have any siblings? Are her parents alive? And where did she go to school? I'll bet that you can come up with something. In the meantime, I'll handle the office. I can take care of the appointments on my own while you dig into Sarah MacAfee's past. I hope you can come up with some useful facts. I'm going to need all the help I can get if this case is going to be brought to a gratifying conclusion."

Molly said that she would be glad for the diversion, but that there were a few things that needed attention first, and that she would start the next day if it was convenient. Doctor Freemont replied that the next day would suffice.

Molly returned to her desk, and Dr. Freemont turned her attention back to the painting of the bluff and once again studied the way in which Sarah MacAfee had captured its essence, trying, if possible, to interpret its hidden meaning. Something was in the painting; she was sure of it. Just looking at the bluff gave her a feeling of dread and a sense of foreboding; it put her nerves on edge, and she began having goose bumps.

Dr. Freemont got up and walked around the room, trying to clear her mind. There was no doubt that the painting was well done. It was very haunting, and she could only study it for short periods at a time. I need a coffee break, she thought. This is almost too much; my eyes are getting strained. After retrieving her coffee and giving her eyes a rest, she returned to the examination of the painting, settling down to the daunting task set before her.

After a tedious hour of searching and with no clear results, she had just about given up but decided to look one more time. So far, the examination hadn't gone very well. The brush strokes were all beginning to run together, and her eyes were out of focus. Then she got up and retrieved a magnifying glass from the desk. "Much better," she said. The brush strokes stood out crisp and clear, raising everything into greater detail. "I should have done this before," she scolded.

Dr. Freemont began paying closer attention to the trees at the top of the bluff. She had gone over them earlier but not with the magnifying glass. This time she went over each area minutely. At first there didn't seem to be anything out of the ordinary, but upon closer examination, something hidden began to stand out.

"It can't be," she exclaimed. "How could Sarah know?" She found the link, the answer to the riddle that had been puzzling her. Reaching for her notepad, Dr. Freemont began writing down her observations in detail. When she had finished all to her satisfaction, she reread her notes, laid them aside, and began to go over it in her mind. Having pondered its contents, she realized that there was still much to do. There were pieces of the puzzle still missing; vital information that was needed to assist in the culmination of the case. Perhaps Molly will be able to provide more insight into Sarah MacAfee's life and enable me to completely solve this baffling mystery, she thought. Doctor Freemont was pleased with what had been discovered, but the case was far from being solved. She couldn't help but be concerned over the final outcome. There was absolutely no telling what might transpire. One thing was certain though. It was clear that Sarah MacAfee was hiding something. Whatever it was must come out into the light of reality, instead of being hidden away in the dark recesses of her mind. Sarah MacAfee seemed in danger of losing her sanity, and Jason had been drawn into the dilemma by the harrowing thought. The longer Doctor Freemont dwelt upon the enigmatic problem, the greater became her desire to untangle the web that had been woven round about Sarah MacAfee and Jason Brennon. She was sure that the painting was the key that would unlock the mystery, but there just wasn't enough information.

Chapter 6


Jason Brennen awoke with a start and bolted out of bed; a look of panic was on his face.

"Now what am I going to do? I'm late for work! Boy, am I going to catch it," he said out loud. Rushing into the bathroom he hurriedly got dressed. No time for breakfast. "That's just great. I'll have to get something from the vending machine. The old man will be beside himself. I can hear him now," Jason thought. Where have you been part time, on vacation? You slug. It's about time you showed up. If I had more employees like you I'd have to shut down. Now, get to work before I fire you. "You slug" Jason shook his head as he thought of what his boss would say. But that was just the old man's way of asking if everything was alright; you had to have a tough hide to work for him. He knew how to push your buttons. Jason was putting his shoes and socks on when a strange sensation suddenly came over him. Something didn't feel right. How late am I? The question lingered in his mind, along with a little bit of doubt. Then it hit him.

"Dummy!" he exclaimed. "I don't work today; it's the weekend." Jason went into the kitchen and put on a pot of coffee. "Oh well," he thought. "It was time I got up anyway."

After his terrifying episode at the bluff, Jason began wondering about Sarah MacAfee. He really wanted to see her again, especially after he had identified her as the woman in his nightmare. Sarah had said he could go exploring anytime he wanted, but he didn't want to push his luck too far, even though he couldn't help but be drawn to her. Jason pondered upon this for a little while, and finally decided to take a chance and go see her, using exploring as an excuse. It was the beginning of a friendship that would turn into love.

At first Sarah would allow Jason to get only so close to her, holding him at arms -length. Jason respected her and kept his distance, not wanting to ruin his chances of getting to know her better. His visits weren't frequent, and he decided to keep it that way until something changed, but he did keep in touch. This cat and mouse game went on for a good while until one day out of the blue Sarah called him up and asked if he would like to have supper with her. Jason was very pleased by this but tried not to act overly anxious. He thanked her and said that he would enjoy it very much. Jason felt like the ice was beginning to break.

As the weeks went by, Jason and Sarah went out quite often. Once in a while Jason went exploring at the old farm house, but he purposely kept things on an even keel; he didn't want to frighten Sarah away. Jason frequently found Sarah at the farm, and soon a bond of friendship formed. It wasn't at all surprising that they began to have deeper feelings for one another. Jason thought of Sarah constantly; he was so glad that they had been brought together. He had lived a rather lonely life and knew little of his parents, for they had died when he was very young. He had been raised by a maiden aunt, and she had passed away only a few years back, leaving a small inheritance that gave him a start in life. What little family he did have was in another state, and they didn't communicate very often. It was just one of those out of sight, out of mind things. They had never been close anyway. He always felt like a stepchild when they were around, so he had learned to live with the loneliness. He had dated some, but no one seemed to fit the bill until he met Sarah MacAfee. Now things were different. The loneliness had subsided, and life was becoming exciting. Sarah had finally accepted him, and they frequently went out together.

One morning, about daybreak, Jason was out and about, puttering around the yard, enjoying the pleasant day.

"What a great morning to go out for breakfast," he said out loud. He didn't think that Sarah would be up and around yet, so he put off calling her until about eight o'clock, then picked up the phone and called.

"Hello," Sarah sounded very cheerful this morning. Jason's prospects were looking up.

"Hello Sarah. I just called to see if you would like to go out for breakfast."

"I'd like to, Jason. But I have to work on a portrait this morning, and it may take a while. Tell you what. How about lunch? I should be just about finished by then."

"Sounds great," Jason replied. "I'll come by the studio around twelve. See ya then; don't work too hard." Jason hung up and thought, "Well, lunch is as good as breakfast. Maybe she won't have any more work to do today, and we can go running around together. What I ought to do is go up on the mountain and check on Jeb. I haven't been out there lately. Sarah needs to get acquainted with him anyway," he rationalized.

Having made his plans for the day, Jason started raking up the fallen leaves that were strewn around. It felt good to be out of doors enjoying the beauty of the day. The weather was cooperating nicely; there wasn't a breeze blowing and the sky was bright and clear. It was a wonderful fall day. Jason began whistling a tune and continued working, killing time until lunch. All was going well; there was finally peace in his life. Sarah had been just what he needed to set things straight. He hadn't returned to Dr. Freemont's office, because it didn't really seem necessary. Since meeting Sarah

MacAfee, all of the nightmares and the bothersome thoughts had completely subsided into nothingness, as though they had never even existed. He was confident that the old trouble was far behind him.

Sarah MacAfee sat at her easel confidently working on a portrait of a dapper elderly gentleman. She had been commissioned to do the picture by his family. It was to be a surprise, so they had brought a photograph of him. Sarah would rather have had a live subject, but the situation wouldn't allow that. It was a challenge to get all of the details from the picture just right, but Sarah liked a challenge. The old gentleman was dressed to the hilt. He wore an old-fashioned suit with tails; a top hat perched on his head at a rakish angle, and held a cane in his hand. His eyebrows were raised and there was a mischievous smile on his face. He looked, as they would say in the old English, like a toff. Sarah continued working away, thoroughly enjoying herself. It was a pleasure to do a portrait like this one. She couldn't help but smile at the near finished picture. There were only a few more details to fill in, and it would be done.

It was almost twelve o'clock when Sarah made her last brush strokes on the portrait. She had been working all morning. Her back was a little sore, and her arms were tired, but the project was complete. A lot of care had been taken to do it right, and a lot of time was involved. The result was very pleasing to the eye. Sarah was sure the customer would like it.

Sarah was glad that the portrait was finished. She put her brushes away, stood back, and observed her work with a critical eye. The detail was perfect. She had captured the essence of the old gentleman, even though she had to work from a picture. It would have been much more enjoyable working with him in person and might have been easier to interpret him in a different light, but that hadn't been possible in this case. She studied the painting a little while longer making sure no detail had been overlooked. A smile creased her face as she nodded her head in satisfaction. The portrait had passed her scrutiny. All that was needed now was a frame, and then it could be hung in a place of honor.

Jason was still puttering around in the yard when his phone rang.

"Hi, Sarah. Did you finish? I thought that it was about time for you to call."

"Yes, I got it done. Jason, I'm sorry for taking so long. I was so caught up in doing the portrait that I forgot the time. Is it too late for lunch?" she asked.

"Of course not," he replied.

"I'll come by the studio and pick you up; see ya in a few minutes." Jason hurriedly put his tools away and went back into the house to freshen up.

It was a little after one o'clock when Jason arrived at Sarah's studio. He walked in to find her signing her name to the finished portrait.

"Wow," he exclaimed. "It really looks just like the photograph. I don't see how you do it. I couldn't draw a stick man."

Sarah blushed, and then replied. "Thank you Jason, I'm glad you like it. Now if only the customer likes it." Jason responded with confidence, "They will like it, Sarah. It is perfect. You are a genius."

Sarah reached out and took Jason by the hand then said, "I thought you were going to take me to lunch. Are we still on?"

Jason laughingly replied, "Of course we are. As a matter of fact, after we have lunch, we are going for a ride. I want you to meet a friend of mine. He lives up in the hills above your farmhouse. I think you will like him. His name is Jeb Rawlings.

He lives by himself and doesn't get much company, so every once in a while I drive up there to check in on him." Sarah said that it would be good to get away from work and do something different, even if it was just going for a visit in the hills. They put a closed sign in the window, locked the door of the studio, and walked down the sidewalk to the café on the corner.

Jeb Rawlings was puttering around the house, doing the few dishes that a man living alone would dirty. He liked to stay busy, not being one to just sit around all day. It could get lonely at times and finding things to do kept his mind preoccupied and his body supple; at least as supple as an eighty- year -old man could be. Getting used to being alone hadn't been easy. It had been difficult to make the transition when his wife Maggie died. He was so used to having her around. She always saw to his needs and had made life so much easier. Maggie was a Godly woman, and lived her life by the good book. He still went to the church and studied the bible, but the loneliness lingered near. He missed her familiar presence. All that he had of her were pictures and memories. There hadn't been any children, so they had contented themselves with family and friends and lived a good life up in the hills. The house they had built together became a home where all were welcome. But now, most of the old friends and family members were gone. Some had died, while others had moved away. His church family checked on him when they could, and that helped. On occasion someone would stop by just to chat. It was always a welcome change that he needed.

Jeb could sometimes sense when he was going to have some company, and this was one of those times. He could feel it in his bones, and so he got out the fixings for muffins and started baking. Maggie had taught him how to make them; when he got out the timeworn recipe, it was just like having her there beside him.

"Well, doll, who do you think will show up today?" he asked out loud. Of course Jeb knew there wasn't going to be an answer, but the memory of doing such a simple thing like baking muffins with Maggie brought her back home. He put on a fresh pot of coffee and put the muffins into the stove and waited.

Jason and Sarah, having finished their lunch together went back to the studio, got in the car, and headed into the hills. It was a perfect day for an outing. The leaves had about all fallen off of the trees, and their bare limbs stood out in dark contrast against the bright blue sky. It was a beautiful scene. Sometimes, Jason would pull off on the side of the road and take a picture of a panoramic view of the trees in the valley below. They continued on in this manner taking their time, enjoying the day until they arrived at Jeb's house. When Sarah saw what looked like old broken down farm equipment in the yard and heard Rouser growling and barking, she became apprehensive about the situation and didn't want to get out of the car, but Jason assured her that the dog was all bark and no bite. With a few last growls and a muffled bark, Rouser turned around, went back to his favorite place on the porch, and laid down again.

It was then that Jeb opened the door to see what the commotion was all about. When he saw Jason getting out of the car, he said, "Come on in, son, and bring your friend with you. That lazy old hound has done his job. You don't have to worry about him, miss; he won't stir from that spot, unless you offer him a pork chop bone. Come on in."

Sarah gingerly got out of the car and walked close beside Jason, being careful to keep him between her and Rouser.

Once inside, she relaxed. The aroma of coffee and muffins was wafting around in the house; it smelled tantalizing.

"Make yourself at home," Jeb said. "Take a seat."

Jason introduced Sarah to Jeb, and he welcomed her with warmth.

"Do you drink coffee?" he asked.

"Yes," Sarah replied. "I'm afraid that I'm hooked on it."

"That's good," Jeb said. "Cause I just baked some muffins to go with it. I had a feeling that someone was coming today. I'll get the cups, and you can help yourself."

Sarah was surprised by the neat and clean appearance of Jeb's house. It was just a natural thing to think that the inside of the house would look as bad as the outside. It pleased her that Jeb kept everything clean and orderly. There didn't seem to be a thing out of place. Jeb ushered Jason and Sarah into the kitchen and served them the coffee and muffins.

Sarah remarked, "Why Jeb, these muffins are delicious. Where did you learn to bake like this?"

Jeb gave her a wry smile and said, "Come on over here, and I will show you."

They followed him over to a small table in the living room where he picked up a photograph of a young couple.

"This is my wife Maggie and me when we were first married. She was a fine woman, a Godly woman. It was from my Maggie that I learned to make the muffins. Many a time we stood at the kitchen counter and made them. But she has been gone a long time now, and so, I keep baking them to keep the memory alive. "Well," he said, "you youngsters didn't come way out here to hear an old man's memories. Let's sit down and drink our coffee, and we'll have a yarn."

Sarah was moved with compassion upon hearing that Jeb had lost his wife and was living all alone. It began stirring deep feelings within. She pushed the feelings aside and tried to concentrate upon the moment; she didn't want to face the reality of the situation. To lose someone you love was such a tragedy. She moved a little closer to Jason and put her arm through his. Jeb's loss had made her feel sad, and it was comforting to have Jason so near.

Jeb could sense the uneasiness in Sarah and began asking her if she was from around the area. In reply, Sarah said, "Yes, I was born and raised here. Did you know any of the MacAfee's?" she asked.

"Why, yes I did," Jeb stated. "As a matter of fact, there used to be some MacAfee's that lived down in the valley just under the bluff. I wasn't all that acquainted with them, but I knew of them."

"That old home place belonged to my grandparents," Sarah answered. "They raised me."

"Well, I'll be," Jeb returned. "It's a small world, ain't it?"

Jason sat listening as Sarah and Jeb carried on their conversation. He would occasionally make a comment, but for the most part he just listened. It was nice to hear Sarah's voice; it was soothing. Jason could feel himself falling deeper in love with her. His hope was that she felt the same. He knew that Sarah was dealing with complex feelings and didn't want to rush her into anything that might push her away. So, for now, he was just trying to be there for her, to help in any way he could.

Jason was awakened out of his reverie by Jeb.

"Son," he asked. "Did I ever tell you of the time that some folks went horseback riding up along the bluff, and like to have fallen off?" Jeb reached for his coffee cup and took a drink, and continued with his yarn. "Well, who in their right mind would ride a horse up there anyway? It's a dangerous place, and horses can do some unexpected things. There are a lot of trails around here that are just right for horseback riding. Folks do it all the time. But once, oh, a good while back, a group of riders went up on top to ride the trails. I don't rightly know all of the details, but you know how it is with stories; the facts can get kinda twisted around. Anyhow, one of our local veterinarians, twas a woman by the way, decided to get a group of riders together and go up there on top and do some trail ridin'. I remember it like it was yesterday. I was a sittin' out there on my porch, when here comes three or four trucks hauling horses. They stirred up quite a commotion of dust as they went by. Well, I didn't think much of it at the time cause, like I said, folks ride the trails around here all the time. As the story goes, they had a good ride for the most part and made a day of it. The problem was that the woman vet and her ridin' partner stayed a mite too long. They kinda got caught up in the fun and forgot the time and had gone farther than they meant to. Before they knew what had happened, it got dark. They had a light with them, but the batteries must have been low, for it didn't last long. Of course they couldn't see where they were going and had to trust to dumb luck and the horse's instinct. They moseyed along in this manner for quite a while, when all of a sudden a very strong gust of wind began picking up leaves that lay strewn upon the ground and swirled them all around their horses. This sudden encounter with the wind and the leaves frightened the horses, and they whirled around and unseated their riders who were then unceremoniously dumped onto the ground. No one was seriously injured, only they were shook up a mite. Well, the two women took stock of themselves and found that they hadn't been injured. Only problem was, those two didn't realize that they had got off on a trail that went right up to the edge of the bluff. They couldn't have been more than ten or fifteen feet from it. It wasn't going to do any good to

71

wander aimlessly around in the dark to try and get the horses, so they just waited and started whistling trying to coax them in. It worked, and presently both horses came back. Instead of mounting up and trying to find their way in the dark again, the vet dug around in her saddle bags, and retrieved some paper and matches to light a fire. After feeling around in the dark for a few sticks, they got a fire going. Can you imagine their surprise when they saw the drop off? Why you could have spit over the edge; they were that close. Well, there they were, scared to death and afraid to move. There was no going forward, and they were afraid to go back along the trail. So they decided the best thing to do was to spend the night right where they were and wait for daylight. Fortunately for them, the moon came out. They managed to gather their wits about them and retraced their steps. From what I understand, it took two hours of riding in the moonlight to find where they started from. Of course all the other riders wondered what had happened to them, but everything turned out all right, and everyone got back safe and sound. Ya know, it's been a long time since anyone has gone up on top to ride a horse along the trails."

All the while that Jeb told his story, Sarah had sat in silence with her head down as though listening in rapt attention. But Jason knew something wasn't right. Sarah had begun fidgeting around, nervously wringing her hands, as though she were under some strong emotion. Jason could see Sarah trembling. Evidently the story had hit a nerve. He was sure it had to do with the bluff but didn't know what to do about it, so he put his arm around her trying to be a comfort. Sarah leaned on him in response and began to cry. Jeb couldn't help but notice what had been going on between Jason and Sarah. It concerned him that Sarah had started crying. Something about the story had touched her;

that much was certain.  He got up out of his rocker and retrieved some Kleenex for her.

Sarah gratefully accepted them and apologized for crying, and said, "I'm alright now. It was just something about the story that touched me," Jeb replied.

"Ya know, Sarah, sometimes we must face our fears; it helps to confront them. If there was something in in my story that frightened you, it needs to be isolated and dealt with. Otherwise it could haunt you for the rest of your life. If it was the fact that those women almost fell off of the bluff, the best thing you could do would be to go up there to face it and get it over with. You don't want to go through life with that kind of fear following you around."

"I don't know if I would have enough courage to do that," she replied to his encouraging remarks. "I think there is something evil up there, and I'm afraid."

As Jason listened to Sarah's voice her fears, his old nemesis began looming large in his mind again.  The thought began trying to assert itself over his mind, trying to get his attention.  Its harassing influence was getting stronger by the moment, and it was all he could do to stay in his seat.  Jason began using some of the old tricks that had worked before, but this time the tricks were absolutely useless. The thought had adapted.  Then he remembered Doctor Freemont's advice of giving in to the thought. It had worked once before, he reasoned. Perhaps it would work again. Jason quit fighting and began letting it have control. As soon as he did this, the thought stopped trying to assert its influence over him, and instead of feeling anxiety, Jason felt calmness take over. It was a strange sensation, but he was glad for it. He knew that Sarah's problem and his were definitely linked somehow. Obviously the bluff played a major role in this drama. It was the centerpiece of the mystery. At the mention of the bluff,

73

the thought came alive in his mind just as the bluff was the focal point of many of Sarah's paintings. Sarah needed to go up on top of the ridge and face her fear. Trouble was, would she?

# Chapter 7

Monday was a day of a lot challenges for Molly, but she didn't mind. "Hmm, I wonder where I should start," she murmured. After pondering on the problem for a while, Molly finally decided to go to the high school first and try to get a glimpse into Sarah MacAfee's past, reasoning that she might be able to talk to some of the teachers. Getting a note pad and pencils from her desk, she headed out the door and went across town.

Molly pulled into the parking lot of the school and parked at the main entrance. She sat in her car looking things over before going in. Presently a bell rang, and students began coming in and out of the doors. "I guess the classes are changing. Wow, does that bring back some memories," she thought. Molly smiled as she observed the coming and going of the students. Some of them were in a hurry to get to their next class, and there were others that didn't seem to be in a hurry at all. They just kind of loafed around, dragging their feet as though they didn't want to go to class. "Typical teenagers," she thought. "I don't remember being that way. I'm sure that I was a model student." Molly silently laughed to herself, knowing better, but it was good to have old memories of her school days come to mind. She sat a while longer, just observing what went on, waiting until the bell sounded again before she entered the building. It wasn't long before it did sound. "Wow, three minutes to get to class. I don't remember class change being that quick... well it was a long time ago," she remembered.

Molly got out of the car and made her way inside. As soon as she went through the door, memories of her school days began flooding her mind. She had forgotten the smells of school. It smelled of window cleaner and floor finish, and there was the bright glow of the many lights in the halls. The school was very clean. Everything seemed to be taken care of.

""May I help you?" someone asked. Molly looked around to see who was speaking to her. A tall dark haired man that had a touch of gray at the temples approached her. "HI" there, I'm Mr. Duncan. How can I help you?"

She was a little surprised to see so young a man with graying hair. There must be a lot of stress in his life, she thought. Molly explained why she was there, and he directed her to sign in at the office. He showed her the library and said that the librarian would be glad to help her. Mr. Duncan hurried down the hall, around a corner, and out of sight. "I wonder why he is in such a hurry," she pondered.

Molly went into the office and asked for the sign- in sheet. The secretary, Mrs. Higgins, a very petite young woman with long black hair and intense looking brown eyes who seemed to be doing three or four things at once, looked up and said, "I'll be with you in just one moment." Then suddenly the phone rang, but she deftly continued her work without missing a beat. This is a busy individual," Molly thought. She was amazed at the way the secretary handled things. "This is the person who really runs things around here," she thought. Then Mrs. Higgins reached for a walkie talkie.

"Carl," she said, "we are out of copy paper. Could you bring some?"

Yes," was the quick reply. "I'll be there as soon as I help Renee clean up a mess in the hall."

Then a gruff voice called out, "Sam, get in here!" A student who had been working at a computer jumped up and went into an inner office. He soon came out with a coffee cup, went into another room, and reemerged with a fresh cup of coffee. What must it be like to work with such an individual, she wondered? Molly pushed the thought out of her mind and patiently waited for Mrs. Higgins to get a free moment.

She presently addressed Molly with, "Hi, what can I help you with?" Molly told her why she was there and that she was told to sign in. Mrs. Higgins gave her the sign in- sheet, told her to sign it, put the date and time, and that she would be good to go. Molly did as she was told, thanked her, went across the hall and into the library.

The school library was not a conventional library. Not at all like a public library. Molly was impressed. It would be very easy to spend some time here. There were comfortable chairs and tables to use. Books lined the shelves as in other libraries, but there were also books displayed on tables for student use. Molly also noticed colorful rugs and end tables at the center of the room that were surrounded by soft cushioned chairs. It made the library very inviting. She felt right at home in this atmosphere.

Molly walked over to the librarian's desk and waited. She could see students moving around in a back room. It was obvious that they were working on a project of some kind. She could hear the sound of scissors cutting paper. Soon the librarian came out of her office, smiled and asked.

"Is there something I can help you find today?" She was a very precise looking individual with long auburn tresses that framed her slim pleasant face. Her name was Mrs. Garrett. Molly explained that she was doing some research and wanted to know if there were any yearbooks that she might look at. Mrs. Garrett replied that there were many yearbooks in her files and that she could go through them as much as needed.

Molly followed her into the file room where the yearbooks were kept, and then it occurred to her to ask if Mrs. Garrett happened to know a Sarah MacAfee.

"As a matter of fact, I do know Sarah MacAfee; she is a local artist," she replied. There seemed to be a questioning tone in her answer.

"Yes, that is the individual I am researching. I am writing a paper on local artists and their crafts," Molly fibbed. There was no sense in divulging her real purpose, she reasoned. This answer seemed to satisfy Mrs. Garrett's curiosity, so she directed her to a yearbook that had Sarah's picture and information in it. After flipping through the pages, she came upon a picture of her in the art room. She was proudly holding a portrait of a landscape. It was of an old white farm house, and in the distant back ground Molly could just barely make out the bluff. It was rather hard to distinguish it in the yearbook, but she was sure that it was indeed there. Interesting, at least we know that the bluff was in her mind at this stage of her life, she thought. Molly wrote this fact in her notebook and continued her research. Yearbooks didn't divulge very much information about an individual. There were the usual pictures of Sarah but nothing much on her background. Nothing was in the yearbook that told about her parents. Molly felt that she had gleaned all that she could from this source of information, so she decided to talk to Mrs. Garrett again. Molly closed the yearbook, put it back in its file, and went to talk to her.

Mrs. Garrett was helping a student find a book to read, so Molly quietly made her way around the library leisurely taking her time. Presently Mrs. Garrett came over to her and asked if there was anything else she needed help with. Molly didn't hesitate, but asked if there was any more information she could share about Sarah MacAfee, stating that it was very important to her research. Mrs. Garrett hesitated a moment before offering anything, and it seemed to Molly, that she was struggling with some doubt. But soon Mrs. Garrett said that although she knew of Sarah MacAfee, she didn't really know that much about her. Other than that her parents were dead, and she had been raised by her grandparents. Once Mrs. Garrett started talking, one thing led to another, and before very long Molly had enough information to help with the investigation. It wasn't quite enough, but it was a good start. It was obvious to Molly that Sarah MacAfee had had a lot of trauma in her life at an early age, and a tragic event was expressing itself through her painting. The mystery was intriguing, and as each new piece of the puzzle fell in place, a little more of Sarah MacAfee's life was revealed.

Molly thanked Mrs. Garrett for her help and left the library. Her next stop she decided would have to be the local newspaper. They should have old papers that could be gone through that might shed a little more light on the subject. She headed over to the Mayfield Chronicle and asked if the archives were available to research. They were, and she was directed to a large room with many files that were full of back issues of the paper. Molly felt overwhelmed by the daunting task that was before her. "Where do I start?" she murmured out loud. "What have I gotten myself into?" She looked around at the files and frowned.

Molly got the notes she had made, and referred to them. She knew that Sarah MacAfee graduated in 1994, so it shouldn't be too hard to find something about her or her parents. There could very well be an article about them, she reasoned. Starting with a paper from 2007, she ensconced herself in a chair, laid the paper on the table, and began to research.

The obituaries didn't have any MacAfee's that might have died that year so she began leafing through the rest of the newspaper but without any success. It was obvious that she was going to be there for a while, so she committed herself to the task and continued. There was nothing of importance, at least not as far as Sarah MacAfee was concerned. There were the usual things found in a newspaper, like the election of a new county judge and advertisements of various kinds.

After having worked her way back to the year 2000, Molly was going over the obituaries when she saw the name Alfred MacAfee. She read the article; sure enough Sarah's name was there as granddaughter.

"Pay dirt at last," she whispered. Molly was elated. "Now I have something to go on," she said. Also, there were the names of her parents, also deceased. Molly began to wonder what happened to them. Did they die together or apart? But Molly knew that more research should bring everything to the light.

Molly was getting a little weary of research, for she had been at it for two hours already. She got out of her chair, stretched her arms and legs, and walked around in the room for a while. Before sitting down she decided something to drink would help. Upon asking one of the ladies at the front desk where she could get a snack, she was directed to the break room at the back of the office. Upon entering she almost collided with someone who was coming out. It was a man who seemed to be in a hurry.

He said, "Excuse me, I didn't mean to run you over." The voice seemed familiar, and looking a little bit closer, she recognized the personage of no other than Jason Brennen. They were both taken aback.

"Don't you work for Doctor Freemont?" Jason asked.

"Yes I do," Molly replied. "I have been doing research in the archives this morning, and I got thirsty. I didn't know that you worked for the newspaper, Jason."

"Yes, I have worked here for quite a while. I am what you might call their go for. I pretty much do everything around here, except deliver papers. I even work in the archives room. Right now I have to go on an errand for Mr. Griswell, our editor.

Molly wanted to ask how he was feeling but thought better of it. It might not be ethical. Besides she was afraid the subject of Sarah MacAfee might come up, and it could spoil Doctor Freemont's plans. Of course, Jason would have to be brought into it sooner or later but not until the timing was right.

When Molly told him that she was doing some research, Jason began to wonder what kind of research it was. His curiosity was up, and he would like to know. After all, she did work for Doctor Freemont. Jason didn't have any more time to chat with Molly, so he said that he had better get going, and that perhaps they could visit later on in the day. Molly was relieved to see Jason depart; for his presence might complicate matters. She went back into the archives room and renewed her research through the newspapers. The year 2000 had proved fruitful. It was a revelation as far as names went. Now she knew about Sarah MacAfee's lineage as far as her parents and grandparents were concerned. It didn't tell her when they all died, but it would make her research easier. It was just a matter of digging out the facts. When and how Sarah MacAfee's parents died might be the real issue. Once she gathered all of the facts and put them together, Doctor Freemont could delve into the mystery a little deeper, until the puzzle was solved.

About an hour later Molly found in the obituaries where Sarah's grandmother had passed away. The date was 1992; her name was Rachel. The grandparents had out-lived Sarah's mom and dad. There hadn't been any mention of siblings, just cousins. So that meant that Sarah was an only child. When and how did the parents die? The question lingered long in her mind, making the research more intriguing. Molly began again with more enthusiasm. Finally in the year 1987, she came upon an article about the death of two people: Sarah MacAfee's parents. "Poor child," Molly thought. It grieved her to think that such a thing could happen to anyone. No wonder she had issues. Sarah's loved ones had suddenly passed away, and her world turned upside down. Molly gathered her material and left for the office to show Doctor Freemont what she had found.

When Molly got back to the office, she went to her desk and began going through all of the paperwork. The adventure of tracking down more information concerning Sarah MacAfee would have to wait until later. It was obvious that Doctor Freemont was with a patient, for the appointment book lay open, and so she began the arduous paperwork before her.

Doctor Freemont was with a harried looking woman. She could see stress on her countenance. It was only her second session, and there was little progress being made, but she encouraged her just the same. "Your anxiety is perhaps brought about by the fear of rejection. Tell me about your parents. What kind of relationship did you have with them? Did you feel loved? Just relax and take your time. Say anything that comes to your mind." The session continued on in this fashion with Doctor Freemont making notes in the patient's file. When the time was up, she set up another appointment, and said, "You are making great progress. If you happen to have another anxiety attack, try to remember the things we talked about, and I'll see you in two weeks."

Dr. Freemont followed the harried patient into the outer office and observed her as she went out the door. It always amazed her at just how sensitive people could be. Of course it all depended upon their situation. What would be normal for one person might not apply to the next. It all came down to what they had been through. It was her job to guide them to the answer, and most of the time the answer was somewhere within themselves. It just took time to probe around with the right questions.

Doctor Freemont came out of her reverie when Molly spoke to her. "Good afternoon, Doctor. Did everything go well today?" she asked.

"Yes, thank you. Very well indeed; that was the last patient. I trust that you had a productive day yourself."

"Actually I did have a good day," she answered. "I brought back a lot of information on Sarah MacAfee. I think that you will be pleased."

Doctor Freemont retrieved the notes on Sarah MacAfee that Molly had done and went back into her office to review it. After going over them, she could see the beginnings of the trauma in Sarah's life. It was obvious to her that the death of her parents had had an effect on her. Although their death would be a hard thing to face at such an early age, it didn't seem to her that her loss would affect her in such a way as to cause her to do different renditions of the bluff. There had to be much more to Sarah MacAfee's story. Molly's research had opened the door to other possibilities; if more probing could be done, the answer might be found. It was proving to be an intriguing problem. Sooner or later, the tangled web of events would come unraveled, and then the true facts would be laid bare before her. She hoped that it would be soon. It would be terrible if she failed to help Sarah MacAfee.

Doctor Freemont poured a cup of coffee and sat down at her desk and began making notes, working her way towards a plan of action. Sarah MacAfee must be drawn into her office by some means. It was doubtful if she would come on her own volition. Jason Brennen hadn't come in for his last appointment, and perhaps it was time to make a phone call. If Sarah MacAfee came in at all, it would no doubt be under Jason's influence. She walked into the outer office and told Molly to give Jason Brennen a call to see if he would come in. "Tell him there will be no charge, and that it is important. Mention that it concerns Sarah MacAfee. Perhaps he will see me on her account."

It was obvious to her that there was a connection between Jason and Sarah because of the events that had been unfolding. She went back to her desk and went over the notes again to try and delve deeper into the mystery. With each new probe, a little more light was shed on the case. It was a beginning; a possibility. But it would take the presence of Sarah MacAfee in order to go forward. Everything hinged on Sarah's past. Where in the past she wasn't sure of, but she did have an inkling.

# Chapter 8

It had been a week since Jason had taken Sarah up on the mountain to meet Jeb Rawlings and now she lay in her bed tossing and turning, unable to sleep. Deep emotions were troubling her. Ever since Jeb told the story about the bluff, Sarah seemed to have come unhinged in her mind. The story had awakened a vague memory from deep down inside, and she could feel it trying to rise to the surface. It was an unknown reality that she didn't want to face because she found it haunting and terrifying. Sarah looked at the clock on the night stand. It was 2:00 am. What an ungodly hour to be awake, she thought. Sarah got out of bed, went into the kitchen, and started brewing a cup of hot tea, hoping that it would settle her nerves. As she waited for the water to boil, she began pacing the floor, trying to fight the turmoil. Disturbing thoughts of ending her life began emerging, tormenting her already harried mind. She began pulling at her hair as she struggled with the unwanted thoughts and emotions. It got so bad that she started to scream, trying to release the frustration. Sarah's mouth opened and the scream began to rise up in her throat, but it never reached her quivering lips, for the sudden shrill whistle of the tea kettle brought her out of her torment. Sarah felt as though she were emerging from a drunken stupor and had to hold onto the kitchen counter for support. The tea kettle was still whistling, so she reached over and turned it off. Her hands were shaking, but she managed to make the tea and began sipping the soothing liquid. It helped a little, but not enough. It was going to take more than tea to settle her mind. Sarah sat at the kitchen table and began to weep. She tried to hold back the tears, but could not.

"Something is going to have to change," she said out loud. "I can't continue on this way. Oh God," she pleaded. "Help me. I can't do this by myself!" The words seemed to comfort her. The shaking stopped, but the tears still flowed down her face. She laid her head on the table and began to sob. All of the pent up emotions broke within her, and she released them with the tears. As she did this, the frustration and tension began to lift. After several moments Sarah reached for a box of tissues and began to wipe her tear stained face. She poured another cup of tea and opened one of the windows and let the fresh cool air flow into the kitchen. She sat and listened to the night sounds. They were a welcome distraction. All of the torment began fading away, and the cloud of confusion dissipated as she focused on the sounds of nature. It was as if her crying out for help had been answered. The thoughts that had entered her mind were still lingering about, but they were not as intense as before. Sarah got up from the table and went into the living room and curled up on the couch. She was afraid to go back to her bed, and so spent the remainder of the night there. Her sleep wasn't exactly fitful. She dreamed and occasionally moaned, uttering unintelligible words that no doubt were a result of her past experience. Sarah slept the night, until she was slowly awakened by the sound of someone's voice. It seemed to be far away, saying, "No, don't. Please I, I." The voice seemed to be coming from a dream. Then she realized that it was her own voice that had uttered those words. Sarah sat up with a start and began looking around to see where she was. It was just daybreak, and she could make out the familiar living room in the dim light. It was a relief to know that she was safe and sound in her own home, but the memories of the night before lingered. Sarah got up and went into the bathroom and looked into the mirror. She looked harried. Her face was drawn from stress, and her head hurt.

It was eight- thirty when she finally got dressed and had her breakfast. Sarah didn't feel like opening the studio; she was still weary and so took her time getting around. An hour passed before she reluctantly decided to open it up anyway. Living upstairs had its advantages, but today it was proving to be a double- edged sword. When Sarah went downstairs and turned the studio's lights on, one of the first things she saw was another painting of the bluff that she had brought in to sell. Sarah had no desire to look at it all day long, so she covered it up. "It would be better if I were to destroy the paintings," she thought. But in the back of her mind Sarah was aware that the bluff held the answer to her dilemma and that at some point in time she would have to face her own fear, just as Jeb Rawlings had said. Destroying the paintings wasn't the answer. Covering them up wasn't either. Sarah felt like a confused little child. She wished that Jason was with her. He had been a comfort from the very beginning. "I should have called him last night, she thought. But Sarah wasn't one who easily shared her burdens. All of the pent up emotions had been held in for so long that she felt as if she were about to lose her mind. She had come to an impasse and needed to confide in someone. Perhaps the story about the bluff was really what she needed to hear, after all. It had moved her like nothing before. Sarah shuddered at the thought and had to get hold of herself once again. She tried to dismiss the dilemma from her mind, and focus on the day ahead. The studio had to be opened sometime, so Sarah put the open sign in the window, uncovered the painting of the bluff, and went about her business as though nothing were wrong. Her face still felt drawn, and her eyes were a bit red from all of the crying, but that couldn't be helped. She wished that Jason would come by. He was only a phone call away, and that in itself was a comfort. Perhaps they could go out for lunch, she reasoned. The thought of having Jason near helped relieve some of the tension and made her a little more cheerful. She had become very fond of him. The way he treated her was special. Jason had proved to her that he was a gentleman in every respect. Deep down inside Sarah knew she wasn't just fond of Jason but that she was falling in love with him. These loving thoughts helped expel the lingering emotions from the night before, and Sarah went about her day's work with more enthusiasm. She occasionally glanced at the clock, hoping that Jason would call. Sarah was anxious to unload her mind's heavy burden and was sure that Jason would listen.

When Sarah looked at the clock again, it was 11:30, and there still hadn't been a call from Jason. By this time Sarah's mind had settled down, and the events from the night before seemed far distant, as though it had only been a bad dream. The turmoil was gone, at least for now, and the fear had subsided. Sarah began having some second thoughts about telling Jason of her personal dilemma; she didn't want to draw him into her troubles. She was too fearful of exposing her emotional scars. The need to be near him overruled her doubts, and so she hesitantly picked up the phone and called him.

"Hello." Jason said. "How are you today, Sarah? I was just about to call to see if you could get away for lunch.
I have to run an errand; but it won't take very long. I'll swing by and pick you up."

"Ok," Sarah said. "But remember, I'm starved." She laughed and hung up. It felt so very good to hear Jason's reassuring voice and made her more anxious to be with him.

Sarah was waiting on a customer when Jason finally came by to get her, so he browsed around looking at the paintings. There was one that he especially admired. It was of a pleasant woodland scene. There was an old abandoned log cabin nestled among large oak trees. There was also a stream of water meandering through the midst. It was fall, and there were many colorful leaves scattered about on the ground. Jason wondered if anyone had really inhabited the place, or if it was just the creative imagination of Sarah at play. The more he looked at the painting, the more he could see himself walking through the woods along the creek bank and up to the cabin. "It looks so real, he thought. I'll have to ask Sarah if it is a real place. If it is, I want to go there."

Jason was so engrossed in the painting that he didn't hear when the customer left the store. The next thing he knew, Sarah had put her hands over his eyes, and said, "Guess who?"

Jason smiled, and answered, "Is it Rembrandt?"

"Close," she replied, "but I'm not that good."

"I don't know, Sarah," he answered. "This painting had me captivated. I didn't even know where I was. It is one of my favorites. I would love to go there if that were possible."

Sarah was pleased that Jason liked the painting. "Actually, that is a real place that I stumbled upon while hiking one fall. I think it is still there. We'll have to make a day of it so you can explore a little. It isn't all that far from here. As a matter of fact, it's at the end of the valley where my grandparents' farm is. We could start from there and go hiking. I could use a distraction anyway, and it would be fun to do something different for a change."

Sarah was feeling the urge to confide in Jason but didn't want to spoil the moment, so she put the thought out of her mind. Jason was elated at the prospect of doing a little exploring, but it would have to be on a weekend, and soon, before the weather changed; the days were getting a little cooler. Sarah had tried to avert her eyes as much as possible so that Jason wouldn't notice their red appearance. She reached for a hanky and started dabbing her nose, in pretense of having a cold. Jason noticed this and asked if she was okay. Sarah replied that everything was alright, but then Jason saw the redness of her eyes.

"Sarah, are you sure you're okay?" he asked. The tenderness with which he asked this touched her heart, and the tears began welling up in her eyes once again. She could feel the fearful emotions rising. Jason reached out, drew her to him, and held her tight. Sarah began to shake, her emotions broke, and she released her tears. Jason led her to a chair and made her sit down until she stopped crying.

"Want to talk about it?" he asked.

At first, Sarah shook her head no in response to Jason's question, not wanting to entangle him in her problems. She was ashamed to have broken down in front of him and felt like hiding somewhere. But of course she couldn't do that. The cat was out of the bag, and there was no going back. She would have to confide in him now. Sarah raised her head and looked into Jason's eyes.

She began her account with, "Jason, when we were at Jeb's house, and he told the story of the bluff, do you remember that it really bothered me?"

"Yes, I do remember that," he replied.

"Well, last night I just couldn't sleep. I kept tossing and turning; I couldn't get the troubling story out of my mind. Something happened to me when Jeb told us that scary story. I became afraid, and I think it has affected my mind. I think that I am having an emotional breakdown, and I know it has to do with the bluff. I just can't stop painting pictures of it, and I don't know why. I am sorry for dragging you into this, but I have no one to talk to. I'm afraid of what will happen if this continues. Am I going crazy? I don't know what to do. I don't know where to go from here; I'm at my wits' end!"

As Jason listened to Sarah's emotional plea, his heart couldn't help but go out to her. It reminded him of his personal dilemma with the thought. He too had been going through an emotional rollercoaster. He knew that the bluff was at the center of both of their plights and that the answer to the problem couldn't be far off. The thought had been quiet in Jason's mind of late as if it were only waiting for the right opportunity to make an appearance. He was a little surprised that it hadn't already woken in his mind when Sarah poured her heart out to him, but for now, it seemed to be dormant. He put his arm around Sarah's shoulders to comfort and reassure her. He talked in soothing tones until she settled down.

"Why don't you dry your tears, Sarah?" he asked, "and then maybe you will feel like going to lunch. I think that you need to get out for a while, and then we can talk about it some more."

Sarah got out of the chair, went into the bathroom, and splashed cold water on her face. It refreshed her, and she started feeling better. It was a relief to have finally talked to someone about her problem. She was glad that Jason had been there for her. It made her appreciate him all the more.

When Sarah emerged from the bathroom, she found Jason standing in front of the painting of the bluff. He was closely examining it, as though trying to decipher its meaning.

"You know, Sarah," he began, "if it hadn't been for finding the bluff I would never have met you."

This statement puzzled her. "How do you mean?" she asked.

"Well," he began. "I have never told you about my own emotional dilemma, and Sarah, I'm not sure if I can explain it so that you will understand, but I will try. It all started with a nightmare I had."

Jason went into as much detail as he could without causing Sarah any undue alarm. He didn't tell her about Doctor Freemont as yet, not wanting to put doubt in her mind about him. As he finished, he said, "So you see, I think that Jeb was right about facing your fear. That is exactly what I had to do, and you must do the same if you want to discover what it is that causes you to paint pictures of the bluff. I think that you need to go up there and put the torment behind you." Sarah wasn't so self-assured as Jason was and didn't say anything for a while. When she did, it wasn't all that encouraging.

"Jason," she said, "that may be easy for you to do, but you just don't understand. I'm very much afraid of that place. There is something about it that I just can't face. I have this overpowering feeling that grips me, and I don't know why. I don't know if I even want to find out. There is something hidden from me, something that I fear."

Jason was disappointed with Sarah's reply. He had hoped that she would agree to face her fear as he had done. Something very bad must have happened in her life that caused her to be so afraid. People are often afraid of heights, but obviously there was much more to Sarah's fear than a fear of heights. What she needed now was to talk to Doctor Freemont. Jason began to wonder if the call from her secretary had anything to do with Sarah's situation. He had purposely missed his last appointment with the doctor because he was sure the cure was complete. Now that Sarah had opened up to him, things were becoming more complicated, and it was going to take a professional like Doctor Freemont to untangle the confusing web that had been woven around them. When Molly had called, Jason didn't commit himself to an appointment but had said that he would think about it and let her know. But after listening to Sarah, he made up his mind to see Doctor Freemont again. It was the only way he could see to be of some help to Sarah. Jason felt very tender toward Sarah and couldn't bear to see her in torment.

Sarah was having a lot of feelings of guilt because of her emotional breakdown and apologized to Jason for what she had just put him through. She looked at him shamefacedly embarrassed at what had transpired between them.

Jason reassured her and said, "Sarah, I would do anything to try and help you through this."

His words warmed her heart, and she began feeling better. The load of doubt and fear lifted, and she said that she was going to close the store for the remainder of the day and try to get some rest.

Jason decided to order lunch to go. It would give him a better chance to talk to Sarah about all that had transpired in his life over the last few weeks. He wanted to explain to her about his struggle with the thought and how it had made his life so miserable. If he could somehow convince Sarah that their two situations were connected, they might be able to help each other overcome the dilemma.

Jason and Sarah spent the rest of the day just lounging around, trying to avoid mentioning the current happenings. Jason wanted to broach the subject but at the same time didn't want to upset Sarah any further. Their troubling difficulty would have to be brought up sooner or later, but the moment would have to be right. As he turned the problem over in his mind, the thought began to slowly make its presence known again. Jason knew that it had not left his mind entirely. He had, in a way, gotten used to its presence and could feel when it was about to make itself known. It always seemed to show up at a critical moment, causing an eerie sensation to run up and down his spine. He no longer felt threatened when it began invading his mind, but it still caused him a moment of panic. It was such an unnatural thing, and it wasn't likely that he would really ever get used to it.

This time the thought became a soothing presence. It was as though it were rewarding him for his actions toward Sarah. Obviously it wanted him to confide in Sarah about his own experience. It was becoming hard not to blurt out what he wanted to say, but the moment wasn't right. The thought began nudging him to take action, but Jason was afraid of what might happen if he spoke out of turn. He decided not to give in, at least, not yet. He would broach the subject when he had made up his own mind. The thought began retreating, leaving Jason in control, but as it departed, it left a shadow of doubt lingering. It was almost as if he could hear it saying, "I'll return." Jason didn't feel threatened, but it was a bit unnerving. It made him wonder if the thought's presence was a friend or foe, reality or unreality.

Everything was coming to a climax. Jason cleared his mind and began to focus his attention on Sarah. She needed him right now, and that was more important than anything. Sarah wasn't in the right frame of mind to listen to his dilemma. It had waited this long; it could wait a little while longer.

The longer he pondered upon these things, the murkier the waters became. There were several places and situations that he could think of that might have caused his torment to happen. It would have to be a process of elimination, and it would take a while; for he would have to do a lot of back tracking. It seemed a daunting task, but it would have to be done if he and Sarah were to be thrown clear of the tangled web.

Evening shadows were lengthening along the ground, and the sun was setting. The fall air was growing chilly, and rain drops were splattering on the ground, forming shallow puddles on the sidewalk. Jason had spent the entire day with Sarah, but now it was time he went home. Before he left, they embraced, for a bond of love was growing between them. Sarah walked Jason to the door and thanked him for listening to her problem because it had helped to unburden herself. They said their goodbyes, and Sarah went back upstairs to her apartment. Jason was reluctant to leave her but knew that she would be okay now. Sarah was in much better spirits, and Jason felt confident that everything would be alright. He still hadn't confided in her about his own problem because he wanted to talk to Doctor Freemont first. She needed to know everything that had transpired, up until now, to best advise him as to what should be done. He didn't want to play doctor, for it was a delicate situation at best. If it wasn't handled properly, anything could happen.

Jason stood under the awning of Sarah's studio, listening to the rain drops fall, taking in the refreshing atmosphere. It was good to know that the darkness that overshadowed them would soon be lifted. They had both been hiding their secret behind masks of pretense, and it was about time to pull them off and face the truth, especially Sarah. She had been carrying her burden for years, and it was past time that her mind found healing and rest.

It was after dark when Jason got home that evening. He had driven around the town trying to rationalize the events of the day. The whole affair was still shrouded in mystery. There was a lot to be explained, such as why did the thought suddenly appear? What triggered it? Jason had never really stopped to reason out his own situation; the thought had been such a tormenting influence on him that he hadn't been able to rationalize anything until now. He was very concerned about Sarah, but he also had to try to grasp the cause of his own torment. Jason began trying to discover the cause, to reason things out in his mind. A thought doesn't just show up without some kind of outside influence. He plied his memory trying to understand what had brought everything about. If he hadn't gone to see Doctor Freemont, he might be in an insane asylum by now, or worse, dead. Jason expelled the disturbing thoughts from his mind, knowing that things had gotten much better for him. He had come to grips with the thought and was no longer afraid of its insistent influence. If anything, it had become his ally. If only he could understand its real purpose.

Jason pondered long upon his dilemma, replaying the nightmares as he remembered them, but to no avail. Something had brought them on. Perhaps it had been something he had seen or heard about. Whatever it was, it had to have been very disturbing and must be hidden deep in his sub conscious mind. He knew that it involved Sarah MacAfee, but what was it?

# Chapter 9

Jason felt drained when he went to work on Monday morning. He hoped that Mr. Griswell was in a good mood. But you never could tell with him, at least not until he got his first cup of coffee. Jason took a deep breath and walked into Mr. Griswell's office. He stood just inside the door until he was recognized. You just didn't walk into his office and make yourself known, not unless you wanted to be berated.

Presently Mr. Griswell looked up at Jason and said, "Well, are you going to stand there all day? Sit down. I've got a lot of work for you today. I have several items, and I want you to use your own judgment. I'll go over them when you're finished." He handed Jason the list of things to be done and curtly dismissed him.

"The old man has certainly got a grump on," Jason thought. He looked at the list and saw that some of the things on the list would take him out of the office, which was always a welcome thing. The other tasks could be performed in house, and it looked as if they were going to take a while. He hadn't been told that they had to be done in a certain order, but only that they had to be done by the next day. Jason looked at the first thing on the list and got to work on it.

Some of the items to be done were a bit tedious and required all of his attention. It was hard to stay focused on the work because his mind wandered back to his own problems. The first half of the morning was a struggle, but he managed to complete several of the tasks. He came to his last thing to be done before lunch; he would have to go to the archive room to do some research on an article for "days gone by." It was one of those articles that Mr. Griswell liked to put in the paper to spark interest in his readers. "Days gone by" wasn't done on a weekly basis, but was only put in every few months or so. This time Mr. Griswell wanted to do past events that had an effect on the present. A wide range of topics was listed, so Jason decided to narrow it down to three of four. That way Mr. Griswell could chose the one he thought was best without getting involved with too many subjects.

Jason started at the top of the list and marked through the ones he didn't want to use. After much consideration he came up with a selection: "Political Issues," "Changes in Agriculture," the "Effect of Deforestation on the Local Economy" and "Tragedies from the Past." It was going to take a while to do the research, perhaps most of the day. It was a very big assignment, and fortunately for him, it wasn't due right away. He might have to work through his lunch hour in order to get a head start, but it was better to do that than to face Mr. Griswell's ire.

Researching each article seemed a daunting task, and after working out the first details of "Political Issues," he decided that the topic of politics was a waste of time. Jason unceremoniously scrapped the few news articles he had collected and went on to the next subject. By one o'clock Jason could no longer ignore the growling of his stomach. He got out of his chair, stretched his tired muscles, yawned, and went into the breakroom to find something to eat. There wasn't much there, so he called Sarah to see if she wanted to eat a late lunch. As it turned out, she had already had lunch and couldn't get away from the studio. She had another portrait to do, and she was doing a preliminary sketch of her subject. Jason said that he would try to call her later on in the afternoon, and that if possible, they could go out for supper. Sarah sounded as if all was well with her, but there was still a lingering doubt in his mind. The day before had been very trying. He was concerned and would like to see if everything was indeed okay, but Jason finally had his lunch delivered. He hastily ate it, promptly went back to the archives room, and took up where he left off.

Jason's back was sore. He got up and moved around the room, trying to work the soreness out of his muscles. Fortunately for him, there was only one more article to finish, the one on tragedies. It had been a long day, but he had accomplished much. Jason had been going through the old newspapers looking for articles that would be relevant to his subject. There were many tragedies that he had found so far, but nothing that really stood out to him.

He had worked his way through the late seventies and had begun working on the eighties when the thought suddenly awakened in his mind. Its presence began overwhelming him, making itself known in a forceful manner. It was as though it had become his old nemesis again. Jason was well aware of what it could do when it took on this form. It was obvious that it was going to have its way with him. Jason had learned that it could help or hinder. It all depended on whether or not he gave in to its demanding influence. It had remained dormant until he had started doing research about tragedies in the eighties. He decided he would rather give in at this point. When he had done so before, all had turned out well. As soon as Jason made his decision, the thought once again became a soothing presence in his mind, encouraging him to continue his research. For some reason he began to think about Sarah, so he began reading the obituaries to see if there were any people who were connected to her. As he progressed year by year, he came upon an article that got his attention. On the front page there was a story about the bluff. As he read the story, he found that there was a dim familiarity about it. He sat back in his chair and then began to ponder trying to remember what it was about. The longer he read, the more he realized what had happened. Now he remembered. He had read this particular story before, probably a long time ago, and had probably dismissed it from his mind. As he studied, he could sense the sorrow of the tragic event. The article clarified everything in his mind. Now he knew what had happened, and he understood. Someone else had also read the story, for it had been underlined. Everything was falling in place, the reason for the thought, and the reason Sarah painted the bluff. Jason felt relieved but also was amazed that something like this could happen. It was time he went to see Doctor Freemont.

It was rather late when Jason left work. He could have finished in the archives room the next day but felt compelled to continue the research until the task was complete. He had the information needed to write the piece for the paper, and now it was up to someone else to put it together.

## Chapter 10

Sarah MacAfee had spent her day in the studio waiting on occasional customers and also working on the latest portrait that had been commissioned. It was a live portrait and would take a while to finish. She made a few more brush strokes and then quit for the day. The image had been fleshed in, but was far from finished. It would take more than one sitting to complete, but it was shaping up nicely. This kind of work was a great distraction for her, and Sarah reveled in it. She had to stay focused on what she was doing. It was good therapy and took her mind off of her dilemma.

As she was cleaning up, the phone rang. It was Jason.

"Hello, Jason," she said. "Sorry we couldn't get together for lunch. I had so much to do, and I knew that you had your hands full, too. Did you finish what you had been working on?"

"For the most part," he replied. "I still have some things that I haven't finished, but they aren't anything like what I did today. About all I got done was research, and it took up the bulk of my time. Tomorrow should be different, unless Mr. Griswell adds to the list. At any rate, I got through it."

Sarah told Jason about her own day, and what a relief it was to have gotten over her confusion and despair. She felt much better after having confided in him. Jason came close to delving a little deeper into her issue, but over the phone would never do. Instead, he said that he was glad she was doing better, and then asked her if she wanted to go out to eat.

"Yes," she replied enthusiastically. "I'm starved." Jason said that he would swing by and pick her up as soon as he made himself presentable.

Jason was glad that Sarah was having a good day. His heart had really gone out to her, and he wanted to make things better. He couldn't stop thinking about her. At first a bond of friendship had formed, and the friendship had grown into love. None of this would have happened if it hadn't been for the thought. He owed it a debt of gratitude even for all of the torment it had put him through.

When Jason stopped in front of the studio to pick up Sarah, his heart began racing because he was eager to see her. He couldn't believe his good fortune. Jason got out of the car and knocked on the door. Presently Sarah came out. She looked very beautiful; he couldn't help but love her. Being in her presence did something to him; it made him feel alive. He wanted to hold her, and so didn't hesitate, but pulled her to him. There under the awning of the studio, Jason kissed her and declared his love. Sarah stood looking into his eyes, knowing that Jason had spoken what was in his heart, and she was glad. She had longed for companionship, and being with Jason took away the loneliness she had felt for so long. Love for him had been mounting in her heart also, and now she could express that love without fear. Jason had proved himself to her over and over again, and she knew that he would remain by her side through every storm. She lovingly whispered the words, "I love you too, Jason."

Their confession of love for each other made the bond between them complete, and Jason no longer doubted that they could overcome whatever life had to offer. He knew from his own recent experience that any obstacle could be surmounted with help. He would walk with Sarah, hand in hand, until they prevailed.

# Chapter 11

Doctor Jillian Freemont sat at her desk going over some of her notes on her most recent client. The individual she was treating had kleptomania, a very interesting issue, but not really unusual in her line of work. Something was urging the person to steal. He didn't need whatever he was taking. There was plenty of money at hand and the inexpensive items could have been purchased easily enough. Sometimes a person steals just for the thrill of it; or perhaps they are bored with life. Whatever the reason happens to be, it is treatable. This person had been banned from certain stores because of the thefts. The police insisted that the individual seek help or spend time in jail. He had opted for help. She closed the folder, sat back in her chair, and tried to relax for a few moments. She closed her eyes and let her mind wander away from the pressures of her work. I could use a day off, she thought to herself. Then her phone rang. She reached over and picked up the receiver.

"Yes, Molly, what is it?" came her curt reply. Molly could hear the tension in Doctor Freemont's voice.

"Doctor Freemont, I hate to disturb you, but Jason Brennen just called and said that he would be willing to come in for a session with you. Shall I call back and set up an appointment?"

"Oh, um, yes. Let's go ahead and do that," came her reply. "Perhaps the day after tomorrow; I may have to take a day off. My case load is getting to me. I know how important it is, but I believe I could think clearer if I had a day off." Molly said that she would cancel her appointments for the next day.

Doctor Freemont had wondered if Jason Brennen would ever call. She was glad when he did, but she was in no frame of mind to tackle his situation just now. Rest and relaxation was needed, even if it was only for a day. Having to listen to everyone else's problems got to her once in a while and this happened to be one of those times. Doctor Freemont wanted to have a clear mind when she did have a session with Jason Brennen. Whenever she was with a client, a positive attitude was a must. All that was needed just now to remedy her weariness was that one day off. Her nerves were on edge. It was time.

It was four o'clock when Doctor Freemont laid down a case file she had been going over. She took her reading glasses off and rubbed her eyes. It had been a long day. Getting up from her desk, she looked out the window at the colorful leaves on the trees. The cool fall wind was swaying the trees back and forth, causing some of the colorful leaves to tumble to the ground. Doctor Freemont watched as they swirled away. The scene was very inviting indeed. Everyone needed some form of therapy once in a while, and she could hardly wait for tomorrow. Even her bones felt weary. "What I need," she thought to herself, "is a long walk through the fallen leaves and a breath of fresh fall air." Doctor Freemont turned from the window, picked up her purse, got her jacket, shut the light off, and quietly closed the door.

Molly looked up from her work as Doctor Freemont entered the outer office.

"Are you calling it a day?" she asked.

"Yes," Doctor Freemont replied. "I've had quite enough work for one day, thank you. I'm beat. Sitting at that desk trying to convince people that all of their troubles can be overcome is really getting to me. Did you cancel all my appointments for tomorrow, Molly?"

"Yes I did," Molly answered. Doctor Freemont then said that she wanted her to take the day off also, stating that the work could wait and that it would still be a paid day. When Doctor Freemont left, Molly put the finishing touches on one of the case files, got her things, set the alarm, turned off the lights, and stepped out into the cool fall air.

Chapter 12

It had rained sometime late in the night, and as Sarah MacAfee opened the studio door, the heady aroma of damp leaves and rain entered the room. The sudden influx of the aromas flooded her mind with memories of her childhood on the farm. She smiled as the images of her late grandparents floated before her mind's eye. She missed them, and it was at times like this that the old memories awoke deep feelings inside, feelings that Sarah didn't understand. It was as though pieces of a complicated puzzle had been lost. There was a vague knowing, and there were details that lingered just out of reach of memory that often plagued her. She had searched her mind, trying to recall what it could be but was never able to grasp the answers. The tragic death of her parents in a car wreck when she was young was only a memory, and it always bothered her that she couldn't remember them in a very clear way. Their faces were etched in her mind; if she sat very still and closed her eyes, she could almost hear their voices, but that was about all. Of course her grandparents had filled in many details, but the details lacked substance for her. Sarah longed to know more about her family, but there seemed to be some kind of barrier separating her from any memories. It wasn't the death of her parents that really bothered her; she had already made peace with that tragic event a long time ago. Still, sometimes, like the other day up at Jeb's house, when heaviness had enveloped her, she had broken down and cried. She had been embarrassed when it happened, but Jason had been there to comfort her. Sarah was glad he was in her life, for he had brought stability and love. The thought of being with him helped change her somber mood, so she went into the studio, retrieved a cup of coffee she had made earlier, went outside, sat on one of the steps, and began to enjoy the morning.

It was around ten o'clock when Sarah finally put the finishing touches on the portrait she had been working on. Standing back from her work, she scrutinized it. "Hmm," she murmured aloud. "Perhaps I should have done a little bit different background instead." Sarah studied the portrait for a while longer, then said, "No, I think it's just right. I believe they will be pleased; it is a real likeness."

As she was musing over her newest accomplishment, someone entered the gallery. Sarah left her study of the portrait to see who had come in. It was an elderly man. Sarah recognized him at once. It was the man in the portrait she had painted a while back.

"May I help you?" she asked. "Well, actually I came in to meet the artist who did my portrait," he replied. "I am Roscoe Delaney. Are you the one who did it?"

"Yes, I am, and I must say that I enjoyed doing your portrait. You made for an interesting subject."

"Why, thank you very much," he returned. "We had to dress up for a party and were having a great time. Someone snapped my picture at an opportune moment, and my family snuck the picture out of the house, unbeknownst to me. They had you paint it for my birthday, and now it hangs in a place of honor. I just wanted to meet you. You're very talented, and I would like to look at some of your other work, if I may."

"Of course you may," she replied. "Look around all you want. I can supply some of the background on the portraits if you wish," she said.

Mr. Delaney walked around the gallery looking at the portraits, pausing in front of the ones that seemed to interest him. It was obvious to Sarah that he liked the ones done of nature.

"My," he exclaimed. "I really like this one."

"Oh, thank you," Sarah said. "It is one of my favorites also."

Roscoe Delaney was looking at a picture of oak and maple trees in the fall. It was a brilliant portrait caught at the height of fall's colorful hues. He stood for a long time observing it, and then said, "I have the perfect place for it in the living room above the fireplace."

"Would you like to take it with you?" Sarah asked.

"Oh yes," Mister Delaney quickly replied. "I couldn't possibly leave without it."

Sarah took the portrait to the sales counter and rang it up. "That will be eighteen hundred dollars. Shall I wrap it for you?" she asked.

"Yes, that will be fine. I can't wait to take it home and put it in its proper place."

Roscoe Delaney hadn't even blinked an eye at the price but had just paid for the purchase as though it were nothing. He thanked Sarah profusely and stated that it had been a pleasure doing business with her. He took the painting, smiled, did a little bow, and left Sarah's gallery.

"Well," Sarah proclaimed, "that was easy. I wish I had more customers like him. I could retire early."

Sarah decided to call Jason to tell him the good news. It wasn't that she never sold any of her paintings; it was just that it had been so simple. She usually had to go into a sales pitch to work up enough interest to sell anything. Sometimes a client would come back three or four times before making up their mind to purchase a painting. She was still elated, and when she called Jason, he could hear the excitement in her voice.

"What has gotten you so worked up," he teasingly asked. "I just made a large sale a little while ago," she said. "Let's go to lunch, and I'll tell you all the details about my big sale."

# Chapter 13

"Furnished apartment for rent, 413 Glenwood Drive; a cleaning deposit is required." The man put the newspaper aside and then began scrutinizing the apartment. It was a nondescript structure at the end of a cul-de-sac; it was just what he was looking for. He walked around looking things over before completely making up his mind. He stood on the sidewalk for a while looking up and down the street as though pondering upon the decision to be made, he looked things over again then walked up the steps and entered the office of the apartment building.

"I'll be right with you," a musical female voice called from somewhere. Presently a rather plump and slightly unkempt older woman came out from a back room. She had rather large blue piercing eyes and red lips that seemed eternally frozen into a smile. Her graying red hair was a bit disheveled, but she seemed businesslike in spite of her appearance.

"I'm here about the apartment for rent," the man said, with a curt tone in his voice, and then he fixed his eyes upon her. Mrs. Farley looked over her glasses at him. He was a bit intimidating in appearance and looked shifty. He wore a brown long- sleeved shirt and black slacks and had cold grey eyes that followed her every movement. The pasty look of his complexion behind the short cropped brown beard gave her the creeps. Mrs. Farley was a good judge of character, and it didn't take long for her to assess this man. In her mind the man looked like someone on the move but seemed clean enough despite his repulsive appearance. It looked like he was hiding something. She could see it in his eyes; the eyes always told. But not wanting to be judgmental, and also not wanting to lose a customer, she replied, "Yes," the apartment is indeed for rent. It has been cleaned and is ready to go. Would you like to see it?"

"All right," was his curt reply. Mrs. Farley couldn't tell too much about the man from his voice, but she did detect a slight nervousness in him. Well, I don't know, she thought. It might be nothing all. There were always characters coming and going; as long as they weren't in trouble with the law and didn't cause a disturbance, she would let anyone rent. Mrs. Farley, having made up her mind that this man would probably be okay, began to show him the apartment.

"I just had every room freshly painted and all of the carpets cleaned," she encouraged. "Take your time and look around; I'll be in the office." Mrs. Farley knew how to sell. She didn't want to follow him around; it might run him off. It was best to let a potential customer make up their own mind. She turned, and left him standing in the middle of the living room and went out the door.

After Mrs. Farley left the apartment, the man began to examine each room. The apartment wasn't very big, but it was big enough for his needs. He wasn't planning on staying there very long anyway. Just long enough to do what he had come to do. "Yes, yes, this will do, yes." Thomas Gilmore's words were whispered as if he were afraid someone might hear what he was saying. A slight smile formed on his face, but as quickly as the smile came, it was replaced by a smirk. "It has taken a long time, but here I am!" This was said to the air, but he spoke as though someone was really in the apartment with him. He smiled again, closed his eyes, and stood very still. The minutes quietly ticked by, and presently he came out of his reverie. He had a dazed look on his face as though he wasn't sure where he was. He looked around for just a moment or two and began to laugh in a coarse voice, all the while repeating to himself. "Yes, yes, yes, I know, I understand." The look on his face was frightening, and had Mrs. Farley been there, she would have refused to rent the apartment.

Having made up his mind, the man went back to the office. Mrs. Farley asked if the rooms were suitable enough, and he quickly replied that they would do. He filled out the paper work, paid what was required, and began taking the few things he possessed into the apartment.

Mrs. Farley, being the inquisitive person that she was, took note of those few possessions. She tried not to be a busybody, but she just couldn't help herself sometimes. But this man was different. "Hmm, Thomas Gilmore, you only have one suit case, a box, and a duffle bag, hmm," she repeated to herself. "He doesn't seem to have much, but he did pay cash," she said into the air. Mrs. Farley made a mental note of the happenings of the new tenant and went about her business of the day trying to put the stranger out of her mind. But the face of the man would invariably come before her. He didn't seem to look any different than anyone else she encountered in the course of a day. But there was just something about him that bugged her, and she couldn't get away from the nagging thought that all wasn't what it seemed to be.

Mrs. Farley had been keeping a close eye on Thomas Gilmore for almost a solid week. As far a she could tell, there wasn't anything out of the ordinary that could be detected by her observations. He came and went just like anybody else, and there was never a peep out of him. As far as she was concerned, he was a model tenant. The only other thing she could think of doing was to go into the apartment and have a look around when he wasn't home. An excuse to do so could be found, but then it wouldn't be ethical, so she put the idea aside. Mrs. Farley turned her attention to the menial tasks before her and tried to forget the puzzling tenant, but for some unknown reason his face kept popping up in her mind. She knew that sooner or later a close scrutiny of his apartment would have to be made. It gave her the chills just thinking about it. She didn't know why, but it did.

Thomas Gilmore parked his rented car on a side street, and observed as pedestrians traversed the busy sidewalks. He was a bit reluctant to get out of the car. Mingling with crowds of people made him nervous, but after waiting for half an hour he opened the car door, picked up his duffle bag, and went down the sidewalk. His shuffling gait kept him well behind anyone, and when he came to a crowd, he crossed the street trying to avoid any contact with them. No one paid him any attention at all, for he just seemed to be another shopper or perhaps a tourist. It took him a while to get to his destination. It had taken some effort to locate the building he had been seeking, but after driving the streets for a day or two, he finally found it. Thomas Gilmore never parked his car in front of this particular building but only made a few experimental passes by to see if it was the right one. It was, and so Thomas Gilmore parked his car and walked two blocks, crossed to the opposite side of the street from the building in question, turned up an alley, went behind an abandoned structure, and began scrutinizing the fire escape he found there. He smiled when he found that it was still sturdy and decided that the setup was exactly what he had been looking for. Without any hesitation, Thomas Gilmore bounded the stairs and ascended to the top. He removed a glass cutter from the duffle bag, cut a hole in one of the windows, reached inside, and unlocked it. The window screeched as it was raised, so he stopped and looked around to make sure he was alone. The alley was abandoned. There

113

wasn't anyone around to disturb his plans, so he entered the building and cautiously looked around. The light was rather dim and cobwebs hung from just about every nook and cranny. It was obvious that no one had been there in a very long time. It was exactly what he had been looking for. He advanced across the creaking floor boards to the front windows and stood off to one side so that he couldn't be spotted from below. A frown creased his face as he watched the comings and goings of the shoppers. Thomas Gilmore voiced aloud. "Go ahead. Enjoy yourself. You don't know, you don't know. You'll see, you'll see!" Then from one of the shops a person came out. They locked the door and started walking down the sidewalk. Thomas Gilmore was beside himself and in an estranged subdued voice began to laugh. The eerie sound echoed through the abandoned structure. All fell silent as he crawled out of the window, went down the fire escape, and quickly went back through the dark alley. He stopped short of the sidewalk, waited for several seconds, then nonchalantly began following the individual who had just emerged from the store.

Thomas Gilmore was just a little bit nervous but also confident as he pursued Sarah MacAfee. He made sure to go into a store entranceway, or just pretended he was window shopping whenever Sarah MacAfee stopped to admire something in a store front. She had no idea that she was being followed, and so went her way, ignorant of the lurking danger behind her.

Thomas Gilmore was enjoying this game of cat and mouse. He thrilled each time he came near Sarah and would smile and mutter to himself at his success. Once, she abruptly stopped at a store front to admire a dress displayed there. Thomas was a little too close and had to walk past her and was forced to enter a hardware store and mill around as if making a purchase. After several minutes of waiting, he decided to take another approach. He left the store, glanced at Sarah, who was still window shopping, and went ahead of her. Thomas looked at his watch. It was eleven forty- five, and so he began looking for a place to eat, thinking that Sarah might be going to lunch. If she was, he might be lucky enough to position himself at a table close enough observe her Thomas began searching for a convenient restaurant. Sure enough, there was a nice sidewalk café just a little way down the street, so he made his way there and went inside. Thomas picked out a table that would give him a clear view of the door and sat down to wait, reasoning that it was a chance worth taking, knowing that Sarah MacAfee might or might not even come in. Either way the odds were in his favor.

Presently a waitress came over to his table to take his order. Thomas was so intent on his purpose that he hadn't even noticed her approach. He jumped when she asked, "How are you today? Can I get you something to drink?"

He looked around as though he didn't know where he was. The waitress saw the confused look on his face and apologized for startling him.

Thomas stammered, "Oh, that's okay, I was just deep in thought."

"Well, I'm Maggie, and I'll be your waitress today. Would you like something to drink?"

"Yes," he replied. "I'll have a cup of coffee."

Maggie noticed the monotone sound of his voice and the way in which he avoided eye contact with her. "This is a strange one," she thought.

"I'll be back in a minute to take your order."

Thomas didn't reply but just sat staring at the entrance of the restaurant, because Sarah MacAfee was standing outside of the cafe.

Sarah stood, lingering, as though she were waiting for someone. Thomas began to fidget with the menu, pretending to read it. He had to restrain himself from looking at Sarah. He found it hard to divert his eyes and had to force himself to look at the menu and choose something to eat. "Maybe she will come inside. That would be perfect," he thought. When Maggie came back to his table, he ordered a sandwich and some chips to eat and then sat back to see what would happen.

Jason had to drive around the block a time or two in order to find a parking place. He waved at Sarah as he went by the first time. She smiled and waved back in acknowledgment. He wasn't long in finding a place to park, and so Jason and Sarah joined hands and entered the restaurant, selected a table, and sat down.

Thomas Gilmore wasn't at all surprised to see Sarah with a man. After all, she was a very beautiful woman. It would complicate matters, but if he played his cards right, he could still achieve his objective. It would take a bit more planning and extra caution, but it could be done. He should have known that she had a boyfriend or perhaps a husband. But that didn't matter to him; at least he had one of her haunts pinned down. The rest would fall into place in time.

Thomas was again jarred from his reverie by Maggie.

"Here is your sandwich. Do you want more coffee?"

"Oh, yes, I'd like another cup," he stammered.

Maggie didn't know what to think of him. "What an odd ball, a queer kind of a duck. You never know who is going to come through those doors," she thought to herself. She

116

poured his coffee, moved on to the next table, and dismissed him from her mind.

When Maggie approached Jason and Sarah's table, she smiled and asked. "Will you have the usual, sweet tea, with lemon?"

"How did you guess?" Sarah replied.

Maggie smiled and said, "If I don't know what my faithful customers want by now, I had better hang up my apron and find something else to do. I'll bring your drinks right out."

Thomas Gilmore had been listening to this exchange, taking notes in a small notebook. He didn't copy their conversation word for word, but only those things that were pertinent to his needs. As far as anyone knew he was only working on an assignment of some kind.

Thomas made sure not to look in their direction; he didn't want to draw any attention to himself. If he were to get caught in the act at this point in the game, it might ruin his plans. He just munched on his sandwich, drank his coffee, and continued to add bits of Sarah and Jason's conversation to the notebook. He decided to linger at lunch as long as possible, for it was a perfect set up. Sarah and Jason were well within earshot, and the notations were adding up; it was proving to be a fruitful day.

Thomas Gilmore finally finished his lunch and decided that he shouldn't stay any longer. He left a small tip for Maggie, walked right by Sarah and Jason's table, paid for his lunch, and went out the door. Instead of going to his car, he went to Sarah's studio in order to find out what her hours were. He went across the street, past the alley, took a roundabout way to the abandoned building, and waited for Sarah MacAfee to return. He got a camera out of his duffle bag and got it ready to take pictures. He adjusted the zoom on the lens and took a picture or two of Sarah's studio. He then began pacing the

117

floor; it creaked at every step, the sound echoing throughout the old building. The result was rather loud and surreal, adding to the already creepy atmosphere. Thomas stopped pacing the floor, stood close to a window, and waited.

Sarah tried to get Jason to stay a while longer, but he said that if he didn't get back to work old Griswell would have his job. They reluctantly left the restaurant, and Jason drove Sarah to the studio and let her out. She stood outside and watched as Jason drove away. If she had looked up at one of the windows in the old abandoned building across the street, she might have caught a glimpse of a man with a camera snapping pictures of her, but her mind was on Jason. Besides, she never even gave the old building a second thought. It was just a part of the background of the neighborhood. Sarah went inside, took down the "gone to lunch" sign, and opened the studio for business.

Thomas watched Sarah's studio to see how much business she had. There didn't seem to be very many customers coming and going. If he could figure out when the slow part of her day was, he might pay her a visit. Of course he would have to be discreet about it; he didn't want to arouse her suspicion. Just the thought of going to her studio sent a rush of adrenaline through his body; he began to smile and mutter to himself, "Cat and mouse, the cat and mouse game. I like that very much!" Thomas Gilmore settled down to a long vigil. Sarah's studio closed at five o'clock. It was now about two o'clock, three more hours to wait, but it must be done in order for him to discover Sarah's daily routine. Thomas entertained himself by watching pedestrians as they came and went up and down the sidewalks, noting when any of them went into Sarah's studio and how long they typically stayed. This information would help him to understand when it would be best to pay Sarah MacAfee a visit.

118

It was late in the evening when Mrs. Farley saw Thomas Gilmore pull up in front of his apartment. Every time she saw him it made her that much more curious. Her intuition told her that he wasn't your ordinary Joe. There was something about him that gave her the creeps. She never had any trouble with him, and he paid his rent on time, in cash. Maybe that was one of the things that bothered her. Most folks paid with a check. Thomas Gilmore was a mystery, and she liked a good mystery. Mrs. Farley pondered upon the situation for a good while before deciding to go ahead and do a little investigating, reasoning in her woman's mind that it couldn't possibly hurt anything. She had been trying to get up enough courage to go into his apartment to have a look around ever since he had moved in, even though she had been a little bit afraid to do so. The longer she thought about it, the more convinced she became that as owner of the apartment it was her right to make sure everything was on the up and up. With her decision made, she went about her business and tried to push the nagging intuition to leave well enough alone and began making her plans. First she took note of Thomas Gilmore's comings and goings, looking for a pattern. The problem with him was that there wasn't really a pattern at all. He didn't really keep regular hours. He always left midmorning and some days was gone for hours. But the next time he went out, he might only be gone an hour or two. It wasn't going to be easy.

## Chapter 14

It was daylight and dark clouds hung low in the sky. The wind had begun to blow, picking up leaves from the ground, swirling them all around, once again forming them into the familiar apparition. Fear began rising within Jason's breast, overpowering him. Then the thought came rushing to the forefront of his mind again, forcing him to stand still and watch as the eerie scene began to unfold. His breath came in ragged gasps, and his heart began to race. Soon a figure emerged from the nearby trees. Jason was quite shocked to see that it was Sarah MacAfee. She began to walk toward the highest edge of the bluff. Jason could plainly see the look of terror on her countenance as she passed by him. He tried to reach out and touch her but was unable to do so. All he could do was stand and watch. She hesitated for a brief moment and then looked at him with pleading eyes, but some unseen force seemed to be guiding her.

The wind was blowing stronger now, swirling the leaves around and around enveloping Sarah in the confused mass. Then the scene changed, and Sarah stood tottering right on the edge of the bluff. She struggled to keep her balance, but then a dark shadow seemed to appear out of the swirling mass of leaves trying to push Sarah over the edge. She began to cry for help as she struggled with the shadow, attempting to free herself from its strong grip but could not. Jason desperately wanted to reach her, but had to stand helplessly by and watch as Sarah MacAfee slipped and then plunged into the abyss below. Jason could hear her screams of agony as she fell to her death.

Jason sat straight up in bed, sweating profusely. His heart felt like it was going to burst. The thought had returned and the nightmares with it. The frightening scene lingered fresh in his mind. When he finally got his nerves under control, he looked at the clock. It was 2:00 am. He felt like someone had just given him a beating. His head hurt, and he felt sick at his stomach. The nightmare had been so real. He wanted to call and check on Sarah, but deep down inside he knew that she was okay. Jason got out of bed, washed his face, got a cool drink of water, and then sat down at the kitchen table to wait for the dawn. He would like to have gone back to bed but was afraid that the nightmare would return.

Jason got up from the table and put on a pot of coffee to try and settle his nerves. As he sat sipping the coffee, the thought began to push its way to the forefront of his mind again, vying for his attention. Jason tried to ignore its presence, but the thought wouldn't give up and persistently tried to pressure him into submission. Jason fought this onslaught for as long he could, but he was already tired; his resistance finally broke down.

Jason took his cup of coffee, sat down on the couch, and began to let the thought have its way. When he did this, the thought stopped pressuring him. Jason closed his eyes and tried to remember the details of the nightmare. Soon the vivid, frightening images began to return. The edge of the bluff appeared in front of him, and the wind began to blow, forming the leaves into the apparition again. But something was different this time. There wasn't a clear face in the apparition; it was only a vague outline. Sarah MacAfee was there, screaming. Then he saw the dark shadowy figure begin to envelop her again. Jason felt the fear return as he relived the nightmare. It was obvious that Sarah was in some kind of danger. This wasn't just a nightmare. It was a warning!

121

When Jason gave into the reality of this, the thought's presence became even more persistent, causing Jason to speak his musings out loud. He heard himself say, "Got to do something about this! Sarah is in great danger, I just know it."

When Jason had voiced these words out loud, the thought suddenly became passive and encouraging as though this had been what it had been waiting for. The thought lingered for only a few moments longer and then slowly retreated into the background of his mind, leaving him in turmoil as to what to do next.

Jason, having come out of his reverie, sat in the silence of the early morning contemplating what had just transpired. He was in a quandary and unsure as to what must be done. He couldn't just go up to Sarah MacAfee and blurt out that she was in some kind of danger. Even though he was now sure that she was. He didn't even know where the danger lay, let alone how to circumvent it. Jason got up from the couch, poured another cup of coffee, and began pacing the floor. His concern for Sarah was real, and his love for her grew with each passing day. He wasn't about to let anyone or anything bring harm to her. She was already emotionally drained, and if Sarah knew what was going on, that alone might push her over the edge. Perhaps when the right moment presented itself he would be able to divulge all that he had been through. As for now, another solution would have to be found to help her, without seeming to do so.

Jason looked at the time. It was 5:30, and he felt drained. The emotional rollercoaster he had been on, plus the lack of sleep, was having its toll on him. He hadn't had a sleepless night like that for a good while. He wanted to call Sarah, but it was still too early for that. So he went back into the bedroom and got dressed. He would like to have stayed home but knew that wasn't possible. It looked as if he was in for a long, tiring day at work. He just hoped that Mr. Griswell was in a good mood and didn't assign him anything too difficult, but you just never could tell with him. One minute he was poking his own brand of fun at you, and the next he would berate you for something that hadn't gone just right. Jason was having a hard time staying in the right frame of mind. He knew that would have to change by the time he got to work, so he headed out the door, got in his car, and went to the nearest doughnut shop. He just couldn't stand the thought of being alone. Jason pulled up in front of the doughnut shop and sat there for a moment or two, observing the comings and goings of the patrons. He began to wonder if any of them were going through anything like he was going through. This last episode with the thought had drained him. He wanted to confide in Sarah, but he knew that she wouldn't be ready to hear what he had to say. Jason got out of the car, went inside, ordered a coffee and two doughnuts, and sat down at a table to eat. It wasn't much fun sitting by himself, and it made him a little jealous whenever a married couple came in. He wanted what they had. Sarah was perfect for him, and he would like nothing more than to be with her always. He knew that although she loved him, Sarah might not be ready for marriage. At least not until her emotional turmoil was healed. Then, there was his emotional perturbation that had to be dealt with. As much as he wanted to get on with his personal life, he knew things couldn't be rushed and that patience must prevail. Jason refreshed his coffee, sat a while longer, and then went to work, putting aside the urge to call Sarah until a little later in the morning.

# Chapter 15

Doctor Jillian Freemont sat at her desk going over her case files, making comments as she did so. It was a bit of a daunting task, for there were many cases that needed a lot of encouragement from her to set things straight. Then there were other cases that were very complex and hard to define. Some of these might never be set right. She had been pondering upon the case of Jason Brennen. When first working with him, she was sure there was more going on below the surface that hadn't come to light. After delving into things further by having Molly do some investigating for her, she was sure that the complex affair would have to come to a head sooner or later. Jason Brennen had made an appointment to see her, and she wondered what had transpired since then. She reread the file on him and noted the progress he had made. As far as she knew, everything seemed to have gone well, but just because a person had a little reprieve from trouble didn't mean that the trouble was over. There was still Sarah MacAfee to be dealt with, and it was obvious that Jason and she were entangled in this together, whether they realized it or not. Doctor Freemont lay the file aside and turned her attention to the picture of the bluff that Sarah MacAfee had painted. She had hung it on the wall behind her desk so that she could study it. It was obvious that the bluff was the key to the baffling case. Sarah McAfee must somehow be brought in, and she knew that Jason Brennen was the answer. Getting him on board might prove difficult. She didn't want to seem to be conspiring against Sarah MacAfee, but something must be done. Her analytic mind just couldn't let it go as it was until the puzzling case was solved.

Doctor Freemont leaned back in her chair and closed her eyes. She let her thoughts wander away from her office. Everyone's problems were her problems also, and there were times when she became overwhelmed. As she rested, her mind drifted to pleasant times. She almost fell asleep, but then the phone rang. It was Molly calling to say that someone was here to see her, and it wasn't a patient.

"Who is it?" she inquired.

Molly said, "It is a certain detective from the police department. He insists on seeing you right away."

"What is his name?" she asked.

"He is Detective Brian Ferguson," Molly replied.

"Oh, okay, Molly, just give me a moment." Doctor Freemont rose from her chair and went to the mirror to make sure that she didn't look disheveled in any way. Then she told Molly to usher him in.

Molly told Detective Ferguson that Doctor Freemont would see him in just a moment and that he was welcome to take a seat if he would like.

He said, "Thanks, but I'll just stand if you don't mind." His voice had the ring of authority about it, a voice that no one would question.

Molly waited until Doctor Freemont told her that the detective could come in and then ushered him into her office. Molly closed the door behind her, went to her desk, and then began to ponder. She wondered why a detective would want to see Doctor Freemont. They did have clients that had some serious issues, but none of them, as far as she knew, were entangled with the law. Molly put the thought out of her mind and returned to her work, but her curiosity got the best of her, and she found it difficult to stay focused.

She got up from her desk, went into the break room, got a soda, went back to her desk, and tried to get something done. The soda was the distraction that Molly needed, and she soon began to complete the paperwork.

Doctor Freemont was always impressed by her good friend Detective Brian Ferguson. He was in his early forties, with dark hair and a touch of grey throughout. He had very piercing blue eyes, and he looked like a detective.

Detective Ferguson delved into his subject, bypassing the pleasantries, by asking Jillian, "Do you remember the case I told you I had been working on and that there might be a link between our two cases?"

"Yes, Brian, as a matter of fact I have been able to gather quite a bit of information about Sarah MacAfee and Jason Brennen and have come up with some interesting facts. Why don't you have a seat, and we will compare notes."

Detective Ferguson began his narrative by saying that it was one of those things that was a little out of his line of expertise but that he had all of the background on the case and just wasn't sure how to proceed with it. The person involved was David Marsh who had walked away from a home for the mentally disturbed, and there was an all-points bulletin out for him. The institution he escaped from said that they didn't think he was really dangerous.

"What I really wanted from you was to see if you could take the time to look at the file and give me your opinion on this individual."

Doctor Freemont said that she would be glad to assist in the case as long as the rights of the individual weren't violated. Detective Ferguson assured her that all of the necessary documents were in order and that they had contacted the family, who had a signed paper giving him consent to proceed. Doctor Freemont agreed to help as long

126

as everything was in order. He passed the case files over to her, and she began to closely examine them. She did this for some moments before looking up from her study.

"Brian," she began. "Do you realize the seriousness of the situation? This person has no business out on the streets. How did this man escape?"

"To begin with," he said, "David Marsh had never really harmed anyone, and so he couldn't be put in a place with hardened criminals. He therefore had been placed in a home with others like him. It was only in the last year that he began to show signs of deeper emotional problems. He had been closely monitored by the staff, but then one night David Marsh just managed to disappear."

"But where did he get his money?" she asked.

"Well, he wasn't behind bars. He was disturbed and seemed quite harmless. The family didn't want him locked up like an animal, so they made sure he had access to his own funds so that he could live as normal a life as possible. No one knew that he would go over the edge!"

"Do you have any idea where David Marsh is for sure?" she asked.

Detective Ferguson said, "We know that he lived here as a boy, but the family moved out of state a long time ago. He owned a car and was allowed to drive it from time to time. Then one day he went out in it and disappeared. The car is the only lead we have on him, and we are on the lookout for that. He is really very intelligent, and it is just possible that he has altered his appearance. So, no, we don't know where he is. I came here to see if you could give me a better insight into his character. If I can find out how his mind works, I might be able to track him down before something goes wrong."

Doctor Freemont said that if he would leave the files she would go over them thoroughly to see what she could make of them. From what she saw so far, there seemed to be some kind of hidden trauma. If that were so, she would possibly need to talk with his doctor or perhaps the family to get more detail from them. As it was, it would take a few days to unravel why he changed and ran away. Detective Ferguson thanked her and said that he would keep in touch and that if she had any more questions, not to hesitate to call. He thanked her for her cooperation and then left.

Doctor Freemont took a long, deep breath and let out a sigh.

"I should have said no. I already have a backlog of cases that need my attention," she groaned. Doctor Freemont got up from her desk and asked Molly to come in.

"Have a seat, Molly. I'm going to really need your help again. I hate to ask you to take on more work, but something has come up and we are both going to have to work a lot of overtime to get it all done." She then proceeded to fill Molly in on what had just transpired, without going into great detail.

Molly didn't really want to work anymore overtime if she could help it, but when Doctor Freemont said there would be a nice bonus, she agreed to this, although somewhat reluctantly.

"Well, Molly," Doctor Freemont replied. "If you could help expedite some of the paperwork on these case files, I think we can get a handle on everything. I know that there is a lot to do, but if you could try and work in some of them, it would free up some of my time to work on this new case. The police need my help, and I feel that I might be able to assist them. It is rather important, or they would never have come to me." Molly agreed to do whatever it took to get the case load caught up. Molly went back to her desk with some of the extra files, added them to her own, and began the process of getting them into the computer.

In the meantime, Doctor Freemont began reading the case file on David Marsh. The detective had given her some insight into what he had discovered and that there seemed to be a correlation between David Marsh and Sarah MacAfee. It all seemed to point to an extremely tragic event in their lives but that wasn't uncommon. Everyone had things happen to them sooner or later. If this individual's mind was already weak, then that could make a difference. It might take years of struggle for whatever had affected him to come out. When it did come to the surface, it could manifest itself in different ways. Perhaps David Marsh was only trying to run from his issue, or it could be that he wanted to confront it. If that was the case, then anything could happen.

Doctor Freemont felt that she didn't have quite enough information to make an intelligent decision as yet. She would like to know when David Marsh had lived here and where he had lived. It would also help if she knew more about his family. If she could come up with some of the answers, it would go a long way in helping the police. She settled down and began making a list of all of her questions. Some of the questions only the police could answer, but there were several that she could take care of. Doctor Freemont began compiling a short list of people to be called, noting the attending doctor's contact information was in the file. She figured that the police had already contacted him, but they might not know what questions to ask. It was going to take a while to fill in the blanks, and perhaps in the meantime, the police would catch up with him. She hoped that they did, because if they didn't, God forbid, anything might happen.

Doctor Freemont worked until six o'clock, put everything aside, went into the outer office, and told Molly that it was time to go home. "Let's start again in the morning at seven thirty. Okay?"

Molly agreed, and replied. "I'd rather come in early and get it over with." So they put things in order and locked up for the night.

Doctor Freemont and Molly stood in the parking lot for a few moments and discussed the present situation. Neither of them looked forward to the task that lay ahead, but once they had started, there was no going back. Molly assured her that she would do whatever was needed to get it done and not to worry about the work load. Doctor Freemont thanked her for the encouraging words and said that she would see her in the morning.

When Doctor Freemont got home, her husband, Bill, had supper on the table. She had called and said that she would be later than usual, so he had everything ready for her. Bill questioned her about her tardiness but didn't probe too deeply; he knew that her line of business was confidential. She did say that the police were involved and that she would have to work longer hours until the case was settled.

Bill was none too happy about this revelation, but she assured him that there was no danger involved. She said, "The only danger I'm in is if I fall asleep at my desk." She didn't tell him that a crazy man was on the loose. If she had, Bill would be camping out on the office lawn, so she only fed him just enough information to satisfy his curiosity. Things were complicated enough without getting Bill upset.

It was midweek when Doctor Freemont finished the last of the research Detective Ferguson had given her. She was able to delve only so deep into the affair, but she had gleaned enough to get some insight. The research had led her to a very tragic event that had happened when David Marsh was younger. The more she discovered about him, the more she understood. There was a story emerging from all of this, a familiar story that seemed to be juxtaposing Sarah MacAfee and Jason Brennen. Doctor Freemont began putting the pieces of the puzzle together and could see the reason for everything that had happened to them. Jason Brennen's nightmares, the insistent thought, and the reason Sarah MacAfee painted the bluff over and over again. It was no wonder that Sarah MacAfee acted so disturbed that day she had bought the picture from her. Years of struggling with her emotions were being played out each time she painted the bluff. It was obvious that she had been hiding guilt and fear, and painting pictures of the bluff was the only release from the torment she had. As for Jason Brennen, the only logical answer as to how he became involved had to be that he must have been doing research for the newspaper and had come across an article that had disturbed him so deeply that his mind had held onto it. The thought was a product of his imaginings. Though it did seem real enough, it was only his mind's way of getting clear of the disturbing article he had read. Doctor Freemont knew that everything must come to a head in order for all of the confusion to stop. Once that happened, she was confident that everything would right itself. She still wasn't sure which direction things would go. She made up her mind once and for all that Jason Brennen must be contacted in order to head off a tragedy. It was obvious to her that Sarah MacAfee was in danger. If she could persuade Jason to get Sarah to come in, they might be able, with the help of the police, to avoid a disaster. She instructed Molly to try and contact Jason Brennon and to impress upon him that it was paramount that he do so. If he wouldn't comply, perhaps a conversation with Detective

131

Ferguson would do the trick, so she called the detective and advised him of the situation as it currently stood.

Detective Ferguson was filling out some reports when he received Doctor Freemont's call. He was glad to hear from her, because he hadn't found any new leads. It was as if David Marsh had vanished from the face of the earth. They had found his car abandoned in a wooded area in another county. There was no trace of him anywhere. The only thing he thought of was that he had caught a ride with someone or had become lost in the woods. At any rate, after hearing Doctor Freemont's report, it became obvious that he would have to redouble his efforts. There was a photograph posted, but it was an older one. A person could alter his appearance in some way if he really wanted to disappear and that might be the case. Just because this person had mental issues didn't mean he was stupid. After learning more about his traumatic background, Detective Ferguson got a glimmer into where things could be headed. If Doctor Freemont couldn't get Jason Brennen to see her, then he would try and persuade him. He couldn't force Jason, but if the situation were explained and if he had any kind of personality about him at all, it should work out. It was the time factor he was worried about. He wasn't all that sure how Sarah MacAfee fit into the picture, but she did and therein lay the problem. Detective Ferguson couldn't just suddenly walk up to her and say that he was assigning a police man to follow her around. From what he gathered, she had her own issues, and according to Doctor Freemont, it wouldn't do to disturb her by saying that a disturbed man might be after her. The situation would have to be handled in a more diplomatic way. Doctor Freemont had filled Detective Ferguson in as much as was ethical, but what had been gleaned from their conversation had been enough to convince him that he needed her expertise  in order to bring the case to a  safe conclusion for all involved.

Jason was at work when he received a call from Molly at Doctor Freemont's office. It was a little unexpected but not surprising at all. He had already made an appointment to see Doctor Freemont, but Molly had been insistent that he should come in now and that it was vitally important. She had been so adamant that he had agreed. The appointment was at five o'clock, and it wouldn't give him enough time to grab a bite to eat with Sarah before going. That meant that he would have to tell her that he had to work over and that they would have to have a late supper together. Jason wasn't too happy about lying, but he didn't want her to know that he was going to see a shrink; she might not understand.

For the rest of the day, Jason questioned in his mind why Doctor Freemont had been so insistent about seeing him. Perhaps she had discovered something else that was causing him to have the nightmares. He went about the day trying to concentrate on his work, but it proved to be difficult. His mind kept wandering back to the conversation with Doctor Freemont's secretary. She didn't really explain why he needed to come in but that it was very important. It was a little puzzling and made him nervous. It would have been better for him if he knew more about what was going on. Perhaps there was more to the situation than he realized, and this was just a follow up.  It seemed strange that Molly had been so insistent.

Mister Griswell could tell something was bothering Jason Brennen but didn't cut him any slack. In fact, a time or two, Mister Griswell called him a lazy slug and admonished him to pick up the pace. This didn't help Jason's apprehension, and he was relieved when four o'clock finally rolled around. He rushed out and went straight home. He called Sarah, fibbing to her, saying that he had to work over. Jason didn't feel that it was time to tell her that he had a problem, at least not yet. First he wanted to see what the Doctor had in mind, and then he would tell her.

When it was time for the appointment, Jason reluctantly got in the car and drove across town.

Molly was there as usual and greeted him with a warm smile and said, "Hello, Jason, it's good to see you again."

Jason acknowledged her with a nod of the head and a muffled hello. He wasn't exactly happy about being there. It wasn't that he disliked Molly or the doctor; in fact, he was grateful for what the Doctor had done for him. It was just that he wanted to put the past behind him and get on with life, and the fear that something else was going to happen played heavily on his mind.

Molly got up from behind her desk and told Jason that Doctor Freemont had been waiting for him; she ushered him into her office. When Jason stepped into the room, one of the first things he saw was an easel with what appeared to be a covered painting, or at least it looked like a painting. Jason thought that was a bit odd, but dismissed it from his mind and waited for Doctor Freemont to explain exactly what she wanted. Deep down inside, he already knew but wasn't ready for what she was going to tell him.

Doctor Freemont greeted Jason with a hand shake and thanked him for coming in and asked him how he had been. He replied that he was fine, considering all he had been through. She began to inquire how he had been getting along with the thought and if it still came into his mind. Jason replied that on occasions, it did indeed show up, but that for the most part, it had been quiet until just recently. Upon hearing this, Doctor Freemont walked over to the easel and removed the covering. Jason was taken aback by what he saw. It was one of Sarah MacAfee's paintings of the bluff. He just stood there, gaping, unable to move, with nothing to say.

Doctor Freemont asked, "Recognize this?"

At first Jason felt a little bit confused and didn't reply. But then he nodded his head and asked, "How in the world did you know about the paintings of the bluff?  Do you know Sarah MacAfee?"

Doctor Freemont related the story of how she had assigned Molly the task of finding out all she could about the artist Sarah MacAfee. It had seemed to her that there was a connection between her and the nightmares that Jason had been experiencing. When Molly had located Sarah and had seen the painting of the bluff and the way in which she had acted, the pieces of the puzzle began to fall into place.

Jason wanted to know what all of it meant, and asked, "All of this is good and well, Doctor Freemont, but where are we going with it, and how is it going to turn out?"

Doctor Freemont then told him about the possible threat to Sarah MacAfee and that the police were involved in order to head off any danger, but that so far the suspect hadn't been found. Jason wanted to know who the man was, but Doctor Freemont said that she didn't think that the police wanted his name divulged as yet. Doctor Freemont said that he was a person that had lived in the area when he was a boy and thought perhaps there might be a connection. Jason wanted to know what he looked like, but Doctor Freemont related that Detective Ferguson thought he could have altered his appearance and that they were having a hard time finding him.

Doctor Freemont, after confiding everything else to Jason, began to impress upon him the importance of getting Sarah to come and visit with her.  Jason, after listening to Doctor Freemont's narrative, wholeheartedly agreed with what must be done but was reluctant to broach the subject with Sarah. He had no idea how she would react. He remembered how she had acted when Jeb had told her that she should face her fear and go to the bluff. Sarah had adamantly refused. How was he going to tell her a crazy man might be stalking her?

Doctor Freemont didn't press Jason, at least not for the time being. Instead, she asked him to look closely at the painting. Jason couldn't see that there was any difference between this painting of the bluff and the other ones, except that they might be done in different hues. Doctor Freemont handed him the magnifying glass and pointed to a certain area of the bluff and told him to examine it closely. At first Jason couldn't find any features that stood out, but after some moments of encouragement from Doctor Freemont, Jason lowered the magnifying glass and stepped back. Tears began welling up in his eyes.

"I don't believe it," he said. "How could Sarah know? I never told her about the nightmare!" Doctor Freemont directed Jason to a chair and made him sit down. The room grew silent as Jason digested what he had just seen. It seemed impossible, but there it was right in front of him, the reality of his fears. Sarah had painted her own likeness plunging from the bluff, or at least it seemed so. But Sarah was alive and well. Did it mean that she was foreseeing her death, or was all of this just madness? Why had he been tormented by the thought? Why hadn't it departed? Did it mean that the drama was yet to climax? Was the torment to end in disaster? The whole thing was becoming a tangled web that seemed to be closing in on him and Sarah.

Doctor Freemont placed her hand on his shoulder and soothingly told him that everything was going to be just fine. As long as Sarah would cooperate and come in, she was certain that the confusion and danger would soon pass. She reminded him that the police were on the case and that they were watching out for Sarah. They were certain the man could be picked up. But Jason wasn't at all that encouraged by her attempt to smooth things over by saying that everything would be all right. Nothing had been all right for months. The only thing that had been right was meeting and then falling in love with Sarah MacAfee, and it looked as though she might be taken away by some mad man. Jason grew silent and wouldn't respond to Doctor Freemont but just sat, trying to comprehend all that had happened.

Doctor Freemont was quite disturbed by Jason's lack of response. If she couldn't get him to talk things out, he might slip into depression. If that happened, everything that had been gained before might be lost. She must get him to respond by some means.

Doctor Freemont began to think about what was really behind the whole situation with Jason and Sarah MacAfee. It was obvious that he was deeply in love with her, and if she worked from that angle, he might open up. After considering this for a few moments, she began by asking him a question. "Jason, are you in love with Sarah MacAfee?" At first Jason didn't respond, but nervously shifted his weight in the chair and cleared his throat. A short moment of silence passed before he answered.

"What does it matter to me?" he asked. "She is probably lost to me anyway. Instead of things getting better, they are getting worse." Jason put his head in his hands and grew silent again.

This was what Doctor Freemont had been waiting for all along, an emotional breakdown. If Jason kept things bottled up inside, he might not be able to go forward and really help Sarah. If only she could get him to open up just a little bit more. She once again spoke to him in her soothing tones, repeating her question.

"Jason," she asked. "Tell me, are you really in love with Sarah MacAfee?" This time Jason slowly raised his head and answered in barely a whisper.

"Oh yes, Doctor Freemont, I love Sarah very much, and I would do anything for Sarah."

This was what Doctor Freemont wanted to hear. She replied, "Well Jason, if that is so, then we have a lot of work to do. Why don't you start from the beginning and tell me everything that has happened since the last time you were here."

Jason was a little slow in starting, but once he began he told everything he knew. The thought was there with its influence, but it wasn't a hindrance at all. If anything, its presence seemed to be weakening. When Jason mentioned this fact to Doctor Freemont, she said that the thought was a thing of his own imaginings, triggered by the need he felt to rescue Sarah, even though he hadn't known her before. Now that the danger to her lay bare before him, the influence of the thought wasn't needed, and it would eventually fade away into nothingness.

When Jason related all of the events leading up to this time, she told him to look at the painting again. He studied it carefully until he had located the figure. Doctor Freemont asked him if it was Sarah. The longer he examined the figure, the more doubtful he became. It certainly looked like Sarah, but he just wasn't sure. Doctor Freemont asked if he had a recent picture of her. Jason got a snapshot out of his billfold and gave it to her. She carefully compared the picture of Sarah to the figure on the bluff edge. The resemblance was striking, but it was obvious to her that they weren't the same person. When she pointed this out to Jason, he gave a long

138

sigh of relief and wanted to know what it all meant. Doctor Freemont pondered a moment on his pointed question before answering. She wanted to collect her thoughts first. When she did answer, it was to say that in order to help Sarah, Jason would have to convince her to come in for a session. Otherwise, they would only be guessing as to what was bothering her. If that could be discovered, then half of the battle would be won, but the entire thing hinged on Sarah's coming in for a consultation.

Doctor Freemont faced Jason and continued with concern in her voice: "Jason, you are going to have to open up to Sarah and tell her what you have told me today. I know that it will be hard for you, but if you care for her as much as you say, you will do it. It is not only for her safety but for her sanity. This thing must be resolved; it has gone on far too long. Sarah will come to a breaking point sooner or later. I think your friend Jeb had the right idea. Sarah must face her fear. If you could convince her to come in and let me talk to her, I might be able to help. But it must begin with you."

Jason could see the logic in Doctor Freemont's words, and so, after pondering on this, he finally said that he would do anything to help Sarah. Doctor Freemont felt relieved when Jason responded in this way. She knew that it was going to take some effort to correct the situation but was confident that everything would be made right.

It was going for six o'clock when Jason finally left Doctor Freemont's office. He sat in the car trying to decide how to broach the subject with Sarah. He felt as though a heavy weight had been placed upon his shoulders and didn't want to face his unpleasant duty. He was a little worried as to how Sarah would respond. She had kept her secret for so long that she might not open up. The fact that he had purposely neglected to call her after work as he usually did left him

139

feeling guilty. How was he going to explain to her that he had an appointment with Doctor Freemont?   Jason was in a quandary. There was no getting out of it; so he took a deep breath, tried to calm his nerves, picked up his cell phone, and called Sarah.

Sarah had been putting some last -minute touches on another portrait she had been working with when her phone rang.

"Hi Jason," she said, "you're running a little late today. Are we still going out for supper?"

Jason could tell by the tone of Sarah's voice that she was wondering why he hadn't called earlier.

"Well," Jason stammered, "I had an appointment with a doctor."

"You had a doctor's appointment! Why didn't you tell me?"   Jason felt sick inside and managed to say that he wasn't feeling very well; he would explain everything when he got to the studio. Jason began to feel like someone had died, and he was the one to tell her the bad news. Jason said goodbye, pulled out of Doctor Freemont's parking lot, and headed across town. As he drove, Jason began to rehearse what he was going to say to Sarah, trying to figure out how to explain what was going on. Sarah was extremely sensitive about the bluff and wouldn't even talk about it. How was he going to convince her to see Doctor Freemont?

Jason took his time getting to Sarah's studio. He wasn't in any kind of a hurry, but the thought was. It kept nudging him to get on with it. Jason fought back the best he could, but it wouldn't let up.  By the time he got to Sarah's, he was a nervous wreck. He pulled up in front of the studio and just sat there, not knowing what to do, but he had to broach the subject someway.

After Jason told Sarah that he had been to the doctor's, Sarah began to feel ill at ease. It wasn't like Jason to hide anything from her. She began to imagine that something was terribly wrong with him, and this seemed to be confirmed since it was taking him so long to get there. Sarah began to wring her hands and to pace the floor. Presently she went to the window and looked out, only to see Jason just sitting in his car. This alarmed her even more. The first thing she thought of was that he must have bad news to tell her. Sarah didn't hesitate but went out and knocked on the passenger window. This startled Jason, and he looked up to see Sarah. She had a very worried look on her face. Jason got out of the car, went to her, and said that there was no need to worry; he wasn't sick. He had something to tell her. Sarah didn't ask what it was because she was afraid to. They went inside, and neither of them said a word. The room was thick with silence. Jason held Sarah in his strong arms, reassuring her that everything was all right.

When the tension of the moment had passed, Jason took a deep breath, exhaled, and proclaimed that he had something important to tell her. He didn't go right into an appeal to get her to see Doctor Freemont, but instead he started with the thought tormenting him and of the nightmares he had right up until his first visit to Doctor Freemont. Then he told her how much she had helped him overcome it all. When he had finished, he felt drained and waited for Sarah's reaction. Sarah was taken aback by this revelation about Jason and didn't quite know what to make of it. Jason let her absorb all he had just told her before going any further; there was no sense in overwhelming her all at once. It had been hard enough telling her his own situation, and he wondered what would happen when she found out that Doctor Freemont knew about her. Jason didn't want to broach the subject yet and so only asked Sarah if she understood what he had been going through.

Sarah had remained silent as Jason told his narrative. But after he had finished, she asked how it was that he had associated her with the girl in his dream. Jason was in a quandary as to how to begin. It was a tangled web at best, and he fumbled around searching for the right words to say. He finally began by asking her if she remembered the woman that came to her studio and bought the painting of the bluff. Sarah didn't answer right away, but just looked Jason in the eyes and asked: "What has my selling the painting of the bluff have to do with anything?"

Jason could feel the anxiety in her voice; he had hit a sensitive nerve, and now he was backed into a corner and would have to try and explain everything as best he could.

Jason took a deep breath and began with, "Sarah, the woman who bought your painting is my doctor, Doctor Jillian Freemont. I honestly did not know that she had been searching for you until my last visit to her office. She has been a great help to me. I told her everything that I have been going through, and I believe she could help you also. I'm so sorry that this had to happen. I would never betray your trust, Sarah, but now the police are involved."

Sarah was quite shocked at this newest revelation and couldn't believe what she was hearing. She quickly replied, "The police are involved! How did the police get involved in my private business?"

Jason then told her about the man, who might be stalking her.

Sarah became very upset. She asked in a quavering voice, "Why, would this person be stalking me?"

Sarah turned away from Jason and started pacing back and forth across the studio. Just knowing that her private life was wide open to everyone shocked her deeply. Sarah felt betrayed. She had fallen in love with Jason, but now she was confused. Did he think that she was mentally unbalanced? Why would a shrink want to talk to her? And was there really some insane man stalking her? Sarah was dumbfounded by all of this. Her life had been so pleasant since she had met Jason; he had brought stability to her mind. He had never pressured her to divulge the reason she painted pictures of the bluff, but now she felt like the walls were closing in on her. Sarah didn't want to face the reality of the situation. She had always been able to avoid any real confrontation about the bluff, but now she was trapped and didn't see any way to get around her emotional dilemma. Sarah ran up to her apartment and slammed the door behind her, but she didn't lock it. She was torn between thoughts of giving up the one she loved or letting go of the torment that she had held on to for so long. The small act of not locking the door was her plea for help from Jason. She needed him to help allay the fears surrounding her.

The thing that Jason was worrying over had happened. Sarah hadn't even given him time to explain himself. It was obvious to him that she wasn't going to cooperate with Doctor Freemont. Her personal struggle would stay hidden away from prying eyes. Of course when he had been struggling with the thought and the nightmares, it had taken a while before he had finally given in and sought some help.

When Sarah left the emotionally charged atmosphere of the studio and went up to her apartment, Jason took note of the fact that she hadn't locked her door. He took this as a sign that Sarah was crying out for his help. Jason waited until he thought Sarah had calmed down before going upstairs; he didn't want to rush her. Jason walked around inside the studio looking at all of the beautiful paintings Sarah had done, wondering at her talent. In one corner of the room where she painted, Jason found a covered easel. He lifted the cover to see what she had been working on. He hardly ever bothered an unfinished painting unless she invited him to do so, but this time he felt compelled to look. To his surprise, it was a rendition of the bluff with his likeness staring up at its craggy edge; the entire background had been painted in bright hues with the sun rising over its crest. It was one of the most impressive paintings of the bluff he had seen yet. Sarah was a true master of art, and the meaning behind this painting was very obvious to him. It was Sarah's way of saying that she had found love.

Jason hesitated before ascending the stairs to Sarah's apartment. When he did decide to go on up, it was with some trepidation. He wasn't sure how she would react to him, but in the back of his mind he was confident that Sarah was going to be okay, even for all of the pent up emotion she had displayed.

The apartment was very still when he entered it. The lights were out everywhere but in the kitchen. Jason was a little afraid of what he would find. When a person was in the kind of condition that Sarah was in, anything might happen. Just thinking about such things made Jason very nervous. He stood still for a moment or two and then softly called her name.

"Sarah," he whispered. Jason did this a time or two and then waited for her to respond. When Sarah didn't answer, he advanced farther into the apartment and listened with bated breath.

Silence, there was nothing but silence. Jason called her again. Still, silence prevailed. He entered the kitchen, but Sarah wasn't there. Jason knew Sarah well enough to understand that she was under much duress but knew that she was okay, so he just lingered where he was. Jason began looking around and noticed that there was a teapot on the table with two cups sitting side by side. The teapot was warm, as though it had just been filled. After seeing this, Jason knew that Sarah was nearby and was probably trying to get up her nerve to face him. He looked down the hallway and saw a dim light under the bathroom door.

Jason waited a few more minutes and then lightly tapped on the door and said, "I'm here for you Sarah; I love you."

She answered back in a half whisper. "I love you too, Jason."

The door suddenly swung open and Sarah rushed into his waiting arms. She clung to him, as though she were a little child.

She pleaded, "Please help me Jason. I don't know how much longer I can go on. I have held this in for so very long, I can't take it anymore! I want to have peace of mind. I'm tired of this!"

Jason held Sarah until her trembling sobs subsided. He continued speaking to her in soothing tones until she said, "I'm alright now, Jason. I'm sorry for all that I said to you. I knew that you were only trying to help me, but I had been holding those emotions in for so long that I just couldn't stop them from coming out."

Jason led Sarah into the kitchen and remarked that it looked like the tea was ready. Sarah gingerly filled the cups, and they sat at the table sipping its soothing warmth. As the tension subsided she began to open up to Jason about the bluff. She told him that as far as she knew, there was absolutely no reason as to why it was so prominent in her mind; only that something was compelling her to paint it and that she couldn't stop.

She said, "Jason, it's a tormenting thing that I just can't get away from. There are times when I have nightmares. And a time or two I almost went up on the mountain to try and understand my fear, but I just couldn't make myself do it."

The more Sarah began to open up to him, the clearer Jason's understanding became as to what might have happened. He was certain that it was so tragic that it had affected her memory. If he could only convince Sarah to give in and see Doctor Freemont, she would begin to mend and could then put this episode behind her. Jason sat quietly listening, letting Sarah tell her story, fearing that the least interruption might cause her to stop the very thing she needed to do. "If only Doctor Freemont were here, she would know how to handle the situation," he thought.

Sarah, as she continued to unload her burden to Jason, began to feel some of the guilt and fear lift. She hadn't felt this kind of relief for a very long time. It was obvious to her that the emotional upheaval she was going through would eventually subside if she continued to talk it out. There was still quite a shroud of mystery that seemed to be hanging over her, and she wished with all of her heart that she could see her way through. Sarah hadn't really told Jason anything terrifying so far. Whatever was behind her renditions of the bluff was hidden away; it all seemed so distant and out of reach, but she did feel better for the telling.

Sarah finally stopped talking and burst into tears again. Between sobs, she apologized for her actions and thanked Jason for listening.

She said, "I have held all of my fear in for so long. I don't know what I would have done if you hadn't come into my life. I just hope that after hearing everything you won't leave me. I really need you right now; I feel like a foolish school girl!"

Jason was relieved when Sarah had finally finished with her story. He said that he wasn't going anywhere and that they would see this thing through to the end. Jason knew that Sarah's underlying problem still needed to be confronted, but obviously only Doctor Freemont could handle that. He didn't suggest seeing her just yet; he wanted to wait until things got back to some kind of normalcy. It would have to be Sarah's idea to make an appointment to see Doctor Freemont. He was confident that she would do the right thing.

# Chapter 16

Thomas Gilmore had been very busy. The pictures he had taken were placed in a manila folder with the dates and times of Sarah MacAfee's comings and goings, so that he could easily study them. Each time he looked at the photographs, he smiled a twisted smile and then touched them. It seemed to do something to him, and he began to mutter to himself in a strange, demented way. So far everything had gone as planned. No one suspected what he was up to. He just came and went as he pleased vowing to accomplish what he had come there to do. He already knew Sarah MacAfee's routine, and he knew her boyfriend also. It was only a matter of timing, and it wouldn't be very hard to put his plan into action. It had been a long time coming, but there was nothing that would stop him now. So far, he had fooled everyone, even the police. As far as anyone knew, he was out of the country. He could work behind the scenes all he wanted without interruption. Thomas studied the photographs once more, pondered upon their images a while longer, and then replaced them in the folder. He wasn't quite satisfied with everything as yet, and so he decided to make another excursion or two before proceeding. He purposely went out at a different time every day in order to confuse anyone that might be watching his movements. The only one who might possibly be a threat to his plan was his landlady. She seemed to be the nosy type, and he kept a close eye on her. He wasn't about to have any last minute glitches foil his long laid plans. "Tonight," he muttered to himself. "Tonight, when everyone is off the streets, I'll get a better look just to make sure." Thomas set his alarm for 2:00 am and then went to bed.

It had been raining hard, and the rain-soaked streets glistened under the lights. Streaks of lightning flashed from the overburdened storm clouds, and the sound of thunder reverberated among the buildings. The alarm clock suddenly sounded and then went silent. It wasn't a fit night to be outside, but a few moments later Thomas Gilmore could be seen slipping out of his apartment and quickly getting into his car.

Mrs. Farley, having been awakened by the ongoing storm, had arisen from her warm bed. She thrust her feet in her house slippers and put her robe about her shoulders. Mrs. Farley didn't like storms. They made her nervous. The last time a storm like this one came through, it blew a tree down in the front yard. She gingerly looked out of the window to see if everything was still intact. The wind had blown a trash can into the street, and it was being rolled hither and yon until it finally rattled on and into the curb. Then she caught a glimpse of a hunched figure running to a car. Mrs. Farley quickly stepped away from the window and positioned herself in such a way that she could still observe what was going on. "Who would be out on a night like this?" she asked herself. The person got into Thomas Gilmore's car and drove off. "That's strange," she thought, "I know that he keeps odd hours, but I have never seen him go out this late. You would think he would stay at home on such a bad night as this!" Her spoken thoughts had emboldened her and her curiosity became aroused. Mrs. Farley had been waiting for such an opportunity to examine Thomas Gilmore's apartment. She just couldn't get away from the feeling that things weren't what they seemed to be.

149

"What if he is a drug dealer?" she reasoned out loud. "Wouldn't it be my duty to find out and turn him in?" The spoken words were more convincing than ever. Emboldened by these thoughts she got dressed, donned her rain coat and galoshes, and proceeded to brave the storm. She lingered a few moments to make sure that Thomas Gilmore was really gone, started down the side walk to his apartment, inserted a key into the lock, and went inside. She had brought a flash light with her and immediately began looking around for anything out of the ordinary. Mrs. Farley was surprised at the neatness of the living room. Normally a single man was sloppy, but Thomas Gilmore had everything in place. It was almost as if he didn't live there at all. She went into the bedroom and took a look around but was disappointed that there wasn't any incriminating evidence. There were only socks, hankies, and underwear in the dresser drawers but no drugs at all. Mrs. Farley was becoming disappointed. She rummaged around for a little while longer and then decided to look in the kitchen. She opened up the cabinet drawers, but they were all but empty. There were only a few pieces of silverware to be seen. The top cabinets held only a few cups and a couple of plates, and they were plastic. It seemed odd to her that he didn't need much of anything to live with. It was becoming apparent that Thomas Gilmore wasn't going to be there very long.

Mrs. Farley looked at her watch. It was 2:30 and time to go home.

"Thomas Gilmore is liable to return at any moment," she thought. She left the apartment, being sure to secure the door and quickly ran down the sidewalk. It was still storming, and by the time she got in her office, she was drenched. Mrs. Farley made a cup of coffee to settle her nerves and to warm her up a bit. She had taken a big chance in going to Thomas

150

Gilmore's apartment. "What if he had come back while I was snooping around?" The thought made her shiver all over.

"At least I got a look around his place. I still think that there is something odd about that man," she said aloud. She had spoken the words with conviction; her womanly instincts were hardly ever wrong. Then a dreadful thought occurred to her. What if she had left watermarks on the floor of his apartment? If he noticed them, he would surely know that someone had been there, and it wouldn't take a very large stretch of the imagination to figure out who that person was. Mrs. Farley began to grow apprehensive at this disturbing thought, and the what if's began to fill her mind. She got dressed for bed, crawled under the covers, and tried to sleep, but sleep wouldn't come. It was a miserable night. The storm was still raging, and she jumped every time a tree limb brushed against the house. Her imagination was running away with her. Every once in a while she got out of bed to see if Thomas Gilmore had returned. After about the fifth or sixth time of this she finally convinced herself that he wasn't coming back at all and that he was probably working somewhere. This helped her to settle down, and finally, about four in the morning, she went to sleep.

Thomas Gilmore had been reconnoitering, making sure that his plan didn't have any flaws in it. The storm had been just the thing he needed to help cover his movements. There hadn't been any further need to use the abandoned building across the street from Sarah MacAfee's studio; he had all of the pictures that he needed from that vantage point. He made his way to the rear of Sarah MacAfee's building, searching for an easy entrance way and discovered a flaw in the old alarm system that he could take advantage of; this he carefully noted for future reference.

151

When Thomas Gilmore finally returned, it was still dark, but the darkness was dwindling away. He entered his apartment and turned the lights on. At first he didn't notice anything out of place. But as he stood looking around, he noticed faint wet marks on the carpet. He stooped and touched one of them. Sure enough, the carpet was just a little bit wet. Someone had been snooping around. Thomas began to wonder if he had been found out, and the thought troubled him. He walked into the living room to see if had anything had been disturbed. As far as he could tell, nothing had been bothered. Next, he went into the bedroom. He opened the top drawer and examined it thoroughly.

"So far so good," he murmured. After looking around in the kitchen he went into the bathroom, turned the clothes hamper upside down, and got the folder that had been taped there. He could tell that it hadn't been disturbed because the hamper had been placed in such a way that he would have known about it. He then added more notes and replaced it under the hamper.

Thomas Gilmore didn't like the idea that someone was snooping around.

"I will find you out, my friend, and when I do." He said these words in a deep husky voice, emphasizing, "And when I do." He had his suspicions, but of course, no real proof. In his mind he was sure it had to be his landlady. She looked just the type to be overly curious. The way she looked at him whenever he had to go into her office got on his nerves. It had to be Mrs. Farley snooping around, he thought. She has all of the keys.

"Well, old gal," he said out loud. "You'll slip up one of these days, and it will cost you."

Thomas went into the kitchen, sat down at the table, and ate the meager breakfast he had purchased. When he had finished, he took a shower and went to bed. It had been a long night and he was very tired, but he had done what he had set out to do. Everything was falling into place. He even had an escape route planned. He had gone over it time and again just to make sure all went according to plan.

Mrs. Farley had a cold. Now, she wished she had never gone snooping around in the rain to check out Thomas Gilmore's apartment. "Ahh choo," she sneezed. Her eyes were throbbing, and her teeth hurt! And the lack of sleep wasn't making her feel better. She was extremely miserable and was constantly reaching for the Kleenex box. Her nose was getting sore, and her throat was scratchy.

"What was I thinking?" she moaned. "I could kick myself." It hurt her to speak, and her voice was coming in a whisper. She got up from behind her desk, went into the back room, and made another cup of tea with honey in it. It helped sooth her throat and loosened her sinuses somewhat, which in turn made her reach for another Kleenex. The process was getting monotonous. "I just hope I have a slow day," she thought. "I had no business going in there in the middle of a storm. It's going to take me a week to get over this cold."

Mrs. Farley didn't even hear when Thomas Gilmore came in. He didn't say a word but just stood there looking down at her. When she did happen to look up, she was very startled to see him.

She stammered, "Oh, Mister Gilmore; you surprised me. I didn't hear you come in. Please excuse me. I have a bad cold today." Thomas Gilmore didn't say anything for a while, and Mrs. Farley could feel the tension building.  Then he asked. "Were you out in the storm last night?"

Her voice quavered as she lied, "Why, no, of course not. I only... I thought I heard my cat crying out on the porch, and I went to check on it. I guess I stayed out longer than I should have and caught a cold."

Thomas Gilmore replied, "Yes, I would say that you were out longer than you should have been. You had better be careful. It probably wasn't even your cat. You know how it can be when you mess around with things that don't belong to you. Why a person might get hurt!" He leaned forward over her desk as he said these last words.

Mrs. Farley, in a trembling voice replied, "Why, why, yes." I see what you mean. I'll try and be more careful and not go outside when it is storming. You were right about the cat; it wasn't even mine."

Thomas Gilmore didn't say another word, but just turned on his heels and walked out the door, letting it slam behind him. Poor Mrs. Farley was in a faint. Thomas Gilmore had just given her a thinly veiled threat. She must have really touched a nerve when he found out she had been in his apartment.

"I must have left some wet footprints, in there just as I suspected," she whispered. Mrs. Farley was in a quandary. It was obvious that Thomas Gilmore was up to something, but what in the world could she do about it? She couldn't go to the police without some kind of proof. She couldn't say that she had been threatened by him. It would be her word against his. Mrs. Farley was at her wit's end as to what to do. One thing she would do for sure was to continue watching him, and the first time he messed up out he would go. Mrs. Farley felt a little emboldened by this thought, and indeed it was only a thought; she had no intentions of having another confrontation with Thomas Gilmore. She was afraid of him and what he might do to her if he found out. There had been confrontations with tenants in the past, but nothing like this. She would just have to hope and pray that he would move

out soon.    Mrs. Farley reached for another Kleenex and
sneezed.

"Oh, I'm so tired of this stupid cold!" she croaked.

Thomas Gilmore didn't like having his well-laid plans
tampered with.

"That old bitty had better stay out of my way. I better not
catch her snooping around again, the old busy body!" He
said this with some force. The more he thought about what
had happened the more convinced he became that his plans
would have to be altered.    It would all depend on the
movements of Sarah MacAfee. If she kept to her usual
routine, he could still pull it off. There had been a lot of
reconnoitering, and he had learned a lot about her. It had
been easily done, and so far as he could tell, she didn't
suspect a thing. With a bit of luck, his plan should come off
without a hitch, unless Mrs. Farley decided to call the cops.
"Well, there are ways around that," he thought. He went
back into his apartment, put on a pot of coffee, and settled
down to rework his plans. He couldn't allow the situation to
get out of hand. It had taken a long time to work everything
out, and it would only take one misstep to ruin it all. He
began to wonder if he should really try and do something
about Mrs. Farley. If something bad were to happen to her
that would just draw more attention, and that was the last
thing he wanted to happen. Suddenly a thought occurred to
him, and a broad smile creased his face.

"Oh yes, yes, of course." he laughed. "I should have
thought of this earlier. It is easier to catch a fly with honey
than with vinegar." The thought of having to warm up to
Mrs. Farley wasn't exactly pleasant. It wasn't going to be easy
to alter his morose personality. But what had to be done had
to be done, for there was a lot at stake. Thomas Gilmore
began to think of how he should go about patching things up

with her. It had been a mistake going into her office like that, but it had made him mad to know that she had invaded his privacy. "What if she had found the folder? I would probably be locked up by now." The thought of it made him disgusted.

Thomas Gilmore didn't like his plans being rushed. It threw everything out of kilter.

"If only that old broad hadn't interfered!" he said aloud. He began pacing back and forth, occasionally pausing to thumb through the folder that was lying on the kitchen table. He was beginning to have doubts about trying to warm up to Mrs. Farley. Sometimes things were best left alone. Besides, he couldn't stand the thought of pretending to be nice; it just wasn't who he was. The more he thought about it, the more he became convinced that he had made the right choice. He would take his chances as they were. If she got in his way again, he would just have to deal with her.

He got the calendar and began looking for the best possible date to set his plan into action. He had chosen a date once before, but with the old bitty getting in the way, everything had to be delayed. The waiting set his nerves on edge, and he was growing impatient. The longer he had to wait, the greater the probability that something would go wrong. The timing had to be perfect with everything in place, or it could mean failure.

He looked at the photographs again and scrutinized every detail of them. It had been easy to acquire them. He had just blended in with the crowd and did as he pleased, and no one was the wiser. Even the pictures of the rear of the building hadn't been all that hard to get, and they had helped him to find a weakness in the security. The building was really quite old, and he had discovered a possible way in without making very much noise. If everything went his way, it could be pulled off with dispatch. He made up his mind as to the date and circled it on the calendar. Now all he had to do was to watch for the opportune moment. His observations of Sarah MacAfee and her boyfriend were very crucial, especially as it got closer to the date he had chosen. It would be best if the boyfriend were out of the picture altogether. He would rather deal with Sarah MacAfee alone, but if it became necessary, he could deal with both. He wasn't about to let anything stop him. His plans had been too long in the making. He continued scrutinizing the notes and the photographs, going over them again and again, paying close attention to every detail. Once he got something in his mind, he followed it through to fruition.

Thomas Gilmore, having satisfied himself as to the probability of his plan succeeding, finally put the folder back in its hiding place. It had been a long night, and he was growing tired. Walking the alleyways and dodging the police was beginning to wear on him. Fortunately, his nightly excursions hadn't been observed as yet, for he never parked his car in the same place twice, and sometimes he just walked to the corner and called a cab. It was just one way of blending in with everyone. It was a good smoke screen. He smiled at the thought of what he had accomplished thus far. Now all he had to do was to wait until the right moment presented itself. The longer he thought about what he was going to do, the more confident he became. He began to picture the whole scenario in his mind. A cruel smile creased his face as he pondered upon his plan. He stood very still, transfixed as he watched the exciting drama unfold in his imagination. It had been a long process with many hours of observation. He was eager to get on with it but knew better than to rush into what must be done. As weariness took over, Thomas Gilmore shook himself from his ponderings, took a shower, and went to bed.

# Chapter 17

Detective Ferguson was in a quandary. He really was dissatisfied by the way things were going. It was as though his suspect had disappeared from the face of the earth. It didn't matter how much the department had searched, they couldn't find him. It was beginning to look like all of the fuss was for nothing. There had been photographs put out, but no one recognized him. Of course if someone really wanted to disappear, they could just alter their appearance and change their name. Detective Ferguson was beginning to think that that was probably what had really happened. But it was one of those things that couldn't be dropped. Perhaps Doctor Freemont could shed a little more light on the subject, he rationalized. If he had more insight into the man's character, he might be able figure out what he was up to. He reached for the phone and dialed Doctor Freemont's number.

"Doctor Freemont's office, how may I help you?" Molly intonated. Detective Ferguson asked if Doctor Freemont was in and said he needed to talk to her. Molly said that the Doctor would be free later on in the afternoon and asked if three o'clock would be okay. Detective Ferguson thanked her, said that three o'clock would be fine, and then hung up. He reached for the current file on the case and reexamined the whole thing. David Marsh had some serious issues and had been under psychiatric care for years. According to his file, he hadn't shown any real tendency to be violent, at least not on the surface, but the mind is a strange place and under the right circumstances violence might be triggered. In the meantime the department would just have to do their best to find him. Detective Ferguson got a cup of coffee and began going over the file again.   He was allowed to delve into a person's personal life while under investigation, and he could do some police work to look into his past without sending up any red flags concerning his right to privacy.

Detective Ferguson, after a discrete inquiry, learned that David Marsh hadn't had any serious run-ins with the law but had gotten in trouble in school when he was in the fifth grade. It was after this that the family had moved away. Whatever had happened from then on was a mystery; except that for some reason or other, he had had a mental breakdown, which had altered his personality.   He hoped that Doctor Freemont might be able to clue him in as to what had happened.

It was just before three o'clock when Detective Ferguson arrived at Doctor Freemont's office for the appointment. He gathered his material, got out of the car, and went inside. Molly greeted him and said that Doctor Freemont would be with him in a few moments. He ensconced himself in one of the comfortable looking chairs, picked up a magazine, and flipped through it as he waited.

The old grandfather clock standing in the corner was beginning to get on his nerves. Its monotonous ticking sounded loud in the quiet office. Detective Ferguson began to squirm. He looked up from the magazine and checked his watch against the clock. "Doctor Freemont must be asleep," he thought. He put the magazine down and reached for another one just as the Doctor's office door opened and a distraught looking woman came out. Doctor Freemont followed her to the door and escorted her outside.  After a few moments she came back in and said that she could see him now. Detective Ferguson picked up his file and followed her into the office.

Doctor Freemont and Detective Ferguson exchanged the usual pleasantries for a few moments before delving into the subject at hand and then she bade him sit down and asked how the search was going.

Detective Ferguson cleared his throat and began by saying, "Not very well I'm afraid. It is as though our friend has disappeared from the face of the earth! I'm afraid that I am going to have to have more information. I have looked at his personal file, and it has given me some insight into his character, but I still need more information."

Doctor Freemont said, "Well, as you already know, he isn't my patient, but I did call my colleague who has been attending to him and asked some questions. I was able find out a few things that might be pertinent to the case."

Doctor Freemont then began to divulge some of the suspect's background. As it turned out, David Marsh had had something traumatic happen, and from that point on he began to change. His grades dropped, and he began to get into trouble at school. Things got progressively worse with each successive year until it got so bad that he had had to be put in an institution. As he got older, he seemed to have gotten better and led a somewhat normal life. He was no longer in an institution per se but had been moved to a home for the mentally disabled. Everything went fine for a few years until one day he suddenly became violent for no apparent reason. He hadn't hurt anyone, and the episode passed. His doctor monitored him for a few weeks, and the episode of violence wasn't repeated. When he recently disappeared from the home, his room was searched, and a notebook had been found. It seemed that he had been writing about his past. His doctor recognized an underlying pattern that had begun to emerge. He had been suffering under strong delusion, and that delusion was coming to life.

The incident of violence might only have been a precursor of things to come. Detective Ferguson, after conversing with Doctor Freemont, came away with a clearer idea of what he was up against. It was obvious to him that David Marsh was a confused but clever man, and he would have to redouble his efforts to locate him. Getting that insight into his past had helped, but it still didn't tell him what was on David Marsh's mind; it could be anything at all. During their conversation, Doctor Freemont told him as much as she knew about him and the incident that had altered his personality. Evidently it had been tragic enough to bring about the change in him. Detective Ferguson was a little better off than he was when he had first talked with Doctor Freemont, but the information he had gleaned still didn't tell him where the suspect was and what he might be up to. If he were indeed going under an assumed name and had altered his appearance, David Marsh would be hard to find.

During their conversation, Detective Ferguson had pointed out Sarah MacAfee's painting of the bluff and commented that it was a foreboding scene. Doctor Freemont said that the painting had been done by a local artist. Detective Ferguson asked who it was that had painted it. When Doctor Freemont told him that it was Sarah MacAfee, a thought began stirring in his mind. There was something he had read once, a vague memory, but for now it escaped him. He filed the thought away to be looked into later. If something occurred to him that might have a bearing on a case, he would not let it go until the lead ran out. Detective Ferguson could be as tenacious as a bull dog, and each new lead would have to be tracked down one at a time. It took a lot of legwork, but that was just a part of the challenge.

It was five o'clock when Detective Ferguson finally sat down to his leftover supper of cabbage and beans. If it weren't for his crockpot, he would have been eating out again a thing he loathed. His wife had died a few years back, and so he had learned to make do. It had been a long day, he was growing weary, and his feet hurt. As he ate his supper, he kept going over the baffling case. His investigation hadn't been fruitful at all, and he didn't really have any solid leads. Every notion had been gone over with a fine toothed comb, but there wasn't anything that gave him a clue. Of course there had been the journal David Marsh had left behind, but it didn't really tell him anything. It just seemed to be the ramblings of a mad man. His doctor hadn't been able to make anything of it at all, at least not yet. And even if he were able to decipher something from it, he might not be able to fully understand what it meant. Detective Ferguson got up from his table, put the dishes in the already half- full dishwasher, then went into the bathroom and took a shower. He was in the middle of shaving when a sudden thought occurred to him. He didn't bother to finish shaving, but just got out of the shower, wrapped a towel around his dripping torso, went over to his desk, and began hurriedly making copious notes. He had remembered something about Sarah MacAfee. A new lead had opened up in his mind, and he fully intended to follow it through. The puzzle was finally coming together. Now he had a better idea of what was going on. The only problem was that he still had no idea of where to search for David Marsh.

Detective Ferguson set his notes aside, went back to the bathroom, finished shaving, and got dressed for bed. It was still rather early, so he turned the TV on and began watching a movie. He needed the distraction to give his mind a rest. It looked as if it were going to be another one of those long grueling days tomorrow. He stayed up watching the movie until his eyes became weary.  Finally, about ten o'clock, he gave in and went to sleep.

Chapter 18


Thomas Gilmore had decided that the time was right to bring his plan into action. There were only a few more details to work out before he made the attempt at what he wanted to do. The first thing on his agenda this day was to get a look at the inside of Sarah MacAfee's art studio. He had already studied the outside of the building and the store next door. If he couldn't get into one building, he might make entrance through the other to achieve his objective. Thomas Gilmore was confident that his plan would go smoothly from either vantage point. It was the inside that had him a little worried. He wasn't sure what he would find, so he decided to take a chance and visit Sarah's MacAfee's studio first. He once again looked over his folder that contained his notes, had another cup of coffee, left the apartment, and headed downtown.

Sarah MacAfee was busy working in her studio getting everything ready for the day. She ran the vacuum cleaner over the carpet and made sure everything was in place before opening. When she was satisfied with the result, she went back to her apartment and made a fresh pot of coffee, poured a cup, and went back downstairs.

It was just nine o'clock and time to open for business, so Sarah put the open sign in the window and unlocked the door. She hardly ever had a customer come in at this time of day, but on this morning someone opened the door and stepped inside. Sarah had just gone into the back room when she heard the bell on the door ring. She went into the showroom to see who had come in. A man was standing at one of her paintings looking it over. He was just an ordinary looking man, but for some reason he seemed to be out of place. Sarah was use to this and thought no more of it. She walked up to him and asked if he needed help with anything.

The man turned to face her, and she immediately felt a twinge of fear. His eyes seemed to be boring a hole in her, and she began to get nervous. Sarah didn't like what she was feeling. This man was giving her the creeps, but she asked the question again anyway. The man quit looking at her and replied that he was just admiring the artwork and wanted to look around a bit. Sarah began feeling more uncomfortable as the minutes ticked by. Her womanly intuition sensed danger emanating from this person. She wished he would leave, but to her dismay he lingered on. Thomas Gilmore had observed a door that was connected to the other building. This was exactly what he had been hoping to find. It gave him another advantage. If he couldn't get in one way, he could get in another.

Thomas Gilmore began walking around the studio acting as though he were interested in the paintings. He would occasionally glance at Sarah as though he were studying her. This made her more nervous than ever and began to wonder if the man could be the one that was supposed to be stalking her. She wanted to run out onto the street but thought better of it. "It is probably just my imagination," she thought, and tried to put the disturbing feelings out of her mind.

Sarah decided to approach him to ask if he saw anything he liked. The way she asked this question proved to be a mistake. The man looked her up and down and said in a silky, insinuating tone, "Yeah, I sure do." Sarah was sure she was in trouble, but instead he suddenly turned away from her and continued looking around the studio. Sarah was relieved by this and went on the other side of the room to put as much space between them as she could. At one point the man stood staring at a painting of the bluff as if interested in it.

165

But to Sarah, it looked as if he were watching her over the top of the painting. She could see his eyes and didn't like what she saw in them. Sarah wished that another customer would come in, but no one did. She could feel the tension mounting, so Sarah did what she should have done before. She picked up her cell phone and called Jason. When he answered, she began talking as though nothing was wrong. Jason could tell that something wasn't right, so he asked if she needed him to come over.

"Yes!" she replied. "I'll see you in a few minutes." The man, upon hearing this, glanced up from looking at the painting, walked over to Sarah, and asked how much the painting of the bluff cost. Sarah's nerves were already on edge, and she had a difficult time answering. She somehow managed to control her nerves and gave him a price.

"That's rather expensive, isn't it?" he asked.

Sarah tried to keep the conversation going until Jason could show up, telling the man that she had put many hours in the painting and that she didn't have any problem in getting what she asked.

The man looked into her eyes and replied in that deep, silky voice, "Well, it's a little too rich for my blood, but I'll bet it's worth it." He gave her an insinuating smile, turned, and walked out of the studio.

Sarah could feel a cold chill running up and down her spine. She locked the door just in case he decided to return. She knew she couldn't stand another encounter like that again. Sarah went over to her desk, sunk into the chair, put her head down, and tried to regain her composure. Presently a knock came at the door. Sarah opened the door and fell into Jason's waiting arms and began to tremble all over.

Jason didn't know what to do. He tried to comfort her as best he could, but nothing seemed to work. Jason waited until Sarah stopped trembling, and then he asked her what had happened. She told him about the man that had come in and that she could tell that he hadn't come in to buy anything. Jason asked if he had made any advances toward her, or threatened her in any way, but Sarah said that the man hadn't really done anything at all.  The way he had looked at her, and the insinuating remarks that he had made scared her. Jason suggested that she close the studio for the day until he could talk to the police, just in case the man came back. Sarah wholeheartedly agreed, for she had no desire to have another encounter with that person again.

Jason told Sarah that he would have to get back to work, because Mister Griswell would be all over him for taking off. Sarah said that she would call the police and report what had happened.  Jason made sure that the door was locked behind him and reluctantly went back to work.

A police officer pulled up in front of the studio. As soon as Sarah let him in, she began to feel a little bit foolish. The officer introduced himself as Officer Smith and asked her to try and remember all of the details of the encounter.  He asked for a description of the man and if she had ever seen him before. Sarah answered his questions as best she could and described the man in as much detail as possible. When the officer understood that there hadn't been an altercation of any kind he stated that there was nothing that could be done. The officer did say that they would keep everything on file and that his description would be posted. He instructed Sarah to call if the man returned. Sarah then thanked Officer Smith and locked the door behind him.

By this time, Thomas Gilmore was long gone from the scene. He had found out what he wanted to know and was pleased that Sarah MacAfee had trembled like a frightened little mouse. It gave him sordid pleasure to know that he had gotten to her. He laughed to himself as he thought of what was going to happen.

When Officer Smith had completely finished taking Sarah MacAfee's statement, he went back to the station and posted her description of Thomas Gilmore. As far as he was concerned, it was just another one of those unfortunate incidents that happens and didn't seem to be anything at all. Later on in the day, Detective Ferguson walked into the station and began going over the new postings. When he came to Officer Smith, he read the recent entry about Sarah MacAfee and asked Officer Smith if he had happened to see the man in question. Officer Smith replied that he had seen no one that fit the description Sarah MacAfee had given him. As Detective Ferguson studied the post again, a memory began to awaken in his mind. There was something about the man Sarah MacAfee described that got his attention. Sarah had described the man as ordinary looking, but that his eyes had held her and that she had felt very uncomfortable in his presence. Detective Ferguson had a feeling that Officer Smith had hit upon something, and Sarah's description of the man seemed familiar. It was becoming obvious to him that the man had been casing Sarah MacAfee's studio. Detective Ferguson decided then and there to have a patrolman watch her art studio on each shift, just in case the man returned. If his instincts were right, he should be able to catch him. Detective Ferguson wasn't exactly sure what the man was up to, but he knew nothing could really be done to circumvent his plans without first getting a good look at him. So far, he had done nothing wrong, but he had a feeling that that was going to change and very soon. Detective Ferguson put out an all-points bulletin explaining the situation, hoping that someone on the force would spot the man and bring him in for questioning. It was a long shot at best and nothing might come of it, but it was worth a try.

When Thomas Gilmore left Sarah MacAfee's studio, he began to have second thoughts about his having gone there. He had gone down the street, had crossed over and went behind the abandoned building across from her studio, up the fire escape, and through the window. He lingered around for a while to see if anyone came after she made her phone call. It would have been much better if he hadn't been so forward with her, but he just couldn't help putting a little fear into her. He had observed when Jason showed up at Sarah's studio and watched as he tried to comfort her. He had watched when Jason left and a cop showed up. He just laughed at this, for he was confident that they could do nothing to him because he hadn't done anything wrong—yet. He waited in the shadows for an hour to make sure it was safe enough to leave. He had donned a different set of clothes to help disguise himself. He nonchalantly exited the old building, strolled down the street, mingled with the other pedestrians, and became lost in the crowd.

# Chapter 19

It was Saturday morning, and the day had dawned bright and clear. There was a decided nip in the air, for it was late fall. Soon the weather would change and winter days would replace the cool pleasant days of autumn. Jason had been pondering upon the dilemma that had been thrust upon him. He had finally made up his mind to convince Sarah to see Doctor Freemont. Jason had put it off for as long as he dared. He was growing weary of dealing with all of the torment that they were going through. The stranger that had come into Sarah's studio that morning had been the tip of the iceberg for him. It was time that something was done before they both went over the edge and into the abyss of insanity.

Jason waited until he was sure that Sarah was awake, before calling to see if she would go out for breakfast. Sarah said to give her a few minutes, and she would be ready to go. Jason could tell from the tone in her voice that Sarah was in a good mood and that was a boon for him, because he was going to need all the help he could get to convince her to go to see Doctor Freemont.

Jason waited thirty minutes before heading to the studio, making sure that Sarah would be ready. It was a beautiful morning, and there was no need to be in a hurry. Besides, he still hadn't decided how to broach the subject. As Jason pondered upon these things, the thought suddenly came back into his mind. It had lain dormant for some time; but now that he had really made up his mind, it began pursuing him with its pestering influence. It seemed to have taken on a rather soothing presence, but even at that, Jason felt put upon and tried to push it out of his mind. The thought would have none of that and began to increase its presence. Jason fought back as best he could, trying to circumvent its growing hold on him. Jason's efforts didn't seem to be having any effect, so he finally had to pull into a vacant parking lot. He sat there struggling, trying to eject it from his mind. He had almost always been able to chase it away, but not this time. Jason finally gave in and allowed it to take over. When he did this, calmness swept over him, and the thought suddenly left his mind. It was as though all it had wanted was to encourage him. Jason pulled out of the parking lot and continued on his way, relieved that the thought's presence had vanished.

Jason parked in front of Sarah's studio and got out of the car. Sarah had been watching for him, and she came out and greeted him with a loving hug and a kiss. They got in the car and went to the restaurant for breakfast. They sat at their table, sipping coffee, enjoying a lighthearted conversation. Jason could hardly believe his luck at finding someone as beautiful as Sarah. He had fallen completely head over heels in love with her, and his pulse quickened every time he was with her. As they conversed, Jason began steering the conversation in a more serious direction, telling Sarah how much he loved her and would do anything for her. Sarah was moved by this and told Jason how much she had come to admire and love him, also. Jason wanted to broach the subject of Doctor Freemont but didn't think the timing was right, so he let the conversation continue as it was. He wanted Sarah to understand how much he cared for her and that he only wanted to help her.

As they sat at breakfast, Jason began trying to find a way to work Doctor Freemont into the conversation. He didn't feel that it would be prudent to broach the subject in a restaurant. So, he began to ponder upon the beautiful fall weather and decided to see if Sarah would like to go for a ride to look at the fall leaves. This she readily agreed to, saying that it would be nice to ride up into the hills for a change and that it was about time that she went to the farmhouse anyway.

Jason and Sarah headed out of town and up into the hills, and whenever they found a good place to pull off of the road, they got out of the car to look at the leaves. The mountains were a cornucopia of color that seemed to rush on and on until finally touching the horizon to mix with the sky. The view was breathtaking, and they would linger enjoying the beauty of nature.

Jason and Sarah held hands all the while, as they observed the colorful landscape. Jason drew her near, but Sarah could detect a slight nervousness in Jason and began to wonder just what it was that caused him to be that way. Was he going to propose marriage? She thought the setting is right. What else could it be?

Sarah looked into Jason's eyes, and she said, "I love you." Jason looked into her smiling face, while the idea of trying to convince her to see Doctor Freemont vanished from his mind. This was the wrong place, and the timing was all wrong. Jason just couldn't bring himself to ruin such a beautiful moment.

Sarah was puzzled that Jason hadn't done what she thought he would do. They lingered a few moments longer, looking at the colorful leaves. She decided it would be best not to get overly anxious, but to let Jason do things in his own way and in his own time. She was sure that Jason really loved her, and if he had asked her to marry him, she would have said yes.

Jason was well aware of the emotional moment that he and Sarah had just shared. He could see her love for him in her eyes. It had been very moving, and his heart reached out to her. He needed Sarah in his life, and knew that she would make a wonderful companion, but that would have to wait until her issues were resolved before he could even think of marriage.

Jason and Sarah lingered a few moments longer enjoying the pleasant scenery and then decided to go to Sarah's farm house to make sure everything was in order. During the winter months she left the heat on so things wouldn't freeze up and made it a habit to check on the house when she could. When the spring came again, she would then open it up to invite the public and other artists out, so they could have a showing.

When they pulled into the driveway of the old farm, everything looked just like it was the last time she had been there, except that there was a manila envelope attached to the screen door. Sarah got out of the car and went up onto the porch to retrieve it. When she opened it, Jason knew from the look on her face that something was very wrong. Sarah stood transfixed to the spot, staring at what had been inside the envelope.

When Jason stepped up on the porch, Sarah handed him a picture that looked as if had been drawn by a child. It was plain to see that it was a rendition of the bluff. Jason didn't see anything wrong with the picture, but then, he wasn't the one who had a fixation.

Sarah said in a quavering voice, "Jason, tear it up. Get it out of my sight! I can't bear to look at it! Who would do such a thing?"

Jason couldn't understand why a childish picture would bring out such a response from Sarah. It looked to him as if some parent had dropped off the picture so that Sarah could look at it. But it was obvious that Sarah didn't think so. She repeated her demand for Jason tear the picture up, but he wouldn't do it. "Sarah," he said, "I'm really not sure what this drawing is doing here, but if it is upsetting you, I think that we should tell the police about it.

Sarah stiffened when Jason mentioned the police, and she adamantly refused.

"It's nothing at all, Jason," she replied. "Give me the drawing."

Sarah reached for the picture, but Jason wouldn't let her have it. This enraged Sarah. She opened the door of the house, went inside, and slammed it shut behind her. Jason was flabbergasted and just stood on the porch unsure of what to next. Then from somewhere inside the house, Sarah began calling his name. Jason rushed in and began searching for her. Sarah's crying was coming from a back room where she kept some of her artwork. Jason found her huddled in a corner of the room. At first he didn't see anything that would have made her cry, but as he looked around the room, he saw that the paintings of the bluff had been slashed from corner to corner and the pieces hung in tatters in their frames.

Jason went to Sarah and tried to comfort her, but she pulled away, saying, "Get away from me Jason! I'm going out of my mind! Leave me alone! You don't want to be burdened with a crazy person. Just go away!"

"Go away!" Jason replied. "Walk away from the one that I adore? I'm not going anywhere; I'm here to stay!" Jason didn't utter another word but just sat down beside her on the floor and let her cry.

When Sarah had exhausted her tears, she slowly reached out and touched Jason's hand. He put his arm around her shoulders and began whispering that everything was going to be all right. They sat still for a long time. He just waited for

174

the right words to come, and the atmosphere in the old farm house became thick with silence.

As Jason waited for Sarah to come to herself, the thought came into his mind again. Its presence wasn't an intrusion this time for Jason had known that it would come back, and he had been waiting. This time, it was welcome; Jason knew that the thought wasn't real and that it was only a figment of his imagination. However it had become a part of him and had merged with his mind. If it took giving in to it to help Sarah, he was willing to do so.

After what seemed an eternity, Sarah finally came to herself and reached for Jason. He held her in his arms, as though he were holding a little child and began speaking comforting words, slowly rocking her back and forth as they sat on the floor.

Presently, Sarah apologized for her behavior, saying that she didn't want him to ever leave her and once again reaffirmed her love for him. Jason was very sorry that Sarah had had to go through such trauma but was also glad, for now he might be able to approach the subject of Doctor Freemont. He was sure Sarah would listen to him and that now was the time to broach the subject.

After Sarah had calmed down, they got up off the floor and began to take stock of their surroundings to see if there had been any more damage done by the intruder. The only thing that they found was where a circle of glass had been cut out of the back door. This was where the person who had left the drawing of the bluff had gained entrance to the house. Jason and Sarah checked every room to see if there was any more damage. The only thing they found was where someone had taken the picture of her grandparents off the mantle in the living room and had placed it on a stand next to the rocking chair. Sarah was puzzled by this, for it looked as if the person had been examining it. Sarah picked the picture up; when she did so, a newspaper clipping fell on the floor. Jason bent down and retrieved it. It was an article from years ago, about someone who had died in a tragic accident. As soon as he had read it, he remembered reading it once before several months ago. Sarah, having seen Jason pick up the newspaper clipping, asked him what it said. Jason wouldn't tell her for he realized the impact it would have on her already stressed emotions. He put the piece of paper in his pocket, telling her that first they must call the police about the break in. Sarah could sense that Jason was protecting her from something and so instead of pressing him about it, she let it go, saying that whatever it was, she didn't think she could cope with it anyway. Jason was relieved that Sarah had said this, for he knew that she might have another break down if she read it. After having read the article, he began to realize what it was that had been tormenting Sarah for so long, and it was imperative that he try and convince her to see Doctor Freemont.

After Jason had called the police about the break in, he reexamined the room where the pictures had been damaged. He left Sarah in the living room on the couch to wait for the police. As he looked around, he was careful not to touch anything in case the police wanted to dust for finger prints. He had probably ruined the newspaper article with his own prints, but it was too late to do anything about that now, so he just carefully looked around to see if the intruder had left anything else behind. As far as he could tell, the only thing that had been disturbed was the damaged paintings of the bluff. As he examined them, he could see that the cuts had been done with some violence. The cuts were not clean, but ragged strips had been slashed from corner to corner, then torn by hand leaving the pieces hanging in the frames. Jason was glad that Sarah hadn't been here when it had happened; the intruder obviously had a vendetta against her. It made him shudder to think of what would have happened if she had been here by herself.

Jason continued looking around, but could find no clues as to who had broken in. He went back into the living room, sat down on the couch, and asked Sarah how she was doing. She didn't reply at first. Jason didn't press her for an answer, knowing that she was still traumatized from the recent events. She remained silent for some minutes before finally answering Jason's question.

Then Sarah said in a rather week voice, "I'm okay, Jason, but I feel a bit foolish. I just couldn't contain my emotions when I saw the damage to my paintings. They have great meaning to me. They are a part of me, a part that I don't really comprehend. It is as though I have been acting out a drama through them. I have suffered many things. It is as though each brush stroke was trying to tell me something."

Sarah then went on to say that there was a hidden meaning behind each painting of the bluff but that the meaning had eluded her all these years.

This was the first time that Sarah had ever really opened up to Jason about what the paintings of the bluff meant to her. As Jason listened, he knew that this was the time to talk to her about Doctor Freemont. He was just about to bring up the subject when a police car pulled up into the yard. A policeman came up onto the porch and knocked on the door. Sarah and Jason opened the door to let him in. He introduced himself as Officer Jefferies and asked if they had reported a break in. He was a rather swarthy man with red hair, and timeworn features. He was very polite in his mannerism, and they felt at ease in his presence. He asked if he could look around a bit and wanted to know where the intruder had gotten in. Jason and Sarah showed him the back door and the damaged pictures. After Officer Jefferies had looked things over, he began asking Sarah questions. He wanted to know if she knew of anyone who might have it in for her, or if she knew of any reason why someone might want do such a thing. Of course Sarah didn't know of any reason why this should have happened. Officer Jefferies said that it looked like the work of juveniles out for fun, but it seemed odd that only the paintings of the bluff were damaged. He said that there might be more to it than meets the eye and thought it prudent to have someone come out and take fingerprints. After he had taken their statements, Officer Jefferies told them not to disturb anything. He then reported in and explained the situation. About half an hour later another patrol car pulled into the driveway, and two men got out of the car. One was a tall, thin, plain clothes policeman with glasses and had streaks of greying hair. Detective Ferguson introduced himself, and immediately asked what the trouble was and that he was there to help them get to the bottom of the problem. Sarah and Jason felt at ease in his presence. They took him inside, and showed him the back door and the damaged paintings. As soon as he saw them, he knew that he was on to something. The paintings were like the one in Doctor Freemont's office. This was the connection he had been looking for. Sarah MacAfee was in more trouble than she realized. As the other officer dusted for fingerprints, Detective Ferguson asked if it would be okay to sit down in the living room so that he might be able to talk to them.

As Sarah and Jason settled themselves down on the couch, Detective Ferguson cleared his throat and began with, "Miss MacAfee, I don't really know how to say this other than to get straight to the point. I have been looking for someone, possibly someone from your past. This person walked away from an institution. Have you had any unusual encounters with anyone recently?"

Sarah and Jason looked at one another in disbelief. Jason spoke up and said that something had happened at Sarah's studio the other day. Detective Ferguson then asked Sarah to explain to him what had happened. She told him about the creepy man that had come into the studio and that he pretended to be looking at the paintings. She knew better because of the way he began to look around the studio and how he looked at her. Detective Ferguson asked Sarah to describe the man.

When Sarah had finished, Detective Ferguson asked if there were any more details she could think of that might be pertinent to the case. It was then that Jason drew the newspaper article from his pocket and handed it to the detective. After having read the article, he put it in his pocket. Sarah thought a while and replied that she could think of nothing else. He then asked if she was sure of the man's description. She said that she could never forget him, and the way he had stared made her shudder. Detective Ferguson said that he had all that he needed for now but that there was one more thing he wanted to talk about. He began by saying that the next question was in no way implying that Sarah was hiding anything or that something was wrong. He wanted her to hear him out, before she said anything. He began telling what he had discovered and that he thought her life was in danger. Jason was quite taken aback by this startling revelation, and he could see the pieces of the baffling puzzle falling into place. Even the tormenting thought that had plagued him seemed to have a reason now. As Jason sat beside Sarah, he sensed her turmoil, and it was reflected upon her countenance.

As Detective Ferguson continued his narrative, he again questioned her about the man that had come into the studio. Sarah said she didn't remember having seen him before, but he had frightened her. Detective Ferguson assured Sarah that everything was going to be all right and that they were watching her place of business. He again asked if she recognized the man. Sarah assured him that she had never seen him before. Detective Ferguson stated that he could be wearing a disguise to hide his features and that he might have changed his name. If that was the case, then they would have to be more diligent in order to catch him.

Then Detective Ferguson looked at Sarah and asked her an unexpected question: "Sarah, do you remember selling a portrait of the bluff to Doctor Freemont a while back?" Detective Ferguson could tell that he had hit a nerve because Sarah stiffened at the mention of the bluff. She hesitated before answering, remembering when Doctor Freemont had come in to her studio. It was one of the few times that she had sold a painting of the bluff, and it had been a traumatic moment for her. Sarah remained quiet for a few tense moments before answering. When she did answer, she avoided looking at Detective Ferguson's eyes and nervously wrung her hands and stammered. "Yes, I remember her coming in and buying the painting. Why are you asking me? Is it important?" He answered with a question of his own "Sarah, why have you... become so disturbed at the mention of the bluff?"

Jason, who had been quietly listening, spoke up in Sarah's defense. "Why are you doing this? Can't you see she is upset? You are treating her like a criminal, not a victim!" Sarah leaned heavily upon Jason's shoulder trying to find some comfort from him. He assured her that everything was going to be okay and that they would get through this together.

Detective Ferguson, having seen the effect of his pointed questions, knew that Sarah was struggling with her emotions.

He turned to Jason and said, "The reason I asked Sarah those questions was to see how she would react to them, and I found out what I wanted to know." Jason was surprise at this. He knew of Sarah's fixation on the bluff and how she reacted to it, but he hadn't expected Detective Ferguson to understand. It was obvious that he had been talking to Doctor Freemont. Then he began to wonder if she had told him of his own struggle with the thought. Things were becoming more and more complicated as time went on, and Jason couldn't see any end of torment in sight.

Detective Ferguson reassured Jason and Sarah that he was on their side and that the questions were very important if he was to understand how to proceed in catching the man they were after. Then he took a picture out of a folder and showed it to Sarah. Sarah took the picture, and studied it. Detective Ferguson said that it was an older picture, because they didn't have a recent one of him.

Sarah looked at it intently for some moments, and then said, "Why now that I think of it, I do seem to remember him. It was a very long time ago, when I was a young girl. I don't know why, but he looks familiar."

Detective Ferguson, smiled and said, "Sarah, I think that we are going to get to the bottom of this after all. He used to live around here as a young man. His name is David Marsh and something tragic happened to him. He just couldn't get over it, so he had to be put in an institution. He got along just fine for years, until one day something set him off, and he ran away. We are certain that he came back here for a reason, and we think that you are the reason!"

181

Sarah just couldn't understand why anyone, especially someone from a mental institution, would be looking for her. The man in the photograph did seem a bit familiar, but she couldn't make a connection with him, although he did look a bit like the man that had come into her studio. Detective Ferguson reminded her of the drawing of the bluff, and the newspaper article, and of the destroyed paintings, and asked her to try and see if she could remember anything from her past that might shed some light on the situation. Sarah said that she didn't know why anyone would want to destroy her paintings and leave a drawing of the bluff. As for the newspaper article, she said that she hadn't even read it.

Detective Ferguson pulled the article from his pocket and read it over. After doing so, he said, "Sarah, this article holds the answers to our questions, and I think that it will reveal a lot of things you personally need to know." Sarah asked him if she could see the article, but Detective Ferguson told her that it wouldn't be prudent to do so, at least not yet. He put the article back in his pocket and said that there was someone that he wanted her to talk to and that he would explain everything to her as best he could.

As Jason listened, he fully understood where the Detective was going. He was trying to convince Sarah to see Doctor Freemont in order to get to the bottom of the mystery.

Sarah ventured a question, and asked, "Who is it that you want me to meet?"

Detective Ferguson answered with another question.

"Sarah, will you trust me? This is for your own good and safety. I want you to see Doctor Jillian Freemont."

Sarah looked at Jason with pleading eyes and moved a little closer to him, seeking his comfort, but remaining silent for a long time. Then she got up off the couch and went out the front door and around to the back of the house.

Jason started to get up and follow her, but Detective Ferguson restrained him saying, "Let her go, Jason, her mind is in turmoil right now, and it would be best to let her think about what we have just told her. She'll come to herself pretty soon. All of this has been a shock to her."

Sarah had gone out into the field in back of the house and was standing looking up at the bluff. Tears were running down her face, and she was whispering, "I hate you! I wish I had never seen you before. You have destroyed my life!" Sarah spoke to the bluff as though it were a living breathing thing. As she stood looking up at its gleaming surface, a cloud passed overhead and cast a shadow upon the bluff. It reminded her even more of the dark pall that had been overshadowing her life. Sarah tried to hold back her tearful emotions but could not. She began to cry out to God for relief from her torment. Just then, the dark cloud moved away, and bright sunshine lit up the surface of the bluff. She began to think of the many times she had done paintings of it. There were days when it had been captured on canvas that were dark and foreboding, and other times it gleamed... with the brightness of the sun as it did now. Sarah began to see the bluff in a different light, and it reminded her of her own life. There were days that were so dark and foreboding and other days that were full of sunshine. Sarah had never thought of her life in this way before.

As she lingered there, Sarah began to think of Jason, and how he had been placed in her life. She began to realize that his coming was of design and not by chance. There were so many things that had happened to cause her to believe nothing else. The more Sarah thought about this, the more she understood. She and Jason had been brought together to help one another. How many times had he been there when she was down? Her life was enhanced because of him. She felt complete when he was near. Sarah wiped her eyes and quit crying. She made up her mind to see things through, no matter what it took to do so. She turned away from the bluff, made her way back to the old farm house, and went back inside.

Jason and Detective Ferguson looked up when they heard the screech of the screen door as Sarah reentered the house. Jason got up off the couch and waited for her to enter the living room.

Sarah, upon seeing Jason waiting, went up to him, and without any thought for Detective Ferguson, began looking into Jason's eyes, saying, "Jason, I don't know what I would ever do without you. I don't see how I got along before you were placed in my life. As I stood outside a little while ago, I was looking at the bluff. I hated what it seemed to have done to me. It was so dark and foreboding, and I was afraid of it. But all of a sudden, the sun began to shine very brightly, and the rock face of the bluff lit up, and I began to see things in a different light. The bluff reminded me of my own life. There have been dark times, but there have been many more times of light. Thank you Jason for being one of those times of light; I truly believe that God sent you to me to help me through this time of darkness. The fear that I have been living with and the unknown reason behind my paintings has to come to an end. I want to put all of this behind me. I am willing to go and see Doctor Freemont. I want something normal in my life. I want peace of mind!"

Jason embraced Sarah. It was a wonderful moment for both of them. Sarah had gone beyond crying; now she was smiling at the knowledge that her troubles would soon be over.

Detective Ferguson, who had been closely watching this loving scene between Jason and Sarah, cleared his throat and said, "I hate to break up this reunion, but there is a lot that we have to do if we are going to get to the bottom of things. I would suggest that you see Doctor Freemont as soon as possible. Sarah readily agreed to this and said that she was willing to do whatever it took to see the harrowing ordeal through.

Before going back to town, Detective Ferguson called the station to see who the fingerprints belonged to. A few minutes later the report came back, confirming what he had suspected. Things were turning out like he thought they would, but there was more going on here than he first thought. In the meantime a constant watch would have to be put on Sarah MacAfee in order to keep her safe. Detective Ferguson looked around the old farm house one more time just to make sure that any clues hadn't been missed in their search. He had an eye for detail, and as he searched, he noticed a little smudge of red clay by the back door. No one had been in or out of the door since he had been there, so it seemed a bit odd. He called to Sarah and Jason and asked if they had used the back door since they had been there. They confirmed that no one had gone out that way at all. It was clear to Detective Ferguson that the person who had broken in had made a mistake in not wiping up that small smudge of red clay. This might be the clue that he needed to help locate him. He told Sarah and Jason that they could go back to town; he had a few more things to do and would lock up.

Detective Ferguson lingered at the farm house searching for more clues. This time he went outside around to the back. At first Detective Ferguson could see nothing out of the ordinary, so he turned his attention to the bluff. He walked toward it, focusing his attention on an area that had a dim trail leading upwards through the trees. At one point he found a spot in a thicket that had been trampled down by someone or something. He went into the thicket, and looked back at the farm house. He had a clear view of the back of the house and could even see the driveway. Anyone might have stood in there and watched as Sarah MacAfee came and went. Detective Ferguson then followed the trail a few yards farther up until he came to where a little stream crossed the trail. There, in the bank was some red clay and a partial imprint of a boot heel.

"I got you," he said to himself. Detective Ferguson turned around and went back to the farm house. It was obvious to him that someone had been watching the house from the thicket and would most certainly return. It was going to be one of those waiting games. So far David Marsh hadn't done anything but break in and damage a few of the paintings. That was bad enough, but he hadn't made any real threat to Sarah MacAfee as yet, although he felt that things were going to escalate sooner or later. Detective Ferguson walked back to the house, took another look around, and went to town. There was much to do if he were to catch David Marsh, but it was beginning to look as if he were gaining the upper hand, although anything could happen when dealing with a mad man.

David Marsh was snickering in a quiet, self-assured way. He had been observing Detective Ferguson making his search of the area at the bottom of the bluff and had also observed Jason and Sarah finding the drawing he had left on the porch. He would have liked to have seen her reaction when she found the paintings of the bluff he had cut up. His face contorted in a twisted smile at the thought of Sarah MacAfee seeing her hard work destroyed. He had known that she would have to come to the old farm house sooner or later, and so he had chosen the weekend to break in, thinking that she might show up. His reasoning had proved correct, and he could see his plan falling in place. Now it was only a matter of time.

No one could see David Marsh for he had located a temporary hiding place under an outcropping of rock, above the bluff. It provided shelter and concealment, and he had also brought in supplies in case he had to stay for an extended period of time. He had rented a room in town close to Sarah MacAfee in order to observe her movements. This gave him a sadistic kind of thrill, and it made him more confident that his plan would come to fruition. Sarah MacAfee was going to pay, one way or another. David Marsh continued in this vein of disturbed thought, biding his time, waiting for the right moment.

When Detective Ferguson had gone back into town, he immediately went to see Doctor Freemont to relay what had just transpired.

As he entered her office, Molly greeted him with, "It's good to see you again Detective Ferguson. How can I help you?"

"I have some business with Doctor Freemont. Is she in?" he asked.

"Yes, she is in but is with a patient right now. She should be finished in a few moments. Can I get you a cup of coffee while you wait?"

Detective Ferguson declined the offer, picked up a magazine, and settled down in a comfortable chair. The magazine was one of those cooking magazines and each time he turned a page, there was a table set with a delicious looking meal on it. He soon got bored, tossed the magazine onto the table, picked up a journal, and settled back down to wait. Presently a muffled cry came from Doctor Freemont's office. Detective Ferguson started to get out of his chair to investigate, but Molly assured him that everything was under control. Detective Ferguson relaxed, shook his head in disbelief, and began his wait again. After another fifteen minutes or so, Doctor Freemont's door opened, and a young, rather large woman appeared in the doorway. It was obvious that she had been facing some kind of emotional trauma, for her eyes were red from crying. Detective Ferguson thought to himself, "There is no way I would want to make my living dealing with emotional people. That would drive me insane."

The woman, after setting up another appointment, thanked Molly, to which Molly replied, "I'll see you next week."

She then spoked to Detective Ferguson and said that she would tell Doctor Freemont that he was here to see her. After a few moments, Doctor Freemont came out of her office, walked over, and sat down in a chair beside him.

Detective Ferguson greeted her with, "I thought that I was going to have to go into your office and rescue you from that woman."

He laughed when he said this, and Doctor Freemont replied, "Oh, yes, my patients do get emotional, but I know exactly how to handle them. I can usually tell if someone is going to be a violent individual, and I don't take on that type. Now, how can I help you?"

Detective Ferguson told her everything that had happened concerning Sarah McAfee and showed her the newspaper article that David Marsh had left behind in Sarah MacAfee's farm house. Doctor Freemont read it with much interest.

Upon finishing, she handed it back and said, "This is very enlightening. It was just what I needed to know; it is perhaps the last piece of the puzzle. It fits into place with what I had suspected all along. Do you have any more information for me?

Without hesitation Detective Ferguson related everything else that was known about David Marsh. He told her that although David Marsh might have a mental issue, he was no dummy when it came to eluding the police. He also told her that he had perhaps changed his appearance and his name, making it difficult to find him.

The papers that David Marsh had left behind and the information she had just received gave her greater insight into putting the baffling puzzle together. To look into a disturbed mind was like looking into a tangled web, but with some careful investigating the tangle eventually began to make some kind of sense. All that needed to be done for now was to get Sarah MacAfee to come in. Detective Ferguson suggested that she call Jason and talk to him about it first because he thought that Sarah would feel more at ease if Jason were there to support her. Doctor Freemont said that it was a good idea and that she would have her secretary contact him right away to set up an appointment.

Detective Ferguson thanked Doctor Freemont for her help, said that he would be in touch, and left the office. A few minutes later, Molly called Jason Brennon to set up an appointment for Sarah MacAfee. He told Molly that he would talk to Sarah after work and set up the appointment. Jason was relieved, and he didn't want to lose any time in getting Sarah in to see Doctor Freemont. He didn't think that she would change her mind, but he didn't want her to back out at the last moment. Jason spent the rest of the day trying to figure out what to say to her. Sarah had been through so much that he hated to bring it all up again, but it couldn't be helped.

Jason had trouble staying focused on the work that had been assigned to him and was relieved when 4:00 clock finally rolled around. He looked at his list of things to be done one last time to make sure everything had been finished, clocked out for the day, and hurriedly left the building. Jason called Sarah and said that he was on his way to take her out for supper. Sarah replied that she had some last minute things to do and that she would finish as quickly as possible.

When Jason pulled up in front of Sarah's studio, there was a swarthy looking man with red hair standing outside peering through the window. At first Jason felt a pang of fear rise up in him. He cautiously got out of the car, walked up to the studio, and went inside. Sarah was dusting shelves and stopped what she was doing when she heard Jason come in.

He immediately asked, "Sarah, did you know that there is a man looking in the window at you?"

Sarah turned to the window and replied, "Yes, I do, but he is gone now. That was Officer Jefferies dressed in plain clothes. Detective Ferguson has him posted at my store. Officer Jefferies doesn't stay very long and walks away whenever anyone comes by. He has been here most of the day, and has been a welcome presence."

Jason said that Detective Ferguson taking that precaution took some of the worry off of his mind.

After chatting for a while, Jason told Sarah that Doctor Freemont's office had called and wanted to set up an appointment with her.

Sarah was a little hesitant at first and said, "Jason, I know that it is the right thing to do, but I'm afraid of what might happen. I have suppressed my feelings for so very long. I don't want to go through such a traumatic upheaval." Jason then reminded her that Doctor Freemont had made him face his fear with the thought, and he was able to overcome his issues.

"Sarah, he said. "I am confident that if I was able to overcome my fears, so can you."

Sarah was still a little doubtful and asked in a half subdued voice, "What if someone finds out that I am being treated by a psychologist? They'll think that I'm insane! What if everyone stops coming to my studio? What would I do then? Oh, Jason, what am I going to do?"

Jason patiently waited while Sarah voiced her fears. When she had finished, he asked her a question of his own: "Sarah, do you really love me?"

She returned, "Why, of course I love you. I don't know what I would have done if you hadn't become a part of my life. How could you doubt my love?"

Jason looked into her eyes and replied, "Sarah, I have told you everything about my mental issues. I opened up my heart to you hoping that you would understand. And you did understand and accepted me as I am. Do you think that I wouldn't do the same for you? I have absolutely no doubt that you will come through this ordeal unscathed. No one is going to care if you went to a psychologist or not. You are a wonderful person and are no different from anyone else who is reaching out for help. I love you Sarah, and I am going to stand by you until we see this through."

Sarah was touched by Jason's commitment to her, and it moved her to think that he would stand by her. It was what she needed to hear and told him to make the appointment.

Sarah said that she wanted to freshen up and then get something to eat before the appointment to help to calm her nerves. As Jason waited, he walked around the studio, admiring the paintings. He came across one of the bluff that had been put in an out-of- the-way place. The painting had been done just as the sun had gone down, and the scene was in half light. As Jason studied it, he could picture Sarah out at

191

the old farm house sitting in her chair, letting her emotions lead her as she painted while working out her frustrations on canvas. Jason recognized Sarah's efforts to understand in the strokes of her brush portraying the bluff. The sun was setting, and dark clouds were rolling in.  There were shadows cast upon the bluff face, and yet there was a ray of light from the sun shining through the clouds. It was as if Sarah knew that there was hope that the bright light of truth could still shine through the darkness. Jason was glad that he had seen this painting for he saw in it Sarah's plea for help. Although the sun was setting and darkness had gathered, a new day would soon dawn bright and clear. Jason remained where he was, engrossed in Sarah's artwork. As he waited, the thought made its presence known again. Jason wondered if it would always remain with him, or if it would eventually fade away. It was a question that he couldn't answer, and so he had learned to expect the thought to come into his mind in moments of distress.

Jason and Sarah went to the restaurant down the street from her studio and settled down in a booth. The waitress came to their table and asked them what they would like to drink. They ordered ice tea with lemon and began looking at the menu.

"Jason," Sarah said, "I'm getting very nervous about going to see Doctor Freemont. I guess it's the unknown that I'm worried about."

Jason replied, "Sarah I felt the same way when I first went to see her, but when I began to voice what had been going on in my mind, I found that I was able to express my true feelings, and things began to turn around for me. Don't be afraid, everything will be all right."

Jason's encouraging words helped her get through the moment of hesitation. She picked up the menu and ordered a ruben on rye. Jason and Sarah lingered in the restaurant, eating their meal, sipping ice tea, and engaging in casual conversation as the minutes slowly ticked by.

When it was time for the appointment, Sarah hesitated and began nervously glancing around the restaurant as if looking for a way to get out of her situation. Jason took her by the hand and gently led her outside and to the car. Sarah had only needed a little nudging to help her stay the course. They got in the car and started to go across town to Doctor Freemont's office. Sarah put her hand on Jason's knee and moved as close to him as the seatbelt would allow. It helped her to know that he was going to be there for her when she went through the traumatic event.

When Jason and Sarah pulled into Doctor Freemont's parking lot, she was relieved. She thought the building would be a sterile looking institution, but instead of a modern building, she saw an old Victorian home with a quaint looking sign that read, "Doctor Jillian Freemont, Psychologist."

Jason put his arm around her, gave her an encouraging hug, and then kissed her, saying, "Sarah, you don't have anything to fear when you talk to Doctor Freemont. She wants to help you with your problem." This further encouraged Sarah, so she got out of the car, took Jason by the hand, and escorted her up onto the porch and into the office.

Molly, upon seeing Jason and Sarah come in, introduced herself to Sarah and said that if they would have a seat, she would inform Doctor Freemont that Sarah was in for her appointment. They took their seats and waited for Molly to return. Sarah wished that the appointment would hurry up and get over with, so she preoccupied her time by looking around the office. There were Victorian looking furnishings in the office that reflected the Victorian style of the house, and the decor was done in very good taste. There was also an old grandfather clock in one corner, and she could hear its rhythmic ticking. It was a soothing sound and helped her nerves to settle down. Soon, Molly called her name, telling her that Doctor Freemont would see her now. Jason walked to the doctor's office door to see if she needed him to go in. Doctor Freemont said that under normal circumstances, she wouldn't allow anyone to come in with a patient but that Jason's presence might be a help. If she deemed it necessary for Jason to leave, she would tell him so. Sarah was relieved to hear that Jason could go with her, for she was walking into the realm of the unknown.

Sarah's first impression of Doctor Freemont was pleasant. Her bearing was one of confidence, and it helped to put her mind at ease. She could tell by her mannerisms that Doctor Freemont had her best interest in mind. She remembered her but said nothing about it.

Doctor Freemont directed Sarah to a chair next to her desk, told her to relax, and introduced herself. Her voice was soft and reassuring. Doctor Freemont didn't hesitate but began the session with a few leading questions about her background and of her business.

Then Sarah said, "We have met before, Doctor Freemont. Detective Ferguson explained everything to me."

"Yes, we have met before, the day I came to your studio and purchased one of your paintings. It was a painting of the bluff in fact." Then Sarah began to feel as if the walls of the room were closing in around her at the mention of the bluff. She started to get out of her chair and go out the door, but Jason wasn't about to let that happen. He... put his hand on hers and spoke to her in as soothing a voice as possible saying, "Don't give up now, Sarah, you must face this. I am

194

right here by your side, and I will see you through this no matter what it takes."

Doctor Freemont nodded her head in approval and said, "Sarah, let me show you something." Doctor Freemont got out of her chair, went into a side room, and brought out the painting of the bluff. Sarah cringed at the sight of it and turned away. Even though she was the one who had painted it, she just couldn't face it under these circumstances. It brought those troubling thoughts to her mind, thoughts she wished to repress.

Doctor Freemont could see what the painting was doing to Sarah, so she put it away again and said, "Sarah, if you will trust me, I can help you, but you must want to be helped. Otherwise you are wasting our time."

Sarah got up out of her chair, walked over to the window, and stood staring out of it. Jason started to go to her, but Doctor Freemont motioned for him to stop. She held up her finger to her mouth, signaling him to remain silent. He sat very still, waiting to see what Sarah was going to do. She remained at the window for a long time as though she were contemplating her next move. When Sarah came out of her reverie, she turned around and faced Doctor Freemont. Jason could see that Sarah had been crying. Her... eyes were red, and there were tear stains on her face.

Doctor Freemont took her some Kleenex and Sarah wiped her face and eyes, and said, "Doctor Freemont, I don't want to live this way anymore. I'm so tired of all the torment that I have been going through. If you think that you can help me, then I am willing to face my problem. I'll do whatever it takes."

Doctor Freemont guided Sarah to the chair next to her desk and told her to sit down. Then she brought the painting of the bluff back into the room and placed it in such a way that Sarah couldn't see it. She then went to her desk and took a sheet of paper from one of the drawers. Doctor Freemont turned the paper over and placed it on the desk. She sat down across from Sarah and began to talk to her.

"Sarah," she said, "I have been doing some research about you, and I have learned a few things that you may not be aware of. I believe I know why you continue to do paintings of the bluff. When I bought this particular painting, I began to examine it closely, and I saw something in it that you had put there. I seriously doubt that you realized what you did. It was your subconscious mind trying to express your true feelings, trying to bring to light the thing that has been hidden away for so long. I think that I have discovered what it is that has been suppressed. I want to explain to you about Jason. You see, Jason, as you know, had been having nightmares about the bluff, and he was also troubled by the thought that continued in his mind. This happened to him because of what he read while doing research at the newspaper where he works. There are times when something disturbing can affect our minds in such a way that it becomes a torment. The mind is quite complex, and there are many things that can't be explained by any rationale that we know of. There are some things that can be explained in only a spiritual sense. I don't know all of the answers, but I do believe that you and Jason have been brought together by a higher power than the human mind can conceive, for there have been too many things in this that I cannot explain. I do know, however, that all of this has come about for a purpose." Doctor Freemont then reached for the paper she had placed on her desk, handed it to Jason, and told him to read the article again. Jason took the paper, leaned back in the chair, and began to read.

Sarah observed Jason's face as he went over the article, curious to see if she could read what she saw there. Jason's eyebrows were knit in concentration, and there was a concerned look on his face. It seemed to Sarah that the more he read, the more concerned he became. By the time Jason had finished the article, Sarah's nerves were very much on edge.

Jason handed the article back to Doctor Freemont, and said to her, "Now I understand about the thought and why it came into my mind; I also understand why Sarah has painted pictures of the bluff."

Sarah was baffled by Jason's statement. How could he understand what she herself didn't understand? Sarah didn't mince any words but spoke up at once.

"What is the big secret? I'm the one that came here for help!"

Doctor Freemont had anticipated this, and was ready with the answer.

"Sarah, I let Jason read the article first, because he came to me first. I wanted him to fully understand what was really going on so that he would be able to help you after you read the article."

Sarah had known by the look on Jason's face that it was a very serious matter. Doctor Freemont asked Sarah and Jason if they would mind setting on the couch while Sarah read the article, so they moved to the couch and sat down. Doctor Freemont handed the article to Sarah and told her to read it slowly and let her mind absorb what she read.

As Sarah began to read, Doctor Freemont studied her face looking for any sudden change that might indicate the struggle going on within. Presently, Sarah began to moan out loud and tears began to trickle down her face. By the time she had finished the article, she was very distraught. Her face was flushed, and there were worry lines in her forehead. Her eyes were tightly closed, and she was shaking as she struggled with her pent-up emotions. Doctor Freemont had been waiting for Sarah's emotional breakdown.

"Sarah," Doctor Freemont asked in a very soft voice, "Have you ever gone up to the top of the bluff?" Sarah didn't respond and turned away. Jason could hear Sarah's half-subdued sobs, and his heart went out to her.

Doctor Freemont repeated the question to Sarah in a different way. "Sarah, I know that this is hard for you to do, but if you really want to get through this, I need you to try and answer my question. You can take your time, but you must try to answer." The conflict in Sarah was apparent, because she began wringing her hands and slowly started rocking back and forth.

After doing this for several minutes, she stopped rocking, reached for Jason, and said in a weak voice, "Oh, Jason, what am I to do? I don't know if I can face what has happened to me. All of the memories have come flooding into my mind, and I'm afraid of what might happen if I have to relive that day all over again."

Doctor Freemont asked, "Sarah, why don't we try to explore what it was that happened to you so long ago? Let's start with the reason that you were at the top of the bluff in the first place. Do you think that you can remember?"

Sarah sat quietly for several minutes, and then asked for a drink of water, and it seemed to help settle her nerves a bit. She was still emotional and started and stopped a few times before she was able to settle into her story as she remembered it. When Sarah did begin, Jason and Doctor Freemont had to listen closely to catch her words because of the weakness of her voice.

Sarah began with, "Now I remember going on a picnic with my grandparents. It was a beautiful fall day. I can remember the bright sunshine and how pleasant it was." Suddenly Sarah stopped and began groaning. Once again the tears streamed down her face, and a look of terror came over her. Then she whispered, "My friend was there. I didn't mean for it to happen, Sally Ann! We were just running and playing in the leaves. It was an accident!" Sarah began to cry out. "It was an accident, Sally Ann! Please forgive me for not being able to save you. It was my fault, my fault." Sarah collapsed on the couch, and the sobbing started all over again.

Jason tried to comfort her, but Sarah wouldn't respond to him. She just lay still quietly moaning. Doctor Freemont motioned him away from her and whispered, "Jason, don't worry; this was necessary. She had to release her subdued memory of that tragic day, and her emotions are part of it. Sarah will come to herself, and when she does, I will be able to help her."

Sarah lay still for quite a while. As the minutes ticked by, Jason began thinking of all that had transpired over the last few weeks. He still didn't understand why things had to happen the way they did, but he was grateful that he and Sarah had been brought together. It didn't matter at all about the circumstances. Sarah was the best thing that had ever happened to him, and he was determined to see her through this difficulty.

"What happened? Where am I?" Sarah slowly sat up on the couch and began looking around. Her eyes were red and swollen from all of the crying. Her dress was a bit mussed, and a feeling of embarrassment came over her. Jason went to her side and sat down.

Sarah reached for him, held him tight, and said, "Oh Jason, I'm so sorry you had to see me like this, but I feel as though a great burden has been lifted from my mind. I think that everything is going to work out. I know that I still have a long way to go, but I feel that I can fully recover with help."

Doctor Freemont had been carefully listening and was relieved to hear her positive words. Putting Sarah through the emotional trauma had been hard on her, but it had been necessary. From this point on, she would get better with the proper guidance. It could take weeks or only days. It all depended on how Sarah responded. If she could get her to face her fear of the bluff and come to the realization that it wasn't her fault that Sally Ann had fallen, then the battle would be won.

Although Sarah was still emotionally distraught, she wanted to know why her mind had been so affected. Doctor Freemont then explained that the death of her friend, Sally Ann, had been so tragic that her mind had tried, in its own way, to protect her from the tragedy. Even though Sally's death was an accident, she had focused on the bluff as though it were at fault. Sarah and Sally Ann knew the danger, but children often look past the danger without realizing it, being caught up in the moment. As Sarah thought on this, the memory of that day began flooding into her already distraught mind.

Sarah and Sally Ann had slipped away without being noticed and had wandered into the area of the bluff. They knew not to go there, but it was such a fine day to play. The wind was blowing the leaves around and around, swirling them into the air. They had made a game of running through them, not noticing that they were close to the edge of the bluff. The next thing Sarah knew, Sally Ann had started to fall. She had grasped her hand in an effort to save her, but to no avail. Their hands had slipped apart, and Sarah saw her tumble over the edge. Sally's scream still echoed in her mind as she remembered that tragic day. She still felt guilt over the death of Sally Ann, and her emotions began to rise up within her.

Doctor Freemont reached over to her and assured her, "Sarah, I know it is very hard for you to remember that day, and you are probably regretting coming here, but if you will trust me, I will help you get through this."

Sarah told her that remembering the death of Sally Ann was difficult to think about, and she wished that the memory would go away. Doctor Freemont said that the memory of that day would always remain and that accepting Sally Ann's death would lead her to the path of healing.

"Death can't be helped. We must all face it sooner or later. It is the acceptance of the death of a loved one that must prevail. When you do this, the healing will come, and your mind will be at ease."

Sarah, although still distraught, began to see a glimmer of hope in Doctor Freemont's encouraging words. It had been good to finally get the death of Sally Ann out into the open. It had cleared her mind and lifted some of the load of guilt. Sarah realized that she couldn't continue holding on to the torment of that tragic day up on the bluff. It might take a while to overcome, but at least she had started down the path to healing.

Doctor Freemont continued encouraging Sarah to accept things as they were and assuring her that progress was being made. She said, "Sarah, there are still the paintings of the bluff that you must deal with, and I don't think that you should stop doing them just yet. As a matter of fact, I believe it would be therapeutic if you continued for a while. I believe that the painting will become brighter and less threatening as you go. At some point in time, you must go to the top of the bluff where Sally Ann fell and face your fear."

Sarah, upon hearing this, shook her head and said, "I don't think that I could. What would happen if I went there? The torment might start all over again, and I don't want to have a complete mental breakdown; I'm already on the edge."

Sarah knew that Doctor Freemont was right, but her fear was great. She would have to think about it for now, because she just didn't have the courage.

Jason and Sarah had been in Doctor Freemont's office for a long while, but much had been accomplished. Before they left, Doctor Freemont told Sarah to look at the painting of the bluff to see if she could find a figure painted there.

Sarah went to the painting, looked at it long and hard, and replied. "I remember painting this, and for some reason it held a great significance for me, but I don't really know why." Jason knew why and wanted to point out the small figure that was obscured in the foliage but restrained from doing so.

As Sarah studied the painting, Doctor Freemont told her to think back to the day Sally Ann fell. At first, Sarah didn't want to do this; she had already faced so much.

Doctor Freemont came to her side, and said, "Sarah, let's do this together. I'm right here to help you. If I didn't think you were able, I would never ask you to do it. I believe that you have enough fortitude to face this." Doctor Freemont placed her arm around her shoulder in a show of support and motioned for Jason to come to her, also.

As Sarah studied the painting, she began trying to remember the day she had painted it, but it all seemed so vague. It was as if a dark shadow hung over her memory, and she couldn't see the painting for what it was. The longer Sarah continued gazing at it, and with the encouragement from Doctor Freemont and Jason, the clearer things became. Presently the shadow lifted, and before she knew what had happened, she heard herself say, "I'm so sorry, Sally Ann. If only I could have saved you." Sarah put her head in her hands and began to cry again.

Jason took Sarah into his arms and held her. Sarah clung to him and after a few moments wiped her eyes and pointed to the small figure in the painting.

She said, "I didn't realize that I had even put Sally Ann in the painting. I guess that all along I had been subconsciously trying to express my grief over her death. After all," she said. "I was only a young girl when it happened."

Doctor Freemont was encouraged by Sarah's remarks and complimented her on the progress she had made.

"Sarah, if you keep this up, you will be over this sooner than you think. Now that you have faced this, I don't think that you will have any trouble facing your fear of the bluff."

When Sarah and Jason left Doctor Freemont's office, they talked about what had just transpired. Sarah felt relieved that she had finally faced the thing that had tormented her for so long. It was as if a great burden had been lifted from her mind; she felt lighthearted but also knew that her torment wouldn't be completely over until she faced the bluff. As they continued to discuss Sarah's successful visit with Doctor Freemont, Jason asked her if she remembered Jeb who lived on the mountain and asked if she would like to go and see him.

Sarah knew what Jason was up to. He wanted an excuse to get her to go up to the bluff. Any other time she would have hesitated, but this time Sarah answered in the positive saying, "Yes, Jason, I think that would be a very good idea. We need to check up on him anyway. He lives by himself, and I'm sure he would like to have some company."

Jason was relieved by Sarah's answer, and he could see the light at the end of the dark tunnel that they were in. If things continued to progress in this manner, they would break out of the darkness and step into the light. Jason suggested that they plan on going to see Jeb on the following Saturday. Sarah said that she would close her studio at noon on that day, and that perhaps they could take a lunch with them to share with Jeb.

# Chapter 20

Mrs. Farley was really worried. It was the actions of Thomas Gilmore that bothered her. He was a strange man, a deceitful man. Ever since she had snuck into his room to satisfy her curiosity, and he had made those thinly veiled threats, she had become afraid of him. There was more to Thomas Gilmore than met the eye. Mrs. Farley suspected that he was up to something. He kept such strange hours. She never knew how long he would be gone, and it hadn't done any good to try and find out. Mrs. Farley always tried to make it a point not to interfere with a tenant, but this was different. She had taken a long time in deciding to report his actions to the police. As far as she knew, there wasn't a thing that he had done wrong, but the nagging sensation that something wasn't right just wouldn't go away. She made up her mind to go to the police station in person rather than call them. She waited until lunch time, put up a "Gone Shopping" sign, locked up, and went downtown.

Detective Ferguson was at his desk when Mrs. Farley came into the station. He heard her ask for someone she could talk to and that it was about a shady character that rented one of her apartments. Detective Ferguson glanced up from his reports and looked at Mrs. Farley standing at the front desk. He could tell at a glance that she was a busybody and was probably sticking her nose into some poor innocent soul's business. As she explained to the officer in charge, he noticed that Mrs. Farley was becoming agitated. He listened to the conversation, and heard the officer say, "Ma'am, you will have to file a complaint on this person. We just can't go out there and investigate because you think that this man is up to something. We have to have something tangible to go on."

Mrs. Farley wouldn't give up. Detective Ferguson heard the insistence in her voice as she continued her harangue, and he began to feel sorry for the officer. After listening for a few minutes longer, he got up from his desk and went to the front.

He asked, "What seems to be the problem?"

The officer replied. "This woman says that one of her tenant's threatened her, but she doesn't really have any proof. It would just be her word against his."

Mrs. Farley, upon seeing Detective Ferguson, began all over again, hoping that he would listen. Wanting to give the officer a break, he told Mrs. Farley to come with him and that he would look into it for her but said he couldn't promise anything. Mrs. Farley followed him to his desk, sat down and told her story all over again. Detective Farley asked her to describe the man as best she could and to make sure of his name.

She said, "His name is Thomas Gilmore." Mrs. Farley said that the way he stared gave her the creeps. It was as if he could see right through her. Detective Ferguson thought that Mrs. Farley was getting a bit carried away but knew that he would have to do something to satisfy her. He asked if the description she had given was accurate.

She replied, "Well, yes, he is one of my tenant's you know."

Detective Ferguson said, "Mrs. Farley, why don't you look through our pictures to see if you can find him? You never know, he might be in there." Detective Ferguson said this as if he believed Mrs. Farley had stumbled upon a plot of some kind, but he was just humoring her hoping that she would give up and go away. He had a lot of paper work to finish and wanted to get on with it. The description she had given could have been any one of a hundred criminals. Although he would like to get on with the business at hand, he couldn't help but think that there was a ring of truth in what she had said.

He listened as she flipped through the pages of pictures, muttering comments under her breath as she studied the photographs.

Finally with a sigh, she said, "I don't think that he is in there; of course, I didn't go through them all. He might not be a criminal, but I just know that he is up to something."

Detective Ferguson, not wanting to offend her, asked if she would describe the man to their sketch artist. It was that ring of truth that made him do this. He had run down many felons on less information than this.

Mrs. Farley settled down with the sketch artist and began to describe Thomas Gilmore all over again. After about an hour of going back and forth, Detective Ferguson heard her exclaim, "Why, that's him. That's Thomas Gilmore!"

He got up from his desk, went over to the sketch artist, and looked over Mrs. Farley's shoulder at the face that had been drawn. The artist handed it to him. As he studied it, there seemed to be something about the man's features that looked familiar, but he wasn't sure. There was something familiar about him.

Mrs. Farley asked, "Is he a criminal? Am I in danger? Are you going to arrest him?"

Detective Ferguson said in a calming voice, "Now Ma'am, I don't want you going around talking about this. Just go about your business. I'm not sure if he is someone we are looking for or not, but we will monitor the situation. I would advise you to stay away from him, and we'll take care of everything."

Detective Ferguson studied the sketch again. There was a little feeling of caution that came up as he scrutinized the picture. He was sure he had seen that face somewhere before, but it was different somehow.

Detective Ferguson escorted Mrs. Farley to the door, continuing to encourage her to stay away from Thomas Gilmore and to just act as though nothing were wrong. He again said that they would monitor the situation and not to worry.

But Mrs. Farley excitedly replied, "Not to worry! The man lives in my apartment building! Not to worry!"

Detective Ferguson said, "Mrs. Farley, we have everything under control. There will be a policeman watching Thomas Gilmore. You have nothing to worry about."

"Well, I am worried! Why don't you arrest him? What if he tries to kill me? He made those threats, you know."

Detective Ferguson sighed and said, "Ma'am, so far he hasn't done anything. Wouldn't you be mad if someone broke into your house and started snooping around?"

This comment got Mrs. Farley's back up, and she went rushing out the door muttering uncomplimentary things about the way the police ran things. Detective Ferguson just shook his head and did a little muttering himself.

"It takes all kinds. We will probably have to go over there and rescue the poor man from her clutches." He said this to no one in particular, and went back to his desk and picked up where he had left off, but a nagging thought lingered in his mind about the sketch he had just seen. He began to... wonder if Thomas Gilmore was using an assumed name.

When Mrs. Farley got back to her office, she cautiously glanced around the street to see if Thomas Gilmore's car was there. It was gone, and this gave her a sense of relief. She couldn't bear the thought of him. It made her nervous just to know that a crazy person like Thomas Gilmore lived in one of her apartments. It gave her the creeps and made her flesh crawl. She wished that she had never let her curiosity get the best of her. Mrs. Farley was thankful that the police were watching her apartments, but that didn't seem to be enough. If only they would just arrest Thomas Gilmore and get it over with. It was going to be hard to sit behind the desk and do her work. She thought about buying a gun, but didn't really know one end of a gun from the other. Mrs. Farley always kept an old baseball bat near at hand and that was a small comfort, but it might not be enough against a determined man like Thomas Gilmore. She tried to settle down and put the fearful thoughts out of her mind, but it was impossible to do. She jumped at every sound and spent the rest of the day in torment.

# Chapter 21

Jason and Sarah had gone to the movies. They had made an evening of it, and it was getting rather late. Jason took Sarah to her apartment at the studio and lingered there as long as he could. Jason glanced at his watch and mentioned that it was about time that he went home, but Sarah looked at him with pleading eyes and said that she wished he would stay a while longer. Even though Jason was tired, he just couldn't resist her pleading and gave in to her. They sat on the couch, snuggled up together, and talked about their future. After a while, Sarah became very quiet, and Jason could sense nervousness in her.

He asked, "Sarah, are you all right?"

"Yes, I'm ok, Jason; I was just thinking about all that we have been through and what must lie ahead. I'm still afraid of going up to the bluff, and it is heavy on my mind. It has been years since I went there, and I'm worried that something bad will happen if I go."

Jason listened closely to Sarah's concerns, trying to find the right words to say. After a while he said, "Sarah, do you remember my telling you how I had to face my own fear of the bluff, and that when I finally faced it, everything began to straighten out for me? It will be no different for you. I think that tomorrow we should pack a picnic lunch and go up there. Remember, we said that we needed to check on Jeb anyway. Why don't we make a day of it? I'll be right there with you. Nothing bad is going to happen. I promise."

Jason lingered a while longer and finally told Sarah that he had better go home and get some sleep if they were going on the outing the next day. Sarah said that she still wasn't fully convinced but said that they could discuss it tomorrow. Jason felt that Sarah would eventually give in and go up to the bluff and so didn't press her any farther.

Thomas Gilmore was getting very nervous. It was time to finalize his plan. He had been in the old building across the street from Sarah MacAfee's studio waiting for the right moment.  He had observed when Jason Brennen... left Sarah's apartment but decided to wait a little while longer before implementing his plan. He wanted Sarah MacAfee to be asleep before going in.

It was 2:00 am, and all was quiet on the street outside of Sarah's studio. At the back of the building, Thomas Gilmore was clipping the wires to the alarm. He halted what he was doing and cautiously looked around to make sure he wasn't being observed.  After having made sure of his surroundings, he reached into his duffle bag, retrieved a glass cutter, deftly applied it to a pane of glass, and cut out a circle. Without making a sound, he set the glass aside and reached in... and unlocked the door. He smiled at his success and thought, "I'll... bet Sarah MacAfee is sound asleep; all the better for... me."

Officer Jefferies, who had been hiding behind a dumpster, watched Thomas Gilmore as he began clipping the wires to the alarm and saw him cut a hole in the glass of the door. When Thomas Gilmore entered the building, he slipped away from his hiding place and followed Thomas Gilmore inside, being careful not to make a sound. This was the moment he had been waiting for. Thomas Gilmore's movements had been carefully watched, and the efforts of the police were about to pay off.

As he entered Sarah's building, Thomas Gilmore's heart began to race as he thought about what he was going to do. A wicked smile creased his face, and he began to grow impatient. It was dark in the back room, and he risked a light in order to see where he was going. He covered the light with his hand so that only a small gleam showed. In front of him was a door, and he found that it wasn't locked. "Sucker," he whispered, "this is too easy." Thomas turned off the light, stepped through the door, and looked around. There was a security light on that lit up the interior of the room. He could see through the windows and out onto the street. There wasn't a soul stirring. "Perfect," he thought to himself, "now, to the job at hand. I'll do what I've come here to do. This is going to be a pleasure." But he didn't know that Officer Jefferies had slipped through the outside door behind him and was following close on his heels.

Thomas Gilmore quietly stepped farther inside the room and looked at the staircase that led to Sarah MacAfee's apartment. He started to cross the room, and as he did so, someone turned on a flashlight and said, "Put your hands above your head."

Thomas Gilmore was quite surprised, and began to curse his bad luck. He tried to run, but he was grabbed from behind. He struggled with his captor for some intense moments but was soon overpowered by Officer Jefferies and handcuffed before he could get away. He just stood where he was and began to berate Officer Jefferies.

"All of the plans and hard work for nothing, stupid cops! Let go of me you filthy pig," he screamed, and began struggling in a futile effort to get loose. Officer Jefferies read him his rights while another officer led him away.

Upstairs above her studio, Sarah MacAfee woke up and looked at the clock.

"2:30 am!" She muttered. She thought she had heard voices, and got up to look out the window. A police cruiser was just pulling away, and from what she could see, there seemed to be someone in the back seat. Sarah didn't think any more about it and supposed that the police were picking up a drunk. She was glad for their presence because it made her feel safe. She got a glass of water, went to the bathroom, and crawled back in bed. Then she heard someone coming up the stairs. Sarah became frightened and didn't know what to do. She started to hide in the closet, but soon there was a knock at her door. It was Officer Jefferies. He was calling her name, asking if she was all right. Sarah gingerly opened the door to see Officer Jefferies and Officer Smith.

She was startled and asked what it was they wanted. They related the break in to her and said that they had the suspect in custody but that someone would have to fix her door. Sarah was overwhelmed by all of this, but Officer Jefferies said that a patrolman would stand by until her door could be secured. Sarah immediately called Jason.

Jason's phone awakened him out of a sound asleep.

"Who would be calling at such an ungodly hour as this?" he murmured. He picked up the phone and saw that it was Sarah.

"Hello," he sleepily said, then asked, "is everything okay, Sarah?"

"No, Jason, it isn't!" she nervously replied. "There has been a break in! But the police caught the man. Can you come over?" she asked. "Whoever it was that broke in removed some glass, and the back door needs fixed."

"I'll be there right away," Jason replied. He hung up, hurriedly got dressed, went to the shed, and got some tools and material to fix Sarah's back door.

When Jason arrived at Sarah's studio, he found a patrolman on guard. Jason said he thought he could temporarily fix the door and that he would stay with Sarah to make sure she was safe. The patrolman reported in and said that help had arrived and that he was going to leave in a few minutes.

The patrolman helped Jason secure a piece of plywood over the glass pane and then left, leaving Jason to finish up. By this time, it was four in the morning, and Jason was tired. Sarah had stayed in her apartment while the door was being made secure and had put on a pot of coffee for Jason. She had become upset by the break in and wondered where it would all end. If the police hadn't been there, anything might have happened. Sarah paced the floor, but surprisingly she wasn't afraid but was sick and tired of all of the upheaval in her life. It was rather nerve- racking, but Sarah was learning that there was nothing she could do but meet her problems head on.

Presently, Sarah heard Jason come up the stairs and knock on her door.

He asked, "Sarah, are you okay?" Sarah opened the door and let him in. He was surprised that Sarah wasn't crying. Jason was glad to see this, and it made him realize that Sarah was on the mend. He did detect a slight nervousness about her, but that was all. Sarah poured Jason a cup of coffee, and they settled down on the couch, discussed what had just happened, and waited for the morning.

It was around eight- thirty, and Jason had called the glass company to come and repair the damaged glass in Sarah's door. When they arrived, Jason showed them where it was, and about an hour or so later the door was fixed. Presently Detective Ferguson arrived. He asked if Sarah was okay and said that the man had been locked away. He had given the officers in charge a rough time; they had to restrain him and put him in a cell by himself. He hadn't been fully processed as yet, but they were working on it. Detective Ferguson said he wanted to come by and let them know that everything was under control and not to worry.

Jason asked Sarah if she thought she was up to going to see Jeb after all that had happened. She said it would do her good to get away and decided not to open the studio. It was Saturday anyway, and it was time she had a day off. All of the drama from the night before was getting to her, and she welcomed getting away with Jason for a little while. There was only one thing that could spoil her day, and it was the fact that she would have to face the bluff. Sarah knew that she would have to go through with it sooner or later if she were to have peace of mind. Even though she had already confronted Sally Ann's death, the very thought of going to the bluff caused fear to rise up in her. If it weren't for Jason and Doctor Freemont, she probably wouldn't go at all. Sarah looked up at the clock on the wall. It was only 9:45 am, so she continued making preparations for the day, noting on her door sign that the studio was closed. Sarah straightened up around the studio, waiting for Jason, who had returned home to put his tools away.

As Sarah worked, she came to the picture of the bluff that had been placed in a corner. She stopped and began looking at it, wondering at the number of times she had been compelled to paint it. Just looking at it made her nervous, but she forced herself to look, trying to confront her fear. She began to think of Sally Ann again. Sarah pulled a chair up in front of the painting and sat down, forcing herself to face the death of her friend. As she did this, the memory of Sally Ann flooded her mind, taking her back to that tragic day.

It had been a warm day, and her grandparents had taken her and Sally Ann on a picnic up to the little park at the top of the bluff. She remembered running and playing with her friend, and she seemed to remember a boy was there too but couldn't recall who he was. The longer she contemplated that tragic day, the clearer things became. As they ran and played, they had gotten caught up in the fun they were having and had forgotten or just plain ignored the admonitions of her grandparents not to go near the bluff. Sarah couldn't remember just how she and Sally had ended up going there, but she did remember the wind swirling the leaves around and around, lifting them high into the air. They had made a game of running through them, not realizing that they were so close to the bluff edge. The next thing she knew, Sally Ann was teetering on the edge, and try as she might she had been unable to save her friend. Sally Ann's screams still echoed in her ears. It was no wonder that she had been affected. Her mind had buried the memory of that tragic day but now had been forced to face it.

Sarah sat a while longer contemplating, wiping the tears from her eyes, trying to regain her composure. The ringing of her phone brought her out of her solemn reverie. She got out of the chair, went to her desk, and answered it.

"Hello."

A subdued voice asked, "Is this Sarah MacAfee?"

"Yes, it is," she replied.

"How may I help you?"

There was a long pause, and then the voice said, "I just wanted to make sure, Sarah!" This last statement was said with strong emphasis on Sarah. Then whoever it was hung up.

This seemed strange to her, and she didn't quite know what to make of it. The police had captured the man who had broken in and was sure that she was safe. Sarah put the call down as just a prank, or perhaps it was probably only someone wanting to know if the studio was going to be open, and so she put it out of her mind.

216

It was almost 10 o'clock when Sarah got a cup of coffee and went outside to sit on the steps. She noticed that there was a yellow envelope in her mailbox. She saw that it was addressed to her, but there was no return address. Sarah took it inside and opened it. There was only one sheet of paper, and when she looked at it, she just dropped it on the floor and walked away. She immediately got her phone and called Jason.

When Jason answered his phone, he could tell that something wasn't right with Sarah, for her voice was quavering, and she was crying.

He asked, "Is everything all right, Sarah?"

She replied, "No, Jason, everything isn't all right. I got a prank call a little while ago, and when I went out on the steps, I found a drawing of the bluff in my mailbox. Jason, what am I going to do? Could you hurry back? I'm scared!"

Jason told her to lock her door, that he was going to call the police, and that he would be right there.

After Jason called the police, he went out the door and headed downtown to Sarah's studio. He got there before the police and knocked on the studio door. There was no answer, so he called Sarah to get her to let him in. Sarah said that she was up in her apartment locked in the bedroom. Presently she came down and let Jason in. Sarah pointed to the envelope and the drawing of the bluff that was on the floor, but Jason didn't pick it up. He didn't want to contaminate it with his fingerprints. The police might find a clue as to who had drawn it.

Jason held Sarah in his arms trying to comfort her. She began to moan, asking, "Will this torment ever end? Am I going to have to face this forever? I want it to stop. I'm going out of my mind!" Jason held her tighter, trying his best to sooth her fears.

217

About thirty minutes later, a police car pulled up in front of the studio, and Detective Ferguson and another officer got out and went inside. The first thing Detective Ferguson did was to tell the officer to bag the sheet of paper with the drawing on it and have it checked for fingerprints. He then asked Sarah if she recognized the voice on the phone. Sarah said that it was definitely a man's voice and that she was almost certain it was the man who came into the studio the other day. He asked her what it was that he had said. Sarah related the brief message to him, and then asked, "Why is this happening to me? Who is this person?"

Detective Ferguson told her that it wasn't the man who had broken in, because as it turned out, the man had been after the jewels in the store next door and was trying to get around the security alarm by going through the door that separated the two buildings. It was Thomas Gilmore who had come to her studio that day and that he had probably been scoping out her studio looking for an easy way in.

Sarah was a little perplexed by all of this, and asked, "Then who left the drawing of the bluff?"

Detective Ferguson answered, "We should know about that when we check for fingerprints." Sarah was becoming weary with all of the cat and mouse games and wanted the torment to end. Detective Ferguson was just as weary as Sarah was but knew that soon or later the entire mystery would come to a conclusion, because he was sure that David Marsh was behind all that had been going on.

Detective Ferguson thought that David Marsh must have a hiding place up around the bluff somewhere and that he could watch the farm house and obviously the studio. He told Sarah that what was needed to catch him in the act was some kind of bait. He stopped talking

218

and looked Sarah directly in her eyes. The pause that ensued was thick with silence.

Detective Ferguson let his concise words sink in for a few moments before continuing, "Sarah, I know that you are afraid of going up to the bluff, but it might be the only way to catch David Marsh. We have been watching the area trying to find him, but so far he has eluded us. We had thought about bringing in dogs to track him but are afraid that if he is chased, he or someone else might fall over the edge of the bluff. David Marsh needs help, and I think you are the one who can help him. We don't want another tragedy on our hands."

Sarah, after listening to Detective Ferguson, could see his point, but the fear she had of the bluff caused her to hesitate before she answered. Jason, who had been closely listening to Detective Ferguson's discourse, thought that his plan left a lot to chance. It would be a very dangerous thing to attempt at best. He didn't want Sarah to have to face the danger it posed. It was one thing for her to face her fear of the bluff, but it was another thing entirely to have to face a mad man.

Jason didn't want Sarah's life to be in danger and started to voice his doubts, but Sarah interrupted him by saying, "Detective Ferguson, I feel that I owe my friend Sally Ann something. If we hadn't gone to the bluff in the first place, none of this would have ever happened. I am willing to do whatever it takes."

Jason was doubtful of the outcome of this proposal by Sarah but also proud to hear that she would be willing to sacrifice her safety for David Marsh. He agreed with Detective Ferguson that the madness had to stop. He only regretted that it had to come about in this way.

He said, "Sarah, I'm sorry to have to see you go through this, but I want you to know that I am proud of you for facing your fear I will... stand by you through it all." Detective Ferguson was relieved to hear Jason say this, because he needed Jason's full support.

It was late in the day when Detective Ferguson finally finished explaining how they would set the trap. It was simple really. All he wanted Sarah to do was to go to the top of the bluff as though she were going to do a painting up there. She was to go alone, for if David Marsh suspected anything, he might not show. At first Sarah was reluctant to do this, because of the danger it posed and because of her fear of the bluff. But Detective Ferguson said that he had thought of these obstacles, and if Sarah was willing, he would take her and Jason to another bluff that wasn't even close to where David Marsh might be lurking. She could get used to the idea, and it just might help her get over her fear. Sarah thought the idea had merit, and so they finalized their plans, intending to put it into action the next day.

It was Sunday morning when Detective Ferguson, Sarah, and Jason met at the police station. They got into a patrol car and headed out of town. The day was a little chilly, but the sun was shining which helped to offset the cool air. It took a while to get to the location, and it was a little hard to find. They had to park on an old logging road in the woods and hike about a quarter of a mile to get there. The bluff wasn't all that easy to reach, and they had to walk through thick brush to find it. When they finally arrived, they saw that it was nothing like the other bluff. It wasn't quite as high and didn't seem as intimidating. Although it wasn't as dangerous, Sarah held back, not wanting to venture too close to the edge. Jason and Detective Ferguson boldly walked up to the edge and peered over into the canyon below.

Jason called back to Sarah, trying to get her to join them. She just shook her head and refused to go any farther. She replied by saying, "No, Jason, it's much too dangerous. You two are making me nervous! Why don't you come away from there?"

Jason and Detective Ferguson walked to where Sarah was standing and began to encourage her to get a little closer to the bluff edge. This she would not do, and so Detective Ferguson asked her if she would at least go a little closer in order to get a feel of what it was like at the edge. Sarah hesitated for a few moments and then agreed to do so if Jason would hold her hand. Detective Ferguson walked about ten feet from Sarah, and Jason led her to where Detective Ferguson stood. They were about twenty feet from the bluff edge, and Sarah had to sit down on the ground because she became dizzy as the memories of the day that Sally Ann had fallen rushed into her mind. She put her head in her hands and began to tremble,

"Jason, if this bluff affects me in this way how will I ever face the real thing?"

Detective Ferguson and Jason sat down beside Sarah so that she would feel safe by their presence. This seemed to help, and Sarah slowly got to her feet, holding onto Jason for support.

She said, "I know that you are only trying to help me face my fear, and I think that I can if you will give me a little time. It is just that I have lived with the fear for so very long that it is going to take a while before I can overcome it."

Detective Ferguson told Sarah that there was no hurry; they would stay as long as it took. It wouldn't be necessary for her to walk up to the bluff edge but only to get close enough so that she could set up as though she were going to do a painting. Sarah stood still and looked across the expanse between her and the bluff, trying to visualize painting the scene before her. It seemed to help some, and the longer she did this, the less fearful she became. After thirty minutes or so, she squeezed Jason's hand, advanced a few steps closer to the bluff, and sat down again.

Sarah had cut the distance to the bluff edge by half and then said, "Detective Ferguson, I think that this is about as far as I can go. I have a very good view of the open expanse of the canyon below, and I can see myself doing a painting of it from this vantage point. If I try to go any closer, I'm afraid that I might faint. It's hard enough as it is, and I just can't go any farther. This will just have to do."

Detective Ferguson said that he was pleased that she had done so well and thought everything was going to work out just fine. Sarah remained right where she was, trying to get used to the idea of being close to the edge. Jason stood with her and made small talk, hoping that it would distract her mind. It seemed to help, for Sarah began to talk about how beautiful the scenery was, but she shivered at the thought of Sally Ann falling to her death and clung to Jason for support.

Detective Ferguson was really encouraged by Jason and Sarah's conversation, for it meant that Sarah would be able to carry out what he had asked her to do. Now all that needed to be done, was to choose the right time to try and pull it off. With a little bit of luck, and if Sarah could hold her own, they should be able to do it.

They remained where they were for a good while longer to make sure that Sarah was going to be okay. Detective Ferguson knew that if Sarah could face her fear for just long enough, it would help them capture David Marsh. Sarah fixed the woods and the panoramic view from the bluff in her mind, lingering until her fear began to subside a little more. When she was satisfied that everything would be okay, they walked out of the woods and drove back to the police station to finalize their plans.

"Monday," Jason said out loud as he got out of bed. "I'm tired." Jason looked at the clock to see what time it was. "6:00 am. It's a wonder I even woke up at all." He yawned and stretched trying to clear his mind of the cobwebs. Jason had had a rough night of it. After the episode with Sarah and Detective Ferguson the day before, he just wasn't at ease in his mind; the thought kept pressuring him to do something. The troubling… nightmare had returned. He kept seeing Sarah at the bluff edge struggling with a shadowy figure. He wished that the torment would end, for it had interrupted his life long enough. It was getting hard to hold onto reality. The whole thing had turned into a waiting game. Sarah feared for her life and had no idea when or where a death blow might fall. The only real comfort she had was in knowing that the police were watching over her. He wasn't allowed to linger around very long at a time because Sarah was being used as bait for David Marsh. This in itself was unsettling; it was a strange situation. It made him wonder about the outcome. Jason tried to shake off the unwanted surmising and got ready for work. He hoped that Mr. Griswell was in a good mood, because he didn't know how much more pressure he could take. Jason started to call Sarah but decided against it. It was still a little early, and he figured that she needed all the rest she could get. He made a cup of coffee, ate some breakfast, and waited around until it was time to go to work. He had a feeling that old man Griswell was going to be demanding, and he just wasn't up to being harassed by him. Everything seemed to be coming to a head, and Jason felt as if he would explode. He was tired of the thought; he was tired of the fear; he was tired of not knowing; he was just plain tired. Jason looked at the clock again and saw that it was time to go to work. He took another drink of his coffee, put on his coat, and went out the door.

When he arrived at work, he reluctantly went inside and looked on his desk to see if there were any new assignments for him. Sure enough, there were. He picked up the sheet of paper and gave it the once over. Jason wasn't impressed but knew that the old man would be on his back if he didn't follow through. He looked at the first thing that had to be done; "more research!" Even though his heart wasn't in it, Jason grabbed some paper and a pen and headed for the archives room. The research had to do with the vintage car show that the town put on every year. Mr. Griswell wanted photos from years past with quotes from some of the old articles from the forties, fifties and, sixties. That meant that he would have to go by the date of the current car show and try to narrow the search. Jason got on the computer and typed in the heading and the year and started searching.

After having worked on the article for two hours or so, Jason left the archives room, went into the break room, and looked for a snack. He found some doughnuts on the table and had just taken a bite when Mr. Griswell called out, "Jason. Get in here, and bring me a cup of coffee!"

Jason winced and muttered under his breath, "I don't need a lecture from the old man today." He poured the coffee and reluctantly went into Mr. Griswell's office.

Mr. Griswell was sitting behind his desk and didn't even look up when Jason came into the room. Jason didn't say a word, but just sat the coffee down on the desk and started to leave.

Mr. Griswell cleared his throat and asked in his usual gruff tone, "Jason, did you get the assignments I wanted done today?"

Jason stiffened. He didn't want to have to have words with him; he just wasn't in the mood for it and only said, "Yes, I got it."

Mr. Griswell could tell that Jason was struggling with his emotions, so he said, "Have a seat Jason. There is something that I want to discuss with you."

Jason wasn't expecting this, because Mr. Griswell was a rather gruff individual, and it wasn't often that he invited you to sit at his desk unless he had something serious to say. He sat down and waited for the worst.

Mr. Griswell didn't say anything at first but just took his glasses off and cleaned them. He put them back on and gave Jason a serious look. Mr. Griswell cleared his throat again and began with, "Jason, I know that you have been having a rough time. It hasn't escaped my attention that you are having some personal problems, but that hasn't stopped you from coming to work and finishing your assignments. I just wanted to thank you for your consistency. You are doing a very good job. I wish that I had more employees like you."

Jason was flabbergasted. He just sat still not knowing what to say, and finally replied, "Mr. Griswell, thank you very much. I have learned a lot since coming to work here. I like my job and hope that I can work for a long time."

Mr. Griswell then said, "Jason, something has come to my attention. We all know that you have had some issues that you have been struggling with. The other day I met a good friend of mine at a restaurant. I think you know him. He is Detective Brian Ferguson from the police department."

Jason replied that he did indeed know him. Mr. Griswell picked up a pencil and began tapping it on the desk. After a short pause he said, "Jason, I didn't realize all that you have been involved in. Detective Ferguson told me just a little bit about what has been going on, and he asked me if I could spare you for one day this week. Jason, you're a good man," he said. "I would like to help you out all I can, and I will on one condition. This newspaper could use a good story, and I believe that you are in a position to give one. It isn't every day that someone working for the paper has a front row seat to something like this. If you will do this, the newspaper will compensate you for the day off and pay you for the article. What do you say to that?"

Jason was very surprised. It made him wonder just how much he knew. But, being in the news business, he knew that Mr. Griswell had a nose for a good story. Jason wasn't sure if he should accept or not. It wasn't just the story that worried him; it was the fact that Sarah was just as deeply involved as he was. She might... not want to have her private business out in the open. He expressed his doubts and stated that he didn't mind telling his own story but that Sarah would have to make up her own mind as to her part in the drama. Mr. Griswell said to get Sarah's opinion and get back to him.

When Jason left the office, he was in a quandary. He didn't want to disappoint his boss, and at the same time he didn't want to put any more pressure on Sarah's already frayed nerves. He was afraid that it might be too much for her. Detective Ferguson wanted to use Sarah as bait in order to catch David Marsh. And now, his boss wanted him to do a story about the whole episode, putting undue pressure on them both. Jason was very worried that something might go wrong. He tried to work everything out in his mind, playing scenarios in his imagination. He was relieved when the work day was finally over, and he was able to clock out and go home. He called Sarah and told her that he had something important to talk to her about. Jason went to his apartment, got cleaned up, and about an hour later went out the door. He could hardly wait to get everything off of his chest. The torment they had been going through was getting to him, and he could just imagine how Sarah felt. Now things were getting more complicated. He was ready for their trial to be over.

Sarah was anxious for Jason to fill her in on their previous conversation, but Jason, not wanting to jump right into the topic, wanted to make sure of what he said. Finally after a few tense moments, he cleared his throat, took Sarah's hand, and began his story. Sarah listened to what he had to say and just nodded her head from time to time.

When Jason finally finished, he looked into Sarah's eyes, trying to determine how she was accepting what he had just told her. The minutes ticked slowly by, and it was a good while before Sarah said anything.

The first words out of her mouth were, "I love you, Jason. I love you very much. I don't know what I would have done without you. Everything has been so complicated, and I am ready to get this over with. It is dragging me down. I don't know how much longer I can go on, but you can tell your boss that I would be willing to do what he asks." Jason was relieved by Sarah's answer but also a little fearful because of the danger involved and admonished her to be very careful and to do exactly as Detective Ferguson said. He knew that she would be watched over by the police, but he also knew that David Marsh was a desperate and clever man.

## Chapter 22

Jeb Rawlings looked up from the kitchen sink where he had been doing the few breakfast dishes, and was cleaning up around the house just to have something to do. Suddenly Rouser began growling and barking. Jeb stopped what he was doing, went to the door, and looked outside. A car had just pulled into the driveway, and a man and a woman got out. Rouser never got off the porch but just continued to growl. Jeb recognized Sarah and Jason at once and went out and stood on the porch, admonishing Rouser to calm down.

"Rouser, you old fool, don't you know friends when you see 'em? Well I'll be, it's Jason and Sarah come to see an old man! Light a shuck and come on in the house; I'll put on a pot of coffee."

Jeb went back into the house and began preparations for his guests. Sarah and Jason walked up onto the porch. Rouser recognized them and began wagging his tail. Jason reached down and scratched his ears while Sarah spoke softly to him.

Jeb admonished Sarah and Jason to come inside and make themselves at home. This they did and soon entered into friendly conversation with Jeb.

"It's been a coon's age since you two came to see me. How have you been doing?" he asked. Before they could reply, he went to the table and brought over a plate filled with muffins. "I made these yesterday. Have one. The coffee will be done in a few minutes."

Jason asked Jeb how he had been getting along all by himself and asked if anyone had been checking up on him. Jeb replied that his church family helped keep an eye on things and that they came over one Saturday and got his firewood in for the winter.

"I don't get around as good as I used to, ya know. It sure helps to have friends close by."

Sarah took a muffin and remarked that she was glad that there was someone that kept an eye on things for him.

Jeb answered, "I don't get many city folk up this way very often, but there has been a strange kind of a duck that stopped by once or twice. He said that he was camping out in this area and was just enjoying the scenery. I didn't like the looks of him, and so I keep my old gun close to hand. He doesn't stack up just right with me. I can tell when a man ain't right in the head, and this one ain't right."

Jason and Sarah began to question Jeb about the man. Jeb described him as best he could and said that the man rode a motorcycle. Jeb stated that he couldn't understand why anyone would want to camp up by that dangerous bluff but that this fellow had been there for a while, and it made him wonder what he was really up to.

"The first time he stopped by, Rouser would have nothing to do with him. That was all I needed to see, and so I keep my gun handy."

Jason asked if he had been seeing the man lately, and Jeb replied that he had seen him go by earlier that morning. This revelation immediately got Jason and Sarah's attention, but they changed the conversation to something else, not wanting to get Jeb involved in their situation any more than was necessary. Sarah asked... "Jeb, that coffee sure smells good. Is it done yet? I can't wait to dunk my muffin in it."

Jeb got up from his chair, went into the kitchen, and brought Sarah the first cup. He went back into the kitchen and returned with cups for him and Jason. They sat for a few quiet minutes enjoying their repast before entering into more conversation.

Jeb, after drinking his coffee, remarked that it had been a while since their last visit. He continued with, "Sarah, as I recall, when you and Jason were here one time before, we had been telling a story about the vet and her friend who had been riding their horses and almost fell off the bluff. If I remember right, the first time I met Jason he was searching for the bluff. It seems to me that there is some kind of connection here. Now if you will excuse an old man's nosiness, I would like to ask a question. I couldn't help but notice, Jason, that you changed the subject when we were talking about the man on the motorcycle. Do you know who he is?"

Jason and Sarah glanced at each other, trying to decide who should answer Jeb's question. There was a short pause before Jason said, "Jeb, I think the best thing for us to do is to be honest with you. We didn't come up here just to visit with you, Jeb, although we did want to see how you have been doing. But, since you have mentioned the man on the motorcycle, we might as well fill you in on a few things that have transpired since the last time we were here."

Jason and Sarah then explained to him exactly what had been going on, but they left out some of the more important details. Jeb said he knew that there was something wrong about the man on the motorcycle. Jason said that they could be mistaken about him, but that the police would have to check things out to make sure if it was David Marsh or not.

When Sarah and Jason had finished their narrative, Jeb sat back in his chair and became very quiet. He remained this way for several moments, but then got out of his chair, went to an old dresser in the hall, and came back with a bit of newspaper, which he handed to Jason. When he saw what it was, he was astonished. He handed it over to Sarah. Her face became flushed, and she just shook her head in disbelief.

Jeb didn't wait for them to say anything but said, "Sarah, I knew the Marsh family. They lived down in the valley not all that far from your grandparents. That first day that you came with Jason to visit me and I mentioned the bluff, I knew that something must have happened that caused you to react the way you did. Do you remember my saying that you must face your fears, and you said that you didn't think that you could ever go up there because it was an evil place? Well, I knew then that something was wrong, but I just didn't know what it was for sure. Of course, I had my own ideas, but I never imagined that you knew the Marsh family. It's funny how things work out sometimes. If you stop and think about it, you can see the hand of God in this. Just look at how you and Jason came together. That in itself is a miracle. You could never convince me that it is anything but a miracle. You two were meant for each other. It's as plain as the nose on your face. And as for David Marsh, he desperately needs help before he does something drastic."

Sarah, who had remained quietly listening, said, "Jeb, thank you for what you have said about Jason and me. I believe that we really were brought together under unusual circumstances, and I also tend to think that it was of the divine. There is... no other way to explain it." Jeb was glad to hear this and began talking about his deceased wife, what a holy woman she was, and how much she prayed. He then said that he would say a prayer for them that everything would turn out all right.

Jason called Detective Ferguson and informed him of the situation, advising him that David Marsh might be in the area. Jason told Sarah and Jeb that Detective Ferguson was on his way with other officers in tow. Sarah hadn't brought any paints with her, so she and Jason said a quick goodbye to Jeb and hastily went to Sarah's farm house to retrieve the paint and canvas.

David Marsh stayed either in the vicinity of the bluff, or in town watching for an opportunity. A police officer had been watching over her, so he patiently waited, knowing that his chance would eventually come. Eluding the police hadn't been much of a challenge, but it had become a fun cat- and-mouse game with him. He had used different disguises to fool them, but now the game was up. He knew that the time had come to work his will upon Sarah MacAfee. He had deliberately broken into the farm house and left the note in order to strike some fear into her heart. He had been a long time planning his revenge upon Sarah MacAfee, and nothing was going to stop him. He had watched as Sarah and Jason made their way out of town and had discreetly followed them. He had gone into the woods, had parked the bike well away from Jeb's, and had watched from the hill overlooking the house. He noted Jason's phone call, and from the animated way in which he talked, he figured that everything was coming to a head. He was disappointed when Jason and Sarah got in the car and drove away. But instead of following them, he quickly hiked through the woods to his hiding place by the bluff. He had a hunch that Sarah and Jason were going to the farm house, so he took up a position nearby and waited to see if his hunch was right.

Jason and Sarah had followed the winding dirt road to retrieve her paints. When they finally arrived, Jason got out of the car to make sure everything was okay. He walked around the house and gave it the once over. He examined the doors and windows, but he couldn't find anything out of place. The glass in the back door had been replaced, so he and Sarah went inside to get her supplies.

David Marsh arrived at his hiding place at the bottom of the bluff a few minutes ahead of Sarah and Jason and observed as they pulled into the driveway. He watched as they got out of the car and went into the house. This is the very thing David Marsh had been waiting for. He quickly emerged from his hiding place and quietly went to the back of the house, waiting for an opportunity to get Jason Brennen out of the way. His heart was racing, quickening his pulse as he waited. The back door had been secured and the windows were locked, so he patiently watched for the right moment to present itself. A few minutes later, Jason came out of the house with an easel. It was the opportunity he had been waiting for. He picked up a stick from off the ground, came up behind Jason and hit him. Jason fell, stunned by the blow. David Marsh went into the house and found Sarah gathering her paints.

She heard who she thought was Jason coming into the room and without turning around said, "Jason, I think I have everything that I need. Let's get out of here and get this over with."

David Marsh laughed, and in a haunting voice, said, "Hello Sarah. It's been a long time."

Sarah jumped at the sound of the unfamiliar voice and turned around. A wild-eyed disheveled man was standing in front of her.

She became very frightened and asked, "What do you want? Where is Jason?"

David Marsh just grinned and advanced toward her. Sarah moved away from him, but before she knew what had happened, he had grabbed her arms and pinned them to her sides. As Sarah looked into his eyes, she read their meaning. She screamed and began calling for Jason to help her.

David Marsh scoffed at her and said, "He won't come to your rescue. I've seen to that; you're coming with me to the top of the bluff. I have waited years for this moment, and you are going to pay for causing my sister Sally Ann's death. You are going over the edge, just like she did."

Sarah tried to break away from him, but to no avail. He had the strength of a determined mad man. He forced her out the back door and shoved her in the direction of the bluff. Sarah protested, begging for her life and trying to break away, but David Marsh only laughed at her again as he pulled her into the woods and started up the hill.

Jason, who had only been knocked out, was slowly coming out of his stupor. He tried to stand up but couldn't. He tried to take stock of his surroundings but was too dizzy. Sarah's screams spurred him into action. Getting a handhold on the car door, he pulled himself erect and leaned against it, trying to steady himself. His head was throbbing from the blow he had received and had to hold onto the car for a few moments to get his balance. He could hear Sarah begging for her life as she fought with David Marsh. Then the thought suddenly came into his mind, growing stronger with each passing moment. Jason felt very weak and nauseated, but feared that if he didn't get moving, Sarah would die. He looked around for something to use as a crutch and there beside the car was the stick that David Marsh had hit him with. Jason slowly bent down to pick it up, and when he did this, a wave of pain hit him. He ignored the pain and started for the back of the house. By the time he got there Sarah, and David Marsh were in the woods. He could hear Sarah protesting, calling out for help. Jason struggled forward and plunged into the trees and brush in pursuit.

Sarah MacAfee was terrified and tried to resist David Marsh's hold as he tried to drag her up the steep path, but she couldn't break his grip on her arms.

"Give it up, Sarah. No one can hear you out here. Your boyfriend is out of commission. I killed him, and I'm going to kill you too. You took my sister's life, and now I'm going to take yours!"

Sarah knew she was going to die. Pleading with him hadn't worked, and it looked as if he had killed Jason. Sarah became infuriated at the thought of this and redoubled her efforts to break away. David Marsh had been holding her arms, while pushing her ahead of him, and so Sarah pretended to stumble and fall. When she did this, David Marsh lost his grip. Sarah picked up a rock and hit him in the back of the head which stunned him for a second or two but not long enough for Sarah to break completely away. She tried to pick up another rock to hit him with, but David Marsh recovered and grabbed her again. This time he flung her to the ground and pinioned her there while he got his breath.

Sarah began pleading with him once again. "David, I didn't mean to hurt Sally Ann; we were just children playing up there. We didn't realize the danger. I would never have hurt Sally Ann. She was my best friend!"

David Marsh grimaced at her. "I was up there, I saw the whole thing. I heard Sally Ann's cries for help, and you did nothing. I can still hear her screaming as she fell over the edge of the bluff. It was all your fault, and you are going to pay!"

Sarah continued pleading with him. "But we were just little girls playing in the leaves. I'm sorry it happened. I tried to save her, but I didn't reach her in time. Do you think that it hasn't tormented me also? Her death has hounded me all of my life."

Sarah began to cry as she thought of Sally Ann falling to her death and gave up her struggle. David Marsh pulled her to her feet and once again forced her up the steep path.

Back at Jeb's house, Detective Ferguson decided to send patrolman Jeffries to check on Jason and Sarah. He didn't like the way things were looking. The situation didn't feel right, so he made up his mind to go up to the bluff. The patrolman reported back to say that Jason's car was in the driveway and that he had found a blood stain on the door of the car. Jason and Sarah were nowhere to be found. He told Patrolman Jeffries to follow the path behind the house and look for them there while he went up to the bluff.

Patrolman Jeffries went to the back of the house and began casting around for the lost couple. When he got to the path, he could hear faint voices, and so he hurried up the hill. After a few moments he came upon Jason, struggling up the steep incline. It was obvious that Jason was injured, for there was blood on the back of his head. Officer Jeffries made him sit down and catch his breath.

Jason protested, "Officer, David Marsh has Sarah, and he intends to push her off of the bluff. Never mind me, I'll be okay, just try to catch up with them." Officer Jeffries ran up the hill in pursuit of Sarah and David Marsh. He paused after a few yards listening for any sound of them, but the voices that he had heard earlier had been silenced. This caused him to redouble his efforts. He finally reached the top of the incline and carefully looked around for any evidence that they had passed that way, but there was nothing to be seen. The pathway split, one path going to the right and one going to the left. After closer examination, he could see that both of the paths had been recently used. Officer Jefferies radioed Detective Ferguson and relayed what he had discovered.

David Marsh heard someone following him, so he shoved Sarah onto the ground, took a rag and a length of twine out of his pocket, and roughly bound and gagged her. Sarah tried to resist, but he had straddled her in order hold her down. Sarah's clothes were disheveled and torn by this time, and her face was scratched and bruised from the rough treatment. He then forced her back onto her feet and shoved her down the path. When they got to the intersecting paths, David Marsh took the one going to the left that led into a denser part of the woods. This path followed the course of the bluff and came out at the overhang that he had been using to hide in. When they reached it, he forced Sarah inside and made her lie down. Sarah lay, wide eyed and trembling, expecting the worse. David Marsh tied her feet together so that she couldn't get away and then went outside and back down the path. Sarah struggled against the cords that had her bound, but to no avail.

David Marsh crept along the path, concealing himself in the brush and observed as Officer Jefferies cast around trying to decide which part of the path to take.

David Marsh smiled when the officer took the path to the right and quickly went down it. Feeling confident that he had thrown the police off his trail, David Marsh went back to his hide out.

When Jason reached the top of the incline, he saw that Officer Jeffries went up the path on the right. He feared that David Marsh and Sarah might have gone the other way, for the path went higher up toward the bluff. He went... to the left, trying to be as quiet as possible. Jason went a few yards and paused to listen, for he thought that he heard footsteps up ahead. Jason went along the path and was just in time to see David Marsh disappear in the overhanging ledge and emerge with Sarah. He saw that she was bound and gagged, but he was too far away in order to help her. He anxiously watched as David Marsh shoved her in the direction of the bluff. Jason wanted to rush to her aid, but David Marsh held a knife in his hand. Jason held... back, afraid that he might stab her. Jason decided to try and get ahead of them, and so he quietly went into the woods. Sarah had been struggling, trying her best to slow David Marsh down, because she knew where they were headed, but Sarah wasn't going without a fight. She made herself fall down again, forcing him to stop his advance.

Infuriated, David Marsh threatened. "Get up, or I will kill you where you lay and toss your corpse off the bluff." He put the knife to her throat and pricked her skin with it, then forced her to get up, and shoved her down the path again.

Jason had been able to get ahead of them and positioned himself in the brush close to the edge of the bluff and waited for Sarah and David Marsh. By this... time Detective Ferguson and several other officers were following the path that Jason had taken earlier and were quickly approaching the bluff.

David Marsh suddenly stopped their advance toward the bluff and whispered, "Listen, do you hear that? Someone is coming, trying to save you. They will be too late. I killed your boyfriend, and now I am going to kill you for what you did to Sally Ann!"

Sarah tried to fall down again, but to no avail. He began dragging her the last few yards to the bluff edge.

Taking the gag out of her mouth, he said, "Go ahead, Sarah. Open your mouth and scream! That's what Sally Ann did when you shoved her over the edge!"

Suddenly, the wind began to blow, picking up the leaves and swirling them around and around until it formed a vortex that surrounded Sarah and David Marsh just the way it had the day that Sally Ann had fallen to her death. Sarah fought

238

to stay where she was, for the bluff edge was only a few feet away. The wind continued to blow the leaves all around them, and then the lingering memory of that terrible day came flooding back into her mind again. She tried to scream, but nothing would come out. David Marsh began to shake her, tormenting her with his words. He kept inching her closer to the edge, repeating, "Come on Sarah, scream for your life. I want you to beg me for your life the way Sally Ann did!"

Jason had been waiting for the right moment to rescue Sarah, so when the leaves began swirling around them, he quickly rushed to Sarah's side and struck David Marsh. He just shook it off and continued forcing Sarah closer to the bluff edge.

David Marsh became infuriated by Jason's intervention and fought for the mastery. As the two men struggled, the swirling mass of leaves obscured them from view. Sarah tried again to break free, and with Jason's help she managed to drop to the ground, causing David Marsh to lose his grip on her. She crawled away from the bluff edge to safety. The wind and the leaves caused David Marsh to lose his balance, and he teetered on the bluff edge, desperately trying to regain his balance. He began clawing the air, seeking for something to hold on to. Jason tried to save him, but the leaves obscured his view, and he couldn't reach him in time. David Marsh slipped over the edge, screaming for Sally Ann as he fell to his death.

Jason fell exhausted to the ground, while Sarah came to him and sat down and wept hysterically. The wind continued to blow, swirling the leaves around and around into the dreadful vortex that had just taken another life. Sarah held onto Jason, sobbing over the tragic event.

Detective Ferguson, who had just arrived, came running up to them and asked, "Where is David Marsh? I thought I heard him calling for Sally Ann."

Jason pointed to the bluff edge. Detective Ferguson walked over and peered into the abyss below. There, sprawled on the rocks, lay David Marsh. Detective Ferguson shook his head and muttered to himself.

"What a travesty, a pointless death." He looked around at the great mass of leaves being born before the wind and returned to Sarah and Jason. Together they walked away from the harrowing scene of death.

As for the thought, it seemed to have disappeared as though it had never been, for it had accomplished the purpose for which it had been sent and had perhaps returned into the depths of Jason's subconscious mind.

# A Dream Unknown

I dreamed a dream
of which I cannot tell
for its meaning
has quite eluded me
and left my mind.

The dream
whether here or there
I cannot say;
it was perhaps made up
of distant memories.

Who can say of dreams
what is true or false,
for the meaning dissipates
as does a vapor
before the sun.

I have dreamed a dream,
a thing most common
unto man;
it has left questions
without answers.

Dreams are perhaps
musings of the mind,
wishes, or bad omens
that in reality
never come true.

I can speculate
but only in a vague way
on the meaning
and purpose
of a dream.

I cannot help but ponder
upon images left behind,
shadowy figures
floating away
just beyond comprehension.

But with surety
this one thing I know,
while I was asleep
my thoughts were at large,
and I dreamed a dream.

R.C. Smith

www.ingramcontent.com/pod-product-compliance
Lightning Source LLC
Chambersburg PA
CBHW020323200626
46814CB00006BB/2385